STEVEN M. ROTH

A SOCRATES CHENG MYSTERY

THE COUNTERFEIT TWIN

The Counterfeit Twin
Copyright ©2016 Steven M. Roth.

Published by Blackstone Press, A Crime Novel Imprint

Cover Design and eBook & POD Formatting: Streetlight Graphics

FIRST EDITION

ISBN 978-0-692-77703-9 (Paperback)
ISBN 978-0-692-77704-6 (ePub)

Visit the author's website: www.stevenmroth.com

MYSTERY AND SUSPENSE NOVELS BY STEVEN M. ROTH

The Socrates Cheng mystery series:
MANDARIN YELLOW
THE MOURNING WOMAN

The Trace Austin Suspense/Thriller series:
NO SAFE PLACE

For Dominica

"They spend their time mostly looking forward to the past."

John Osborne

PART ONE

CHAPTER 1

THE FIRST TIME I EVER heard that the much revered Confederate general Robert E. Lee was born a black slave who passed for white was when I sat across the desk from the director of the Museum of the Golden Knights of the Confederacy in his office in Richmond, Virginia.

"You're kidding," I said.

"Do I sound like I'm kidding, Mr. Cheng?"

He didn't. I shook my head.

"Why haven't I heard this before?" I asked. "I read a lot of Civil War history when I was younger, including some well-respected biographies of Lee. None said anything like that. Didn't even hint at it."

"Of course not. There are only eight people alive who know this secret," the director said. "Seven trustees of the Museum and me."

"Nine then, including me."

"Point taken, Suh. Nine."

The circumstance leading to my meeting with the director began when he called to ask me to come to Richmond to meet with him. He wouldn't tell me why on the phone. He only said he believed I would be intrigued by the case he wanted me to investigate on behalf of the Museum.

Although I ordinarily would not have driven several hours to meet with a potential new client on a speculative case without first knowing more about it, these days, with the economy still soft and our PI business down, my partner — Ralph Harte — and I could use the work. So I drove the ninety-plus miles from Washington to Richmond, and entered the director's office at the appointed hour.

* * *

The director met me at the entryway door. As I stepped into the vestibule, he pushed the heavy iron door closed behind me and locked it.

I looked around for typical museum indicia, but didn't see any. No visitors' help desk or informational posters or marketing display posters reflecting past or upcoming exhibits, not even a coatroom such as most museums provide. In fact, I didn't see any indication to suggest the public would be welcome in this building.

The director smiled at me with what looked like a well-practiced impersonation of humility. He abruptly poked out his arm in what seemed to be an afterthought, and perfunctorily shook my hand without any warmth in his grip or facial expression.

I followed him through several dimly-lighted hallways until we arrived at an office I assumed was his. He instructed me to step inside, and pointed me to a chair in front of the desk across the room. He closed the door behind us and engaged the door's lock.

He was younger than the mid-fifties-age his telephone voice had suggested to me, probably about thirty-five or so, but because of his broad mid-girth and his alcohol-reddened, desiccated skin and bulbous nose, he could easily have passed for sixty-five or more. He clearly liked his liquor.

The first thing he did when we both were seated was to hand me a legal document to sign. I recognized it as a routine confidentiality agreement, the kind of document signed every day in business transactions. When I signed it, as I inevitably would just to hear what he would have to say about the Museum's problem, I'd be promising to keep confidential everything I learned in the course of our conversation and, if I accepted the case, learned in the course of the investigation.

I skimmed the document to make sure it held no surprises, signed it, then slid it back across the desk. The director, in turn, put the document in a drawer and replaced it with a thumb drive he set on the desk midway between us.

"Everything you need to know to get started, Mr. Cheng, can be found in the files on that memory drive," he said, tilting his head toward the tiny object sitting between us. He spread his hands, palms up, in what seemed to be a well-rehearsed gesture of resignation.

I nodded, and said, "Call me Socrates."

"Yes, Suh, Mr. Cheng."

I watched as he took a deep breath and held it briefly. He seemed to be performing an imitation of indignation as he decided what to say next. He sighed softly, as if embarrassed by what he was about to tell me.

"There was a burglary here at the Museum, Mr. Cheng, the night before last."

"I hadn't heard that," I said, trying to make polite conversation.

His face darkened. "Of course you haven't," he said, his tone suddenly truculent. His eyes narrowed. "We haven't reported it to the authorities, Suh, and we don't intend to. We're not looking for publicity." He paused and looked away as if attempting to regain control of his emotions before he spoke again.

I was duly chastened.

He put both hands on his desk and made a tepee with his fingers. He looked hard into my eyes and maintained contact.

"The thieves, Mr. Cheng, stole dozens of documents from our restricted, closed archival holdings. Among all those artifacts taken — and there were many — they stole a journal written in the 1870s by a former negro slave. They also made off with several letters sent from two very important — one distinguished and one scurrilous — late-eighteenth and mid-nineteenth century Virginia women."

I continued listening without comment or question in my chastened state.

The director leaned forward as if to make sure I knew he was confiding in me. He dropped his voice to a lower, almost conspiratorial level, and proceeded to take a long time to tell me very little.

"It is essential, Mr. Cheng, that you find the stolen documents and return them to the Museum before the information in the journal and letters becomes public knowledge. Understand?"

I nodded, and continued to hold my tongue.

He continued, still sotto voce. "I cannot stress this point more than to say that the revelation of the information contained in those documents would be catastrophic to the Museum and to many lives were it to become public knowledge." He nodded sharply once as if to underscore his point.

I decided to ask some basic questions to see how forthright

he would be with me. This was one measure Harte and I often used to gauge if a prospective client was one we would want to represent.

"This is awkward," I said, "but I need to ask a question and get it out of the way." I paused to compose my thoughts. "Since you suggested the contents of the documents are so inflammatory, why didn't you just destroy them when you still had possession of them?"

I watched as the top of the director's head strained to come to a point. You might have thought I'd just revealed to him that I was having a love affair with his mother.

"We don't do that, Mr. Cheng," he said, using a condescending tone that should have put me in my place, but did not. "We are archivists. We protect and preserve historic artifacts, not destroy them, no matter how odious their content." He shook his head as if to banish the question from his memory bank, and sighed.

I nodded again and asked an innocuous question. "Are you positive the documents are genuine?"

So much for *innocuous*. The director looked stunned by the implication of my question. Indeed, almost angry.

"Of course I am, Suh. There's no doubt in my mind. None at all. You can drop that line of inquiry and put that empty notion to rest."

"Okay," I said, "but I had to ask." I paused to give him time to cool down. I changed direction again, wondering if I could come up with even one routine question that wouldn't offend him.

"I'll want to talk with the guard on duty at the time of the burglary. When can I do that?"

"There was no guard. We never needed one before."

"What about the alarm system? Did it go off? Who was alerted by it?"

"There was no alarm. We just now are installing a system." He looked uncomfortable as he made this admission. "It will be operative later today or early tomorrow after it's set up and tested."

This next question should be a waste of time, I thought. "Were there cameras? I'll want to see the footage for the night of the break-in and possibly for some days before that night, too."

He shook his head as if to say, *Why are you wasting time with these questions?*

"No cameras either, Mr. Cheng. Not then there weren't." He looked away from me as if embarrassed by the Museum's naivety.

I dropped the topic of pre-theft security, and decided to throw him a question that had concerned me since his phone call to me.

"Why are you hiring me?" I asked. It made no sense to me. "There must be dozens of competent private investigators here in Richmond? It's not practical or efficient to use a PI based ninety miles away. Besides," I added as an afterthought, "in addition to paying me for my investigative time, you'll be paying me for travel time you could avoid by hiring someone local."

"Confidentiality, Suh. Confidentiality, is why. And you, Mr. Cheng, come highly recommended by our colleagues in Washington at the Smithsonian Institution. They said you not only are a skilled private investigator, but are also absolutely discreet, a quality that is of the utmost importance to us.

"The fewer people in Richmond who know what is going on, the better for everyone involved. That's why we looked for help outside Richmond, and so here we are with you." He nodded again once, sharply this time, as if adding a final punctuation mark to his statement.

Better for everyone involved or better for you? I wondered.

"What specifically needs to be kept confidential," I asked, "the fact there was a theft at all, knowledge about which documents were stolen, or information that might disclose the contents of the stolen documents?"

"All, Mr. Cheng, all. Everything you said. But of the three, most important of all, critical in fact, you must recover the documents before the thieves learn the content of what they have taken, and before the information becomes public."

He paused, looked down at his desk, then said in a voice I had to strain to hear, "My job, Suh, my entire career as the director of this organization, is also at stake if any of this gets out. Any of it at all."

He looked away from me as he said this, as if embarrassed to admit it.

"Tell me specifically what it is you don't want the thieves to learn, what it is the documents contain that's so incendiary." He had whet my curiosity beyond easy retreat.

Again, the director's face darkened. He clearly was losing patience with me, but I didn't care. I wouldn't work for a client I didn't feel was fully on board with us, was candid and truthful with me. He was slipping below the waves as we talked, going down for the final time.

"I told you, Mr. Cheng, everything you need to know is on that thumb drive you're going to take with you." He tilted his head toward the memory stick still sitting on the desk. "I don't need to tell you right now, Suh."

He paused a beat, then added, "You are wasting valuable time by asking questions, time you could be using to locate the stolen documents."

So now you're going to tell me how to run my cases? It was time for a showdown.

"Actually you do need to tell me," I said, "and you need to tell me right now if you want me to consider handling this for you. I might have questions for you based on what you say or don't say." I paused to let that sink in, then added, "I don't work for clients who don't cooperate with me."

I wanted to hear his version of the facts so I could compare my initial reaction to them with my reaction later when I would read the documents on the thumb drive. I also needed a sense of how well he would work with me if we accepted the case. His candor now, or his lack of it, would help me judge that. This could be useful over the next few days when Harte and I discussed the case to decide if we would represent the Museum.

I crossed my legs, folded my hands on my lap, and waited while I watched the director silently struggle with my demand. I would give him all the time he needed to answer my question and fill-up the silence I'd just imposed on him.

After a few seconds, he grunted and shook his head, apparently resolved to humor me. "All right, Suh, have it your way. It will be wasting time telling you what you can read for yourself, and it won't help you find the stolen artifacts, but all right." His eyes had narrowed and his face had become blotchy.

He waited a beat and looked beseechingly at me, as if

silently pleading with me one last time to change my mind. When I failed to take his bait, he shivered once. After a few more seconds he apparently accepted that he could not talk me out of my position.

"Well, Suh, there are reputations at stake here, not only at the Museum, but historically, too, reputations affecting some of Virginia's finest and most venerable old families who are the very backbone of our historic culture. That's why haste and discretion in resolving this unfortunate incident are so important."

I made a show of looking at my wrist watch. "Tell me your version of events and your summary of the information in the files on the thumb drive. Specifically, what it is you don't want made public?"

"As I said, Suh, I would rather you read the files yourself in the privacy of your office. Then I will be happy to answer your questions. I implore you, will that be satisfactory?" He looked at me over the top of his half-lens eyeglasses, and raised his eyebrows.

You're not getting off the hook that easily.

"No, Sir, it won't do," I said. I stared into his eyes and held his gaze until he broke it off and turned his head away. Then I said, "Look, I signed your confidentiality agreement so the Museum's protected. Now you have to decide if you trust me and are willing to let me run the case my way. Meanwhile, I'll decide if I'll take your case. If you don't tell me what you know about the contents of the documents right now, then we're done. We won't be working together." I paused, then said, "It's up to you."

That was when he told me General Lee's secret.

CHAPTER 2

TWENTY-EIGHT YEAR OLD CALEB LIVENGOOD held the heavy woolen greatcoat at arm's length — using his left hand to firmly grip its collar — and, applying a stiff brush he held in his right hand, swept the coat from top to bottom with long, graceful, repetitive strokes, as if he were brushing the fine coat of Traveller, Robert E. Lee's favorite war horse. The gray topcoat was the final piece of costume in Caleb's orchestrated ensemble which, when slipped into by him, transformed Caleb from his workaday, ordinary role as an automobile mechanic into the persona of his hero, General Robert E. Lee.

Livengood was big, slightly north of 6' 4", and solidly built. His two hundred—forty pounds were mostly hard-earned muscle. He wore a full, well-trimmed beard that masked a face marked with past troubles and the promise of more to come.

In addition to the greatcoat, Livengood owned other Robert E. Lee replica gear: Lee-type riding boots, the General's black string bow tie, his gray woolen slacks, Lee's gray, broad-brimmed hat, and a faux gold-plated watch chain that looped down from Livengood's right-side pocket, as it did in the post-Civil War, late-life photographs of General

Lee. To complete his illusion, Caleb had bleached his hair and beard white to mimic the General's own beard and hair at the end of the Civil War.

Caleb slipped his arms into the greatcoat, wiggled his shoulders until the garment settled comfortably over him, and carefully placed the hat on his head, tilting it slightly to the right and forward, as Lee had done in his posed tin-type photographs.

Caleb stepped back and admired himself in the full-length mirror, nodded once at his reflected image, and said, as he looked into the eyes of the contrived, aged soldier gazing back at him, "I am ready to do mah duty, Suh, for Virginia and for the South." He saluted the mirror, and then stepped away from his self-induced mirage.

CHAPTER 3

DARRYL POOLE SAT IN THE black Escalade SUV he'd stolen an hour earlier from a Metro-train short-term parking lot in Northern Virginia, and waited for the mark to show. The vehicle's engine was turned off; the windows were tinted dark. Poole was not concerned about being heard or seen by any passerby.

He was parked in the last row of the outdoor parking area, as far away from the Wheaton, Maryland, high-rise apartment building as he could be, with the vehicle facing the ten-foot-high brick wall that enclosed the apartment complex on three sides. He faced sideways in the driver's seat so he would be able to see the mark and his leashed boxer when they emerged from the building, as they prepared to engage in their twice-around-the-perimeter walk, as they had done every night between 10:30 and 11:00 p.m. over the past six days.

The mark's dog-walking practice had not varied either in its timing or its short route. The mark would emerge from the building with his boxer on a chain-link choker leash, would walk on the grass along the wall, and would stop from time-to-time to allow his dog to sniff items or to do his business. The mark never stooped to pick up and bag his dog's droppings, as he was supposed to do, and as other dog walkers Poole had seen in this apartment complex had done.

That, in itself, Poole thought, *was sufficient reason to take out this arrogant asshole.*

For some reason Poole could not discern, the mark and his dog walked this circumscribed route twice each time, even if the boxer had seemingly emptied itself the first time around. Probably for their mutual need for exercise.

———

When Poole saw the man and his dog emerge from the apartment building's lobby, out onto its front patio, he turned back to face the steering wheel, and started the vehicle's engine, allowing the SUV to idle quietly. He did not turn on the headlights.

Poole patiently waited as the man and his boxer, half-way through the completion of their first loop, approached the area of the wall faced by the SUV. Poole looked around for pedestrians or for people in nearby cars. He didn't see any.

Poole gripped the steering wheel, but left the headlights turned off. As the man and his pet neared the target area along the wall, Poole slipped the vehicle's gear-shift into drive. He rested one foot firmly on the brake pedal and touched his other foot lightly on the gas pedal.

When the man and his dog stepped into the imaginary bull's eye existing between the wall and the SUV, Poole, in one fluid motion, released the brake pedal, flicked on the headlights' high beams to startle, blind, and freeze the man, and crushed the gas pedal to the floor.

The man and his dog abruptly looked in Poole's direction — fixed in place like a startled deer — and took one step each to flee before Poole waffled them between the wall and the SUV's radiator grill, partly extruding both the man and his boxer through the grillwork, into the engine's housing.

Poole turned off the headlights and engine, unfastened his seat belt, pushed aside the airbag that had deployed, and stepped out of the vehicle. He looked around, feigning injury in case anyone was watching. When he was satisfied he was alone, he brushed the wrinkles from his slacks, peeled off his latex gloves, and placed them in his jacket's pocket. He would dispose of the gloves later near the Metro station.

He looked briefly in the direction of the crushed, steaming front of the vehicle, then quickly walked from the parking area through one of several pedestrian openings in the wall. As he left, he glanced back and noticed people beginning to congregate near the building's entrance, looking into the parking area as if trying to locate the site of the noisy crash.

Poole felt no injuries, having braced himself for the impact. He quickly walked to the Metro station to board a Red Line train to ride from Wheaton to Metro Center in the District. Once there, he would change trains for the Blue Line train ride home to Arlington.

CHAPTER 4

THE MUSEUM'S DIRECTOR SQUIRMED IN his chair, adjusted his bow tie, and shook his head once as if resigning himself to the inevitable. He cleared his throat, then used his finger to flick some lint I couldn't see off his jacket sleeve.

"Well, Mr. Cheng," he said, "you are now part of a small, élite group of people who know that Robert E. Lee's biological mother — his actual mother — was one of Light-Horse Harry Lee's concubine slaves at Stratford Hall." He squinted at me as if trying to measure my level of misgiving about what he'd just said.

I maintained my professional, inscrutable, partly-Chinese facial expression, although I wasn't entirely sold on the truth of what he'd just told me.

"And this is verified by the stolen documents?" I asked. I tried to keep my voice neutral to mask my skepticism.

The director nodded.

"The general's putative mother," he continued, "Mistress Anne Carter Lee, raised young Robert as her own child, even though she was fully aware of his bastard, mulatto birthright."

"Why would she do that?" I said. "Didn't she have other children?"

"The answer, Suh, is suggested in Mistress Anne Lee's stolen letters. It is all there on the thumb drive, as I said before." He pointed to the memory stick still on the desk between us, as if to say, *See, I told you to read the files on the thumb drive before wasting my time asking unnecessary questions.*

"Summarize it for me."

"It's just a theory, mind you," the director said. "The letters aren't explicit, Suh."

"Tell me anyway."

"Of course, Mr. Cheng, of course." His severe frown belied his seemingly upbeat verbal response.

"From my readings of Mistress Anne's letters," he said, "I believe she never emotionally recovered from the death of her first son, Algernon Sidney Lee, in 1796, when Algernon was only fourteen months old, and Mistress Anne was barely twenty-three.

"When we look back at her correspondence, we can see that the poor woman was in a continuous state of the blues. The birth in 1807 of baby Robert Edward to Light-Horse Harry's concubine slave was a blessed opportunity for Mistress Anne to heal her festering wound and to replace her loss with young Robert. That, Suh, was not unheard of at that time in our culture, among the very best families of Virginia, in case you didn't know that."

Be nice, Socrates. Curb your tongue. Do not make a wisecrack. "Okay," I said, "now tell me about the stolen journal."

"The journal — actually a memoir, not a real-time daybook, although the director referred to the artifact as a journal — was written by General Lee's mulatto, twin brother, Isaiah, sometime after the end of the War of Northern

Aggression, when the General's brother was a freedman living in Washington, DC. Its narrative continued into the 1870s. Isaiah's journal was not a contemporaneous diary written day-by-day as events occurred, but was a look back at events, as later recalled and described in the book.

"Isaiah's account of events was based on family lore and on plantation tradition, as well as his own experiences while he still was a bondsman, and then afterward when he'd been freed. The journal was indirectly confirmed by Mistress Anne's letters."

"And what about the other letters?" I asked. "You said there were letters from two well-known Virginia women."

"The other letters, Suh, are only three from that despicable traitor, Elizabeth Van Lew." He shook his head in apparent disgust. "That pernicious Yankee spy whose actions during the War sullied her home state, Virginia, and her home-city, Richmond. Her letters are important only because they corroborate the journal and Mistress Anne's letters. Otherwise, the Van Lew letters are abominable, just as one would expect from a craven woman who sold out her birthright."

I let his editorial rant slide without comment. "What is it you want me to do?"

"As I said, Suh, if you were paying attention before, I want you to recover the journal and letters before the thieves or someone else find out what they contain."

"That assumes they don't already know."

"Yes, Mr. Cheng, you are right, and that certainly is our fervent hope." He looked away briefly and stared off into space. Then he turned back toward me. His face had taken on a hangdog expression.

"There is one more thing, Mr. Cheng, that is of the utmost importance. It addresses the point you yourself so astutely, but indirectly, made just now."

"Which is?"

"There is one final condition you must agree to, besides confidentiality, before I can permit you to pursue this."

Permit me to pursue this? Cute.

"Another condition? What is it?"

"Since we cannot assure ourselves, Suh, that the thieves have not already learned General Lee's secret, and since you will not be able to assure us they haven't, you will be required to take all necessary measures to make sure they cannot ever divulge that information, should they know it."

I didn't like the sound of that at all. It smelled to me like the solicitation of a contract-to-kill.

"There's only one way to assure that," I said, "assuming, of course, the damage hasn't already been done by the time we find the thieves."

The director smiled. "Exactly, Suh. I'm glad you understand."

I didn't comment on the director's invitation to commit murder, but before I left him I did ask to see the room where the documents had been stored, the entrance the burglar (or burglars) had used to enter the building, and several rooms adjacent to that site, all to give me a sense of context concerning the crime scene.

I told the director I'd get back to him in a day or two to let him know if we would handle the Museum's case. He wasn't happy with my timetable or with my refusal to accept the assignment right then, but I didn't care. Our firm has procedures to follow when we're offered a new case, and I intended to follow them.

CHAPTER 5

LEFT THE DIRECTOR'S OFFICE AND slowly drove back to Washington in the new Lincoln MKZ I'd purchased three weeks earlier. I was a bit apprehensive as I drove because, although my SUV was brand new, it had shown some signs of having an undiagnosed electrical issue that had resulted in my headlights going dark the second night I owned the vehicle as well as some problems with the windshield wipers. The problem, however, had not occurred again. So far.

It rained hard all the way home, so the drive was not as easy as it had been in the morning on my way to Richmond. But the extra time I spent in my vehicle gave me the opportunity to think through the odd meeting I'd just left. There was no doubt in my mind that if Harte and I took on this case, we would be entering into a strange new world, a world wholly unfamiliar to us.

The first thing I did when I returned to DC was drop my vehicle off at my condo's below-surface garage where I owned a parking space. Then I went upstairs to my condominium apartment to copy the files from the thumb drive onto my desktop computer and onto another, backup, thumb drive. I intended to put the backup device in our office safe.

As I copied the files, I thought about the reading I'd done

in Civil War history when I was in high school and college. I tried to recall what I'd read about Robert E. Lee.

Very little in the way of specifics came back to me. What I remembered, however, in general terms, was how so many established historians had seemed to worship Lee, both as a military leader faced with sustaining a hopeless cause and as a virtuous symbol of the imagined, antebellum South. This, of course, was before the era of historical revisionism that swept academia in the late 1970s and early 1980s, when Lee occasionally was knocked off his tall perch by young, ambitious historians looking to make names for themselves. Up to that time, it seemed that historians, such as Douglas Southall Freeman and others, had treated Lee as if he were a marble, unfathomable God-like figure in search of a pedestal from which to overlook his legacy.

———

As I indicated, much to the annoyance of the director, I'd left the meeting without having agreed to accept the case on behalf of our firm. I told him I would review the files on the thumb drive, consult with my partner, and then call him during the next day or so with my decision. That was all I was willing to commit to at that point.

If we decided not to take the case, I promised to destroy or return the thumb drive and to continue to be bound by the confidentiality agreement I'd signed. I made a mental note, too, that if we refused to take the case, I also would destroy the hard drive files and the backup thumb drive copy I'd made.

When I arrived home from Richmond, after I copied the thumb drive, I showered and changed into fresh clothes. When

I finished, I called Clotille at her office at the Commodities Future Trading Commission on 21st Street, where she worked as a management analyst. Clotille — specifically, Clotille Berenson Harte — was the woman I'd been dating for about one year. I called her now because I hoped we could get together for a drink and dinner after work, but I was told by her secretary that Clotille was in a meeting. I left word for her to call me when she was free to talk.

Next I called my mother. I hadn't visited her in almost a week and wanted to check in to see how she was doing.

My mother had reached the age and temperament such that missed or delayed visits with her by me were received as momentous failures on my part. I recently noticed, too, that she had started to show some early indicators of dementia, frightening signs similar to those my mother and I had watched take control of my father years ago, signs that signaled conditions that eventually laid waste to him before he died.

Notwithstanding these infirmities on her part, I wanted to run aspects of the case by her. Although my mother wasn't as sharp as she used to be and, in any event, had never been a great listener or necessarily impeded by her lack of facts when she formed a definitive opinion, from my point of view, my mere act of stating my concerns out loud to her might prove helpful to me. It often had in the past. And, in spite of her emerging mental frailty, I believed she still possessed great, natural instincts, and I intended to respect her gift while it still functioned.

Unfortunately, she wasn't home. I left a voicemail message saying I had tried to reach her — so I would receive some bankable, if fleeting, credit on her maternal balance sheet for having tried to get in touch with her — and said I would call her again soon.

Since I was on my own until I heard back from Clotille or my mother, and I wasn't yet ready to talk to Harte about the case, I decided I would go to our office, place the backup thumb drive in our safe, and then open the files stored on the director's thumb drive to take a quick look at the former slave's journal. That's the document that interested me the most.

I booted up my computer and inserted the thumb drive into one of the USB ports. I entered the password the director had given me and navigated to the file containing the first journal entry.

I read the first page.

> My name is Isaiah Lee. I was borned in Westmorland County, Virginny, at Stratford Hall, on January 19, 1807. I belonged to Massa Henry Lee who I learnt later from my mamma was also my father.

> My father was knowed to white people as Light-Horse Harry Lee. I don't know why. There was nothin' that looked light about that big horse he rode around on at our place. It looked like everybody else's horse who had dem a horse.

> My mamma was one of Massa Harry's bondswomans, one of his slave womans.

There was two of us borned at de same time from de same mamma. We was called twins by the other cullud folk except we didn't look nothin' alike. Not at all. My brother's name became Robert. He was taken from our mamma shortly after him and me was borned.

Robert was raised in de Great House by de Massa and Missus as dere own flesh and blood son. His skin was enough white he could pass for one of dem. I was coffee color, what dey called *café-au-lait*, a mulatto, not enough white looking so I could pass. So I guess dat's why I lived with our mamma in de slave quarters at Stratford Hall until I was 10 years old, while my twin brother Robert lived in de Great House.

De young massa Robert was raised as a member of de Massa's own family as if de Missus had borned him. I was put out in de fields with our mamma to work with a hoe.

I don't actually remember much of dis, or even some of what I will write later in dis writing book dat was gived to me by a friend of our mamma, but as I growed up I was told all dese things many times by older cullud folks who was der at de time. Dey said that what I just wrote on dis page here was de way it actually happened (although dey

ain't here to see dis page). So dat's all dat matters
to me all dese years later as I write dis.

Although Massa Harry was always kind to me
and to our mamma, I made sure enough, as our
mamma always reminded me, never to forget dat
although Massa Harry was my father, he was my
owner too.

Even though I'd been obliquely forewarned by the director,
I was stunned by what I read. If this journal was genuine,
its revelation would cause a tidal wave of controversy among
historians, academics, journalists, African-Americans, Civil
War buffs, Civil War reenactors, proponents of the various
myths associated with Robert E. Lee, descendants of the
Old South, southern heritage advocates, and descendants of
Confederates.

I logged off the computer and locked the thumb drive in
my desk drawer. Then I tried Clotille and my mother again,
but didn't reach either woman. I decided that what I needed
was an afternoon drink so I could think through what I'd just
read.

CHAPTER 6

CALEB LIVENGOOD SAT WITH HIS live-in girlfriend, Celia Pomeroy, beneath the replica Confederate battle flag tacked to the wall above their second-hand couch, and shared a longneck beer with her. He had met Celia when they were patients at the Meadow Woods Drug & Alcohol Rehabilitation Center, located in Ashburn, Virginia, a small community approximately thirty-five miles southeast of downtown Washington, DC. Celia had been one week into her rehab program when Caleb arrived. They'd met in a group therapy session.

Both Caleb and Celia had emerged from the program drug free. Neither had been a heavy drinker before entering the program, so alcohol was not an issue for them. Their separate, but vicariously shared burdens had been methamphetamine and heroine. Celia also was not a heavy cigarette smoker, but indulged occasionally. Caleb, a chain smoker before he entered the program, had not had a cigarette the entire time he was at Meadow Woods, but resumed his smoking habit within hours of leaving the program. He now consumed cigarettes at an unbroken pace.

Celia, at thirty, was two years older than Caleb. She came from a family tradition of Civil War reenactors, who performed on behalf of the South's glorious cause, for as far back in memory as Celia could recall. She'd introduced Caleb to reenacting shortly after they started dating. He took to these contrived theatrics as if he had been searching for reenacting all his life.

CHAPTER 7

I LEFT OUR OFFICE AND WALKED to *Stan's Restaurant and Lounge*, located one story below street level at the intersection of Vermont Avenue and L Street, NW. I decided I'd have a drink or two, think about the issues in the case, then go back to the office and read the rest of the thumb drive's files, while I waited for Clotille to return my call.

Stan's had become my hideaway over the past year. It was a comfortable neighborhood bar/restaurant where the drinks were generously poured to the lip of the glass, with a free beer back. The tender on duty behind the stick when I entered — the secular priest of *Stan's* mahogany — was a woman named Danika, an old friend who typically and patiently allowed me to bend her ear when we were alone at the bar. Danika was part of the comfort and refuge offered me by *Stan's,* and it seemed she was always on duty when I showed up, never some other tender. I knew this was a coincidence, but even its anticipation was comforting.

I settled onto a bar stool across from where Danika was performing one of the sacred, time-honored rites of tending

— rinsing glasses before putting them into the dishwasher. She smiled when she saw me.

"The usual?" she said. She barely looked up from her task as she asked this. She punctuated her question by raising her eyebrows.

I nodded, said yes, and waited while Danika retrieved my drink.

— a Glenlivet 12-year-old single-malt Scotch served neat with a water back. When she set the drink and the water down on coasters in front of me, I leaned in and took my first hit. The drink felt warm and comforting.

I chatted-up Danika for a few minutes until it became clear from her anomalous reticence that she was focusing her attention on preparing for the upcoming Happy Hour, and could not spend time standing across from me idly chatting. I realized I shouldn't be taking advantage of her good manners, because Danika would never tell me she was too busy to talk with me.

I swiveled away from the bar and, using my cellphone again, tried to reach my mother. This time she answered. I paid my bar bill and left *Stan's* to walk to my mother's condo apartment, located in the Mount Parnassus Condominium on Kalorama Avenue, near Connecticut, not far from the National Zoo and the former site of the Embassy of the People's Republic of China, before it relocated to its new address.

I used the key my mother had given me to open the entrance door, but then knocked loudly, twice, and called out, "Hello, Ma!" before actually entering. I wanted to give her a heads-up

I was there and that I'd be heading back toward the kitchen, the place I would almost certainly find her. I didn't want to suddenly appear, unannounced, and startle her.

I inhaled slowly and deeply as I walked along the hallway leading from the foyer to the kitchen. The blended aromas of basil, eggplant, ground beef, tomato, cheese, and béchamel sauce caressed my senses. The fragrances announced to me that I was back home, if only figuratively, and that my mother was baking a *Moussaka* casserole. I could also smell the coffee she always had percolating on the stove, the *ellenkikò café* she served in demitasse cups, with a glass of water on the side, in the traditional Greek manner.

As I stepped into the kitchen, my mother's refuge, I saw her at the counter near the sink, with her back to the doorway, exactly as I expected her to be at this time of day. She was holding a long, narrow, wooden rolling pin as she flattened out a lump of dough.

"*Yia sou — Hello*," she said, without turning around to face me. "*Ti kánis, Socrates — How are you?*"

"Good, Ma, and you?" I walked up behind her, put my hand lightly on her shoulder, and kissed her cheek. I could see her smile as I stepped to her side, although her lips never moved. Her smile was in her eyes.

"You have time for coffee, Socrates?" she said. "I just put on a fresh pot. Sit."

"I'll get it, Ma," I said. "You sit. Let me do it for you."

This time I saw her lips smile, although she would never admit to me, if asked, that I gave her pleasure by waiting on her. *Her lips were made for smiles,* I thought. I watched as she briefly became younger.

I poured two cups of coffee, placed them on the table

so we could sit across from one another, and set out two glasses of water. Meanwhile, my mother cut a large piece of *Moussaka* for me although she'd never asked if I was hungry. There are some things a mother's radar always knows without her asking.

We had no sooner settled across from one another when my mother frowned and said, "What's bothering you, Socrates?"

She had read my body language with her usual, unfailing accuracy.

I described my meeting with the Museum's director, using vague, circumspect terms to avoid disclosing confidential information, and told her I was trying to decide if Harte and I should take the case.

My mother wasn't happy with this. She instinctively knew I was hiding something from her.

And, to make it worse, I knew she knew, without her saying so.

"I can't go into the details, Ma, but I've been asked to recover some documents stolen from a museum."

I watched as she worked her way through her usual repertoire of eye rolls, minor shoulder shrugs, and exaggerated sighs — all this as she patiently endured my reticence, and assumed the mantle of motherly martyr, a role she so often and so skillfully recreated for me.

"Oh, Socrates. It sounds just like your Mandarin Yellow fountain pen case you worked on a few years ago. Is that becoming your specialty now, finding stolen things? Can you even make a decent living doing that?"

"It's part of what I do as a PI, Ma, but it's not the same case this time except on the surface. This case is far more complex and potentially more controversial than the other one."

"So what's the problem then?" she said. "If the pay's good, take the case. If the pay's not good, don't take it. It's that simple."

If only it were that simple.

"There are some complications I can't go into," I said, "but they bring aspects to the case I have to come to terms with before I decide what to do, before Harte and I decide what to do, that is."

"Then resolve them, Socrates, and make a decision. If you find out you made the wrong decision, rethink it and move on, but don't just drift. Like I always told you ever since you were a little kid, don't worry so much like you always do. Whatever decision you make, if it's wrong, remember that the worst rarely happens."

That's one of the things I loved about my mother. Not only would she attempt to set me on the right path without knowing the facts, she didn't care that she didn't know them. She never had a problem nudging me in the right direction, as she perceived it to be, nudging me to make a decision, one way or the other.

CHAPTER 8

THIRTY-FOUR YEAR OLD DARRYL POOLE sat on the front lawn of his Arlington, Virginia, single-family detached house drinking Gatorade as he cooled down from his six-mile run.

Poole worked hard keeping himself in top physical condition, running almost every day, watching what food and drink he introduced into his body, working out with weights four days each week, and practicing advanced *Kobudo*, the first thing most mornings, with a Grand Master of this ancient Chinese martial art.

Poole was a computer programming security consultant who hired himself out as a freelance, white-hat hacker specializing in network security. It was his job to act like an unlawful, nefarious hacker, and then find and fix actual or potential security vulnerabilities in his clients' trusted corporate and government computer networks.

He was good at this work, or so it seemed, because when Poole took on a contract he always, without fail, found the network's weakness. At least that was what his clients believed.

On those occasional instances when he was unable to find a vulnerability, Poole would clandestinely insert hostile, malware code into his client's network to create a digital problem, which he would then discover, take steps to quarantine, and, with contrived fanfare, finally eliminate. His clients invariably were grateful to him, having been led to believe by Poole that, thanks to him, they had just dodged a dangerous, if not lethal, digital bullet.

Poole felt free to mess with his clients this way because he didn't care about his computer work or, for that matter, care about his computer-based clients. Computer consulting served one function, and only one, for him. It was his cover.

Poole relied on his network-security projects — his seemingly legitimate cover — to justify his frequent, if unglamorous, travel, his moderate income (being that part of his actual income he reported to the IRS, and did not hide off—shore), and to explain his manner and standard of living, all in anticipation of anyone who might come around and take a look at him.

In the unlikely event that law enforcement agencies, Homeland Security, or the IRS were ever to come snooping, Poole reasoned, he would be able to rationalize his modest lifestyle by pointing to his successful national computer consulting business. His other line of work, his role as a professional contract killer, and the substantial undeclared income he derived from this latter line of work, would remain unknown.

CHAPTER 9

I WAS TIRED WHEN I LEFT my mother so I decided to postpone going back to the office. Instead, I walked to my condo on 22nd Street, near O, to wait for Clotille's call. The files on the thumb drive would have to wait until tomorrow before I would read them again.

Although I hadn't made up my mind about accepting the case for our firm, and wouldn't until I consulted with Harte, and we made a joint decision, I was certainly more interested in the case now than I'd been before, now that my appetite had been whet by the opening entry in the former slave's journal. I had never read anything like that before. I hadn't even known such memoirs by ex-slaves existed.

In the meantime, I thought it might be useful to get a feel for whatever collateral facts I would be dealing with if Harte and I did become involved with the case, so when I arrived home I booted-up my desktop computer, and went online. I started by researching the Golden Knights of the Confederacy and its namesake museum.

My research revealed some interesting information, none of which gave me much comfort, nor motivated me to accept the case. In fact, reading the results of my Google search left me with the feeling I had stepped back in time to a day when narrow-minded, bigoted, all-white male membership organizations were generally accepted as a fact of life, or, subconsciously, were even envied by people who aspired to belong to them, but by definition could not.

What I learned was that the Golden Knights of the Confederacy had been founded in 1867 to preserve, foster, and protect the public image of General Robert E. Lee as the hero of the Confederacy and as a symbol of a genteel, antebellum Southern society that existed, if at all, mostly in the minds of its present-day disciples.

The Golden Knights had been established as an historical lineage organization that used a system of primogeniture to continue and control the purity of its membership. Only eldest sons, who were direct descendants of Robert E. Lee, or who were descendants of a member of Lee's general staff in the Army of Northern Virginia, were eligible for membership. This hadn't changed all these years later.

The organization's museum in Richmond, I learned, was a private museum not open to the public, except by invitation. Only Golden Knights members and their occasional guests were permitted to visit the premises. That explained the absence of typical museum-type trappings I'd noticed on my visit.

The Museum's staff were few in number and were carefully preselected, too, for societal and genealogical purity. The director, I learned, was a longtime employee of the Museum, grandfathered-in for some reason not disclosed online. He did not qualify for membership in the Golden Knights. From what I could tell from my limited research, no staff member had ever done anything that publicly discredited the Museum.

Based on its membership restrictions and composition,

the Golden Knights of the Confederacy was comprised of people I would easily dislike in any other situation, without having to actually meet them. They were people I could readily do without, people who were dedicated to worshiping ancestors who had fought to preserve a repugnant way of life that involved the enslavement and debasement of other human beings. I had no doubt that if members of the Golden Knights were to meet me, they would disparage me as a Chinese/Greek mongrel, not pure American, not pure Greek, not pure Chinese — someone who even the Chinese themselves looked down upon because of my lack of racial purity, someone the Chinese had frequently referred to, when I investigated the case of the missing Mandarin Yellow fountain pen, by the derogatory Mandarin phrase, *low faan*.

Yet I also could see, from my point of view as a private investigator, the challenge that would exist in recovering the stolen documents and preserving the organization's secret about Robert E. Lee's clandestine lineage. That dual endeavor was something I could readily sink my teeth into as a professional challenge, while still despising the Golden Knights and its contrived, antiquated, self-serving ethos.

I shut down my computer and thought about what I'd just learned. I couldn't just glibly dismiss my negative feelings about the Golden Knights and accept their case with the rationalization that it would challenge me professionally. Nor could I unilaterally refuse to accept it. I was getting ahead of myself. I would neither accept nor reject the case — nor could I in all fairness — until I had consulted with Harte. That was our tacit understanding about all new work. That would be my next step in this unappealing, but challenging endeavor.

CHAPTER 10

CALLED CLOTILLE AGAIN. HER SECRETARY said she still was in the same meeting she'd told me about earlier. It was clear I was pushing the limits of the woman's patience so I apologized for bothering her again and decided not to call Clotille again this afternoon. I would wait until the end of the workday when Clotille generally returned her calls. In the meantime, I decided to make good use of my time. I would return to the thumb drive and would read more of the former slave's journal. I headed back to my office.

Before I scrolled to the journal's second entry, I made a few notes about what I'd observed when I first looked through the document. I noted, for one thing, that none of the entries had a date attached to it. Also, the handwritten entries were child-like in appearance — no surprise there — and the grammar, spelling, and syntax were primitive.

I poured myself a glass of wine from a bottle Harte and I kept in the conference room, then scrolled to the second journal entry.

I is writing dese words in the year of de Lawd

1872. I now live in Washington City where I came after de surrender by Massa Robert to the army from up North. I came here to get away from de Ku Kluxers and to search for work. I is in my 65th year after my being birfed.

I found this entry interesting, but innocuous. It gave me a date, however, and therefore some context in which to understand and appreciate the entries, but not anything I could necessarily rely on or in any way use in the investigation. I suspected the rest of the journal might do the same. After all, memories are not static. They fade and evolve with the passing of time, then return as something falsely recollected, rewriting history to suit the world as we preconceive it.

The only way the contents of the journal could possibly be useful to me in the investigation would be if the thief had also read the journal (before the burglary) and for some reason had based his crime on the journal's contents. Why he would do that and, more to the point, how could the contents even have helped him if he'd wanted them to? I couldn't imagine an answer.

I turned the digital page to the third journal entry.

When I was ten years after being birfed I put down my hoe for good like dey told me to do and was taken from de fields and brought to de Great House where I was dressed differently and taught good manners. I also was taught how to serve at de Massa's and Missus' eating table, and how to help other bondsmen and bondswomans who was more older den me. For many years I stood by and held de tray of food or pot of soup while de older bondsmans served de victuals to de Massa and Missus, to my brother Robert, to de Massa and Missus other chillins, and to dere guests at de table.

I liked working in de Great House. I had plenty to eat, clean clothes, and a comfortable room to sleep in with five other housemen.
Another thing I also liked was dat we took baths every Saturday night, put on special clothes, and had our hair combed and picked for lice. On Sunday we housemen also was given a special breakfast in de big room.

While we ate in de big room on Sunday, de Massa and Missus sat in chairs and watched us. I later lernt dat by watching us eat dey could see who was healthy and who was needing fixing by de doctor.

One thing I didn't like was when de Missus used to call us chillins to de Great House to give us a dose of garlic to keep us healthy and make us grow good for de slave sale market in de town knowed as Richmond.

I turned the page to read the next entry.

Another thing I liked about Sunday was we ate biscuits because de womans received dere weeks flour, hams, bacon, lard, cornmeal and coffee on Sunday. De only 'ting I can say about dat is nobody ever goed hungry at dat place, Stratford Hall, while Massa Harry Lee runned it.

We slaves dat ate in de Great House each carried a mussel shell with us to use as a spoon. De Missus did not like us eating with our fingers although I did dat when she weren't around to see me.

Sometimes at night when all de candles was out in de Great House, we housemen would set around de fire out back of the Great House and eat cracked nuts and potators. We'd pick out de nuts with a horseshoe nail and cook dem potators in de ashes until dere skins was brown and crisp like our mamma used to cook dem.

At night we all just went to bed in our rooms in de Great House or our cabins. We wasn't allowed to sing at night. Most of our singing was done in de fields so I never sung again once I moved to de Great House. But sometimes on Sundays we could listen to de white folks singing to de Lawd from outside dere church.

Although de Massa and Missus treated us good, we was not allowed to learn to read and write, although I secretly learnt the alfabet and writing later on, and we couldn't have no paper. I was told dat dis was de law in Virginny. But we was allowed to learn to count, and by de time when de surrender for de war happened I could count numbers on my fingers up to number 100, and also add some numbers together. Dis helped me later when I looked for work in Washington City because I could show de boss man I could make change for customers when dey paid dere bills.

Just as I finished reading these entries, Clotille called.

"Hi, Socrates, you. Sorry I'm so late callin' back. I've been in a meeting all day, me."

Even after more than a year of dating Clotille, I still found her Cajun accent and phrase structure refreshing and cute. In fact, I found it hard not to imitate her when we talked, but I knew she might think I was mocking her if I did that, so I mostly avoided it. Sometimes I couldn't resist.

"No problem," I said. "If you have time to have drinks and dinner tonight, I'd like to see you and talk over a new case I'm thinking of presenting to Harte and possibly taking on."

I had earlier received some good advice from my mother about coming to a decision, and likely also would get helpful advice from Clotille, although, like my mother, she would be advising me with one hand tied behind her back since I could not reveal the salient details of the proposed investigation.

The real test would come in the morning when I called Harte and walked him through the case. Because he and I were partners in the PI business I would disclose everything to him, things I could not disclose to my mother or to Clotille. As far as I was concerned, the confidentiality agreement did not preclude me from discussing all aspects of the case with Harte, my alter ego in the private investigation business.

Because it was close to 5:30 p.m., Clotille and I decided we would meet at her office and walk from there to a nearby restaurant.

CHAPTER 11

Whereas Caleb Livengood became Robert E. Lee, on those days when he assumed the fictive mantel of the Old South's beloved riddle, Caleb moved far away from his daily, drudging function as an auto mechanic at Blankenship's Auto Shop, on West Broad Street in Richmond, and stepped back in time to an imagined glory he readily adopted.

Caleb had become a committed Civil War reenactor although, if you were to ask him, he would say he actually had evolved from being a mere reenactor — a Farb, in the vernacular of reenactors, who did not take reenacting seriously — into the real deal, into what his group called a Hardcore, thanks to the persistence and influence of Celia who, herself, was already a Hardcore when she and Caleb met in rehab.

Caleb demonstrated all the attributes of a Hardcore. When he became Lee, he sought absolute fidelity to the 1860s in his authentic and archaic speech patterns, in his *bona fides* diet, in his personal hygiene, in the clothing he wore, and even in the utensils he used to eat and shave.

On those infrequent times when the re—enactments occurred — as opposed to the two weekends each month when the group drilled and practiced — Caleb wore foul-smelling underwear and socks he never washed between reenactments. His well-brushed General Lee greatcoat sported bronze buttons Caleb had soaked in urine to give them patina. He wore riding boots that looked like Lee's boots and were the General's boot size, but did not fit Caleb since the General's boot size was considerably smaller than Caleb's own. And, to further advance his authentic semblance, he desisted from brushing his teeth for the entire week before the reenactment day until the day after it concluded. His attempts at verisimilitude were supported — indeed, were encouraged — by Celia, who lived her own agenda of authenticity.

All in all, having incorporated the participation of Celia — she re—enacted as a Hardcore field nurse — into his illusion, and having responded to the period-rush his Hardcore semblance of authenticity provided him, Caleb, with each reenactment, experienced his own time-travel high. It sometimes took him days after a field performance to come back down to reality and to emotionally return to his true role as an auto mechanic.

CHAPTER 12

I FIRST MET CLOTILLE WHEN HER father, Ralph Harte
— then a District of Columbia detective on leave
of absence because he'd been wounded in the line of
duty — informally assisted me with my investigation of a
series of crimes that had occurred at the Mount Parnassus
Condominium. Clotille, it turned out, was the illegitimate
by-product of a one-time liaison between Harte and a Cajun
hooker he'd met while he was attending a law enforcement
convention in New Orleans during his rookie year as a cop,
approximately thirty-four years ago. Neither Harte nor his
wife, Rosie, had known about Clotille until she was ten years
old and her Cajun mother had died, leaving a letter in which
she claimed that Harte was Clotille's father. Once Ralph and
Rosie learned about Clotille and had confirmed her mother's
claim with DNA testing, they brought ten year old Clotille
to Washington to live with them, and gradually established
a warm and loving relationship among the three of them.
Eventually Harte and Rosie legally adopted Clotille.

Clotille and I started dating last year shortly after we
met. We've been at it ever since. If there was one hitch in
our otherwise excellent relationship, it was that Clotille was
growing restless with the status quo, that she wanted more

from our arrangement, that she wanted to marry me and have children. Unfortunately, I wasn't yet ready to take that plunge because of some baggage I still carried from an earlier time in my life. I did worry, however, that if I didn't move forward along the path toward marriage, didn't at least make a tangible effort in that regard, I might eventually lose Clotille. I did not want that to happen.

I hooked-up with Clotille on the sidewalk on 21st Street in front of her office building. We hugged so long and so tightly, it seemed we did not need to say anything in greeting one another.

"What are you in the mood for," I said, as if I didn't know. Ever since she moved to Washington, Clotille craved foods she had never had in Cajun country, in New Iberia, Bayou Têche, Louisiana, her home for a good part of her early life. She especially liked Tex-Mex fare, a cuisine Washington offered in abundance.

Clotille blushed. "You know, the same as I always like, me. My all-time favorite." She smiled.

Clotille was right. I did know. I didn't have to ask. Before I could acknowledge what I knew, however, Clotille said, "I would love Mexican, if you don't mind, you. Y'all know I'm always in the mood for a tortilla." She giggled.

I laughed. I had even nicknamed her *Ms. Tortilla*, she craved eating them so often.

We caught a cab to *Cactus Cantina* at Macomb Street and Wisconsin Avenue. Ms. Tortilla would have her Tex-Mex way.

We were seated immediately, snacked on chips and salsa

dip, ordered two Dos Equis XX longnecks, and promptly and silently toasted one another with our beers when they arrived, clinking our bottles together for good measure.

Clotille again held up her bottle, but said this time, "Good health, Darling, you."

"*Yasou — To your health,*" I said in Greek, as I smiled, then once more clinked my bottle against hers.

The waiter stopped by, dropped off menus, then left, giving us a few minutes to read the menus. He soon returned and recited that day's specials. He took our orders and left us alone again.

"I'd like to brainstorm about a case your father and I've been offered," I said.

Clotille nodded, and said, "Okay." She smiled and slowly lifted her beer to her lips. She kept her eyes locked on mine.

I walked Clotille through the gist of my meeting in Richmond and the general sense of the former slave's journal I'd read on the thumb drive, but did not tell her about General Lee's secret or that he even had one. I tried to be as vague as possible to comply with my confidentiality restriction, even as I attempted to convey the general sense of what we would be involved with if Harte and I accepted the case. I described the proposed investigation as a search and recovery case involving some stolen historic documents for a client whose core values profoundly offended me.

"Is there more, Socrates? Something you're not telling me, but I should know if I'm going to be able to help you?"

I said nothing and refused to look into Clotille's eyes. It dawned on me that Clotille, without me saying anything, understood that I would tell her no more for now, yet that I still would look to her for advice.

Clotille stared at me without saying anything. Her gaze was so clear that I realized neither of us was fooled by our shared silence. Nonetheless, we silently agreed that we both would stay in our respective roles until we'd finished with the scene: I would withhold critical information, and we both would act as if I had not.

Clotille finally broke the ice. "It sounds interesting, Socrates, but why are you hesitating to take it on, you? Your instincts usually are good. What bothers you about this case?"

Though her words were light and upbeat, I knew Clotille well enough to know that her expression hid a felt burden I had set upon her. I now regretted having done that, and tried to dance away from this with my candid response.

"I'd be helping an organization I find repugnant. It would be sort of like helping the American Nazi Party recover Goebbels' stolen diary."

Clotille nodded, then became pensive for a few seconds before she shook her head, seemingly reversing the implied message of her previous nod, whatever that message had been. I watched her decide to say nothing, her silence staking out her position on the matter. I was glad I knew her well enough to know when to remain quiet.

For a moment I forgot what we'd been talking about. When I remembered, it was with the uncomfortable realization that I had been hoping that Clotille would justify for me my refusal to come to grips with possibly representing the Golden Knights.

Clotille did not take on my burden.

I marveled at how Clotille, a person who was spontaneous in so many ways, could also lead the highly principled life she led. I stared at her for a few seconds to see if she would say anything. She didn't, so I decided to speak.

"And there's another thing," I said. "Most, if not all, of the investigation would take place in Richmond. I don't know that I want to spend the next few weeks away from you."

Clotille rolled her eyes, a response I've always detested, ever since I first noticed my mother doing it when I was a child. Clotille reached across the table and took my hand. She gently squeezed my fingers. She knew what I was really thinking right now, that I was fond of options and that I wanted to keep them as plentiful as possible.

"Besides," I said, "there's a practical problem, too. I don't know Richmond all that well. I barely know my way around the city. And I don't have any contacts there to look to for help if I need it."

"Okay," Clotille said, producing a long-suffering smile. "Those last things sound like legitimate reasons not to take the case. But that makes me wonder why you've considered taking it at all. Those considerations have been there since the beginning, haven't they?"

I nodded. "True." I could feel my face grow warm.

"What's my father think?" Clotille said.

"Nothing because I haven't brought it up with him yet. I wanted your take on it first to see if you thought I might be overreacting."

The corners of Clotille's mouth turned up in the hint of a smile. "You, Socrates Cheng, overreacting?" She placed her hand on her chest and mimicked a swoon, paused, and then smiled big. I saw that eye roll again. "Do you actually think you could be over-reacting, you?" she said. She giggled and shook her head.

I almost responded with a wise-ass remark, but decided to hold my tongue, to prudently remain silent. I was a man who had learned patience in the household of my Taoist father. I would let Clotille engage in her little theatrical exercise, without any comment by me, because I knew she had my best interests at heart.

She didn't disappoint.

"I think you need to talk with my father, him, about this, and you and Harte make a decision. I can't help you with that." She bobbed her head as if to underscore her point. Then she said, "Let's eat," as she signaled the waiter we were ready to order. The subject was closed for now.

CHAPTER 13

T HE NEXT MORNING, AFTER CLOTILLE left my condo and headed home to shower and change clothes before going to work, I took a short run in Rock Creek Park, showered afterward, and ate a late breakfast. Then I returned to the office and opened the files on the thumb drive to continue reading the former slave's journal.

I won't talk against de Massa and Missus like some cullud folk do now we be freed. Massa and Missus were kind white folk and always treated us slaves good except when they had a reason not to.

One reason to treat us bad was if a cullud done somebody mean and de Massa told him to stop doing dat. If de slave ain't then listened, de Massa sold him. I remember one time a cullud called Patrick sassed de Missus. Massa told Patrick if he did dat again he would put Patrick in his pocket. I axed my mamma how de Massa could put Patrick in his pocket because Patrick was a full growed man. My mamma said dat meant de Massa would sell Patrick and put de money he got from de sale of Patrick into his pocket. Once I learnt what dat saying meant, I never wanted to be put in de Massa's pocket so I was always careful from den on to obey him.

I turned to the next entry.

My mamma married a bondsman named Ned when I was eight years after being birfed. He was a kind man. Ned was not owned by de Massa. He belonged to a man name Culbertson over on a farm not far from our place. Culbertson used to come visit de Massa and Missus, and he would bring some slaves with him. One time, Ned was one of dem slaves he brought.

After dey was married, Ned was allowed to come visit my mamma on Tuesdays and Saturdays if he finished his work at Culbertson's place. When he visited, and him and mamma was done being alone together, Ned secretly taught me de letters in de alfabet and how to write and read words even though culluds was not allowed to learn dis. Ned used a book he brought under his shirt to do lessons from. It was called de New York Primer, whatever dat means. Ned wanted to teach our mamma to read and write de letters, too, but she said no. My mamma, however, did not stop Ned from teaching me, I is glad to say.

A year or more after mamma and Ned married,

our mamma birfed a baby sister for me. Dey
named de baby Anne after de Missus. One day
when Anne was two, Anne took sick with fever
and den went to live with Jesus.

One Tuesday Ned came to be with mamma
like always, but he did not come back de next
Saturday. Den Ned didn't come back to our place
any day after dat. We later heared dat Ned was
sold by Culbertson to a speculator man who took
Ned down south to sell him again. We never did
find out if dis was de troof, but it seemed it was
because we never heared about Ned no more. We
never talked about Ned after dat, mamma and
me.

After Ned was gone, mamma never did marry
again, but she birfed four more chillins, three
girls and one boy. I don't remember their names.

I put aside the journal and retrieved a soda from the
office refrigerator. Then I called Harte, who hadn't come into
the office today, and arranged to meet him for dinner. It was
time to take him through my meeting in Richmond, and to
get his take on the case. We would have to make a decision
soon whether or not we would accept the investigation. I still
was feeling ambivalent about it.

CHAPTER 14

As I was shutting down my computer so I could leave to meet Harte, he called to say he was running behind schedule, that he would meet me an hour later than we'd planned. That was fine with me. I wasn't particularly hungry yet, and I would be happy to use the extra time to sample the other files on the thumb drive, specifically the letters, before returning to Isaiah's journal. It might help to have a rounded picture of the various files when I met with Harte.

I started with the first letter written by Elizabeth Van Lew — the woman the Museum's director had called scurrilous — to her friend Philomena Clarke in Philadelphia, Pennsylvania. There were three Van Lew letters on the thumb drive.

April 07, 1869
My Dear Friend, Philomena,

How nice it was for me to receive your letter this Tuesday past. I am happy you and your family are in good health.

I must above all else apologize for my neglect

of our friendship these past several years after the Rebellion was brought to a happy end in Richmond by General Grant. Since that otherwise felicitous occurrence, my life and the lives of my dear mother and stalwart brother have gone through many unhappy vicissitudes. But now, I am glad to report to you, our lives have begun to repair themselves and even improve thanks to my friend and patron, President Grant, who, having taken the highest federal office himself just a few weeks ago, recently appointed me to be the Post Mistress of the City of Richmond.

Although I did not respond to your four caring letters you sent me by covert carrier during the Rebellion, I saved them and I reread them this morning. I will try to respond to your questions in this and subsequent letters. Hopefully, you will recall your former questions when you read my responses in my letters to you.

I am content now with my life as I grow older, and do not regret what I did during the Rebellion or dwell on the villainous actions of my neighbors near the end of and immediately after that time. We all did what we believed to be right at the time, and I leave it in the hands of the Almighty to decide whether my path during the Rebellion was the righteous one or if my neighbors' paths were the righteous ones.

I paused in my reading, fetched a beer, and then returned to my computer to finish Van Lew's first letter.

You asked me in your last letter why I became a spy for the Union while living in Richmond. The reasons were many and complicated, but in the end, I remained loyal to our country because of the values I learned as a young girl. Specifically, dear Philomena, I took up the cause of the Union because of the beliefs instilled in me when, as an adolescent, I attended the Quaker Meeting school in Philadelphia with you and your lovely cousin, Charlotte. As you might recall, too, when my father died before the Rebellion, my brother, John, and I freed the nine slaves our father had left to John in his Last Will and Testament. This act on our part did not please our Richmond friends and neighbors, but there was nothing they could do about it. Most of the slaves we freed stayed on with us in our home as paid servants and friends.

Because John and I believed slavery was a blight upon this Earth, not a condition sanctioned by the Lord, we hoped the Union would prevail against the Confederacy in the Rebellion. And so my dear friend, I tried to help the Union's cause in every way I could, first by bringing food and writing supplies to Union military prisoners captured by the rebels and held at Libby Prison in Richmond, and also by offering these prisoners such material comfort as I otherwise could.

Occasionally I learned useful military information — such as rebel troop movements when I visited the prison. I wrote this information I learned in a cipher I'd created, and hid the papers in empty egg shells I glued back together. I then smuggled the egg shells down the James River to Aiken's Landing where I passed them on to Captain Moses Bagley, the Master of the Flag-of-Truce boat, the *New York*. Captain Bagley carried the egg shells and the information they contained to Fortress Monroe. After that, I don't know how the papers traveled, but after the Rebellion General Grant told me that the information I sent was critical to his ability to seize Richmond and the peninsular area.

I checked my watch. I wouldn't have to leave to meet Harte for another twenty minutes. I continued reading Van Lew's first letter.

One of the slaves John and I set free before the Rebellion was a young mulatto named Mary Bowser. She not only was a great aid to me in furthering my clandestine activities on behalf of General Grant, but Mary also instilled much colored-folks' lore in my head, including the secret story of General Lee's true birthright.

At first I couldn't believe what Mary told me, but as time went on other freedmen and their freedwomen living in Richmond confirmed the information for me.

I must end this letter now as I have work to do in my very busy job as Post Mistress. More from me later about Mary Bowser and this interesting topic in my next letter.

Your dear friend,
Bet

I still had some time before I would meet Harte, so I turned to another file on the thumb drive.

CHAPTER 15

ONTRACT KILLERS, NO MATTER HOW outwardly adjusted and congenial they might appear to be in their other, non-working lives, are nothing more than certifiable psychopaths, serial killers by another name, who murder their fellow humans for pay.

They wear many stripes, but underneath their skins, contract killers share certain characteristics.

They might appear to be detached from emotions and to be pragmatic as they perform actions that would horrify most people, but there is nothing detached and practical about them. Peel away the many layers of their skins, peak into the primitive lizard depths of their brains, and you will find someone who is driven by rage.

Hit men — and hit women, for that matter, for there are many hit women, too — use a variety of weapons to perform their work. In many cases, the choice is dictated by the circumstances of the kill — the ease of getting the weapon to the target, the likelihood of avoiding detection when using the weapon, and the ease of escaping after the kill.

In some instances the choice of weapon is dictated by the personality of the assassin. Like all working tradespeople, each hitter has his or her favorite tools, depending on the nature and circumstances of the contract assignment. Some contracts require that the hitter execute the contract at a remote distance from the mark, yet the contractor might still want to see the kill occur. These are hitters who derive pleasure from the very act of killing. In those cases, the hitter might use a sniper rifle to distance himself, while still observing the takedown.

In other instances the hitter might want to be as far away from the target as he can be at the time of the kill, and might not want to see the kill occur. These hitters seem to enjoy the process of devising the means of popping their target, the cognitive operation of puzzling-out how to implement the hit, more than they enjoy the act of killing itself. These contractors tend to use a remotely detonated explosive device or a time bomb, or, sometimes, a slow acting poison to fulfill their assignments.

Other contractors savor not only the process of setting up their kills, but also enjoy the very act of killing itself, and crave immediate, even tactile, participation in the event. These hitters prefer to do their work up close and personal. Their means of performing the kill and their weapons of choice, among others, might be a knife or their hands or a ligature — both for strangulation or to break the mark's neck — or a plastic bag to throw over the target's head to use to suffocate the target.

Sometimes these contractors use a small caliber handgun at close range, placing the first bullet behind the mark's ear, and the next two in the mark's chest. In short, these contract killers use any weapon that will enable them to be close to the target when they perform their kill.

Darryl Poole was flexible. He almost always let the

circumstances of the contract determine his choice of tool to use. Poole didn't care if he performed the hit close up or long distance. He didn't care if he saw the mark die or not. His concern was always to make the kill, fulfill the contract, escape undetected, and collect his fee.

Yet he, too, had favorite weapons.

Poole's preferred array of tools for close work were a piano wire garrote, a two-edged throwing dagger, sometimes a slim stiletto, or a small, Ruger Mark II .22-caliber semi-automatic revolver.

For distance work, he favored a H-S Precision Pro Series 2000 HTR long—range sniper rifle with a telescopic sight — the sniper's weapon of choice used by the Israeli Defense Forces. When all else failed, although it rarely did, Poole fell back on his most intimate weapon — his bare hands — which he used silently and quickly to dispatch his target, just as he had learned to do in his advanced *Kobudo* classes.

Poole also used other weapons from time to time to avoid creating a signature that could be established by authorities and ultimately traced back to him. To do otherwise would be stupid and, likely, deadly for him. So, in one instance, Poole had resorted to folding ground glass into a fancy dessert favored by the mark. On another occasion he'd used his computer programming and hacking skills to cause a heavy garage door to come down on his mark and crush her chest, suffocating her. And another time he used the heel of his right palm to forcefully flatten his target's nose, sending bone shards deep into the mark's prefrontal cortex, killing him.

Poole prided himself on his flexibility.

CHAPTER 16

I NOW TURNED BACK TO ISAIAH'S journal, and set aside
Elizabeth's two remaining letters to read later.

There never was no whippin' done at our place
except for one time I remember good like it just
happened. De Massa had a cullud overseer named
Jim dat was de meanest devil ever lived, far as
I knowed. Massa and Missus never allowed Jim
to beat us slaves except one time when de slave
Samuel runned away from our place. He was
caught after three days by de hounds and mens,
and brought back to be punished.

All us slaves was marched to de back of de Great
House to stand around and watch Samuel be
whipped. Massa Robert was der in de back of our
place, too, up on his horse looking down at all of
us. He said we was to watch de punishment to
make a lesson what would happen to de rest of us
if we ever runned away.

De overseer Jim laid de lashes with a whip on
Samuel's bare back until Samuel was covered with

blisters and swelled up like a dead horse two days gone. Den dat Jim put down his whip and beat dem blisters with a cat—o—nine tails, breaking dem blisters and making dem bleed something awful. When de cullud Jim was done with dis, dat Jim picked up a bucket of salt water and throwed de water on Samuel's bloody back. Samuel screamed with dat pain, den he passed out. He looked daid to me.

Before he sayed we should all go back to work, Massa Robert gathered us up in a group and stood in front of us up on his horse. He told us to remember de lesson we learnt dat day by watching, and what would happen to us if any of us slaves tried to run away. Then Massa Robert rode off on his horse around de corner of the Great House until we couldn't see him no more.

After dat, no other culluds runned away from de Massa and Missus dat I can remember. We never even wanted to try because we was afraid of de whip and because we was afraid we might not be able to take as good care of us selves away from our place as de Massa and Missus did for us. We didn't know what would happen to us if we was off our place.

This entry stunned me by its matter—of—fact description of a bone—chilling beating. I needed to rest my emotions before I continued with the journal, so I put this file aside and turned back to Elizabeth Van Lew's letters.

CHAPTER 17

ARRYL POOLE SAT AT HIS kitchen table drinking coffee and pondering a contract he'd just been offered by his Richmond—based handler, the elderly, gray-haired, very plump woman he called, for reasons he no longer remembered, Aunt Marge.

Ordinarily, Poole would have reflexively turned down this contract without any other consideration because the target lived and worked in Washington, DC, and this was too close to home to suit him. He had always lived by the credo that you never perform a hit in or nearby the city where you live or where you work your cover job. Too many things could go wrong as you set up the kill, got close to the target, performed the contract, and then escaped. But these were not prosperous economic times, even for contract killers, so he did not dismiss Aunt Marge's proposal out—of—hand.

Fortunately, he thought, *the mark isn't a well-known or influential politician or a high-level federal employee, so killing her shouldn't create extra pressure on the local cops to solve the case. It would probably go okay.* This was exactly how Marge had rationalized the assignment when explaining it to him.

The mark was an unmarried female who lived alone and taught tenth grade at Woodrow Wilson High School in the District. If he did his job well, the schoolteacher's death would be ruled an unsolved homicide resulting from a mugging gone bad.

Poole poured a second cup of coffee, broke off a piece of the apple tart he'd been holding, and planted it in his mouth. His gesture reminded him that even hitters had to work to eat. He would reluctantly accept Aunt Marge's home-field contract.

CHAPTER 18

OPENED ELIZABETH VAN LEW'S SECOND letter. It, too, was addressed to her girlhood friend in Philadelphia, Philomena Clarke.

My dear friend, Philomena,

I felt much better after mailing my recent letter to you because I know I am taking steps to repair our injured friendship which resulted from my neglect of you. As I write these words, I look forward to unburdening myself to you and, then hopefully, visiting you in November after the passing of the Yellow Fever season in Philadelphia.

To pick up where I left off in my prior letter, when the Rebellion ended in 1865, my mother, brother and I were destitute, having spent all our resources to purchase and free slaves and to provide food, medicine and other necessities to Union prisoners held at Libby Prison.

Just before General Grant took possession of the

city, my neighbors and former friends assembled in the front yard before our home and threatened to burn it to the ground. They did this because of the aid my family and I had rendered to the Union cause, and because I had run a United States flag up the pole in front of our house in anticipation of General Grant's imminent arrival.

As the mob became more and more unruly and the shouts to burn down our house became more frequent, I walked out onto the second floor veranda overlooking the front lawn and faced the mob. I pointed to various people and shouted, "I know you, and you, and you," and so forth, and added "If you set our house afire, when my friend General Grant arrives in the city, I will tell him you were involved, and he will burn your homes to the ground."
That mollified the mob who cursed my mother, brother and me, but they then dispersed without doing us or our home any harm.

When a few days later General Grant entered Richmond, he came to our home for tea and thanked me for the information I had passed to him during the Rebellion, and for the flowers I occasionally sent him from our garden when he besieged the city.

I am growing tired, Philomena, so I will bring this letter to an end. I will write again in a few days.

I want to tell you what happened when I went to Washington to tell President Lincoln what our friend Mary Bowser had told me about Robert E. Lee's secret. You will be shocked when I tell you what the secret is. I know I was shocked.

Your dear friend,
Bet

Bet I was anxious to turn to Elizabeth's last letter to learn what occurred when she went to Washington and told Lee's secret to Lincoln, but I realized I had to leave to meet Harte. The letter would have to wait. I shut down my computer, locked the thumb drive in my desk drawer, turned out the lights in the office, and set the office's burglar alarm. Then I left to meet my partner.

CHAPTER 19

HARTE AND I HAD AGREED to meet at *Stan's*. As I reached the last step down from the sidewalk my cellphone rang. I looked at the CallerID readout. Harte was calling.

"Sorry to do this to you, but I have to cancel."

"No problem," I said. "What's up?"

"I've been painting my living room all day and the fumes have gotten to me. I feel like hell. I need to go to bed and sleep it off."

"We'll reschedule when you're back at the office," I said.

I turned around and climbed back up the steps to the sidewalk. I decided to return to the office to continue reading the thumb drive's files.

I headed toward the office, walking along the L Street corridor, heading toward 18th Street, flanked on both sides by darkened, closed, and mostly empty office buildings. L Street was deserted except for an occasional vehicle that raced by. An errant page from the *Washington Post* blew against my leg and wrapped itself around my calf as I walked.

I'd covered two blocks when I developed the feeling someone was following me. I slowed my pace and listened for footsteps, but didn't hear anything, not even the sound of the wind any longer as it tunneled along the cavernous street. It was as if the air, too, had paused to listen.

I was spooked by the quiet emptiness of the avenue, but I sucked in my breath, dismissed my instincts, and trudged silently on.

I walked another block and, although I heard no one behind me, I still couldn't shake the feeling someone was there. I abruptly turned and looked back, but again saw no one. I drew in a slow, deep breath, held it briefly, then let it seep out between my clenched teeth for a very long four seconds. This well—practiced Taoist exercise should have calmed me, but did not.

When I reached 18th Street, I turned right to walk north to Dupont Circle, but before I left L Street I dropped to one knee, pretended to tie my shoe, and furtively glanced around. Again, I didn't see anyone. Either my imagination was playing tricks on me or the person following me was a pro.

I didn't think my imagination was playing with me.

CHAPTER 20

WHEN I ARRIVED BACK AT the office, I poured myself two fingers of single-malt Scotch, then set up the thumb drive so I could continue reading the letters. As much as I wanted to continue with Elizabeth Van Lew's letters and find out what had happened when Van Lew told Lincoln about Lee's secret, I knew I needed to sample Mistress Anne's letters to round out my picture of what the case might involve. If I finished Anne's letter early enough, I then would read the last Van Lew letter before calling it a night.

The digitized folder titled ANNE CARTER LEE contained seventeen letters, each numbered as a separate sub—file.

I opened each sub—file and skimmed its letter to develop an overview of them.

Anne Carter Lee had written the letters to her oldest son, Charles, when he was living in Boston and she was living in Fairfax County, Virginia. Most were written in 1829, near the end of her life. The letters all had a breathless, confessional, almost remorseful tone to them. At this point I didn't know much about Anne Carter Lee except that, according to accepted tradition, she was Light—Horse Harry Lee's wife and Robert E. Lee's mother.

Before I turned to the letters themselves, I decided to learn more about Anne so I could read the letters in a meaningful context. I went online and brought up Google's search engine. I entered Anne's name in the search box and launched my inquiry.

I learned that Anne had been the daughter of one of Virginia's most prominent and wealthy colonial families, and that she had grown up near Richmond at Shirley Plantation, on the south side of the James River.

As a young child, and even later as a young woman, Anne had not been physically strong, She'd suffered from the condition we now recognize as narcolepsy. As a result, Anne lived most of her life with the chronic fear of being mistaken for dead when she had a spell, and then being buried alive. This had happened to her when she was eleven years old, but she'd been rescued in time to save her life and prevent her premature burial. But the emotional damage had been done. This manifested itself in various forms of melancholia and hypochondria that afflicted Anne for the rest of her life.

Anne and Light—Horse Harry married in 1793. It was his second marriage, but Anne's first. Lee was thirty—seven years old; Anne was twenty.

Their first child, Algernon Sydney, died when he was fourteen months old. After his death, Anne gave birth to five other children — including, according to plantation tradition, Robert Edward. She and Harry named these children Charles, Sydney, Anne, Robert, and Mildred, all of whom lived beyond infancy.

Plantation lore also had it that after the death of Algernon Sydney, Anne developed a condition that today's physicians would call postpartum depression, or what lay people sometimes referred to as the postpartum blues. But in the late eighteenth and early nineteenth centuries, Anne's condition was neither diagnosed, named, nor treated. As a result, although she gave birth to other children after Algernon Sydney's death, Anne's unhealthy fixation on her first infant persisted, her emotional deterioration continued, and her hypochondria increased in scope and severity.

In 1807, Light—Horse Harry, likely at his wits—end over his wife's steadily failing health and spirits, suggested to Anne that they raise as their own child the white—appearing twin fathered by Harry with his Stratford Hall concubine slave. He suggested that he and Anne act for all purposes as if Anne had herself given birth to the light-skinned boy.

Anne resisted at first, but Harry persisted. Eventually, Anne agreed. They named the infant Robert Edward. Robert's twin brother, his mixed—blood, slightly darker, mulatto twin — a boy their biological slave mother had named Isaiah — was left by Light—Horse Harry and Anne to work in the fields with his and Robert's biological mother.

Satisfied I now knew or surmised enough about Anne to read her letters in some meaningful way, I closed Google and read her first letter.

June 16, 1829
My dear son, Charles,

I regret I have not written to you sooner in answer to your most recent letter, but I have not been well.

I trust that you continue to find the city called

Boston agreeable to you, and have no regrets in having settled there, so far from your mother and siblings, to raise your own family. I recently relocated from my home in Georgetown to Ravensworth in Fairfax County, thanks to the kindness of the widow of William Henry Fitzhugh.

Dr. Farnsworth, a prominent local physician, visited me today to treat my melancholy and my uncontrollable shivering, a condition the doctor called the ague. To do this, Dr. Farnsworth spent the otherwise lovely afternoon bleeding me. Unfortunately, the leeches have left me very weak, and so this missive to you must be brief.

I have much to tell you as I fear the end of my days is near, and I wish so much we were together to talk. But since your choice of habitation means we cannot be together, I intend to write several letters to you over the next few weeks, such as my failing health will permit, being letters that will disclose and explain to you a certain family secret that never has been revealed before to you, but which you, as the eldest son among my loving children, should be aware of. So you know, your father, were he alive, would forbid me from disclosing this secret to you.

I must finish this letter now and give it to the slave boy Phillip who will place it with the driver of Van Horne's stage to begin to carry my letter on its journey to you.

Please write at your earliest convenience. Until next time, I remain,

Your loving mother

CHAPTER 21

C ALEB, CELIA, AND THE ELEVEN other active members of their re—enactment group regularly met on the second Friday of each month at the home of one of the members. The practice was for the hosting member to provide a light meal and drinks for everyone, and to give a presentation with respect to some aspect of the Civil War or with regard to some aspect of reenacting. The group was congenial for the most part, and tolerated novice as well as experienced reenactors, although, thanks to the influence of Caleb and Celia, the group had gradually weeded-out the so-called pretenders and dilettantes — the Farbs — and retained as members only genuine reenactors — the Hardcores — and others still less sanctioned by the group, but who aspired to become Hardcores.

This month's meeting was hosted by one of the newer members of the group, Janet Bonnard. She presented a PowerPoint talk she called *Authenticity vs. Convenience in Reenacting.* This was the type of topic generally eschewed by the group because it invariably led to heated arguments between the novice reenactors and the Hardcores, causing the precarious façade of goodwill that cloaked the divisions among the members to be in danger of being wrested from the group, breaking-up the meeting.

Janet's talk addressed recent scholarship concerning such matters as the cloth used to make period-like underwear and jackets, and used to recreate authentic-looking trouser buttons. She also spoke about the dye used by the Confederacy for officers' uniforms.

Much to Caleb's amusement, Janet's talk gave rise to a heated argument between Celia and a new member of the group who had the temerity to state that allegiance to authenticity in reenacting was merely a narcissistic, compulsive conceit. Celia fumed and argued heatedly, but eventually held her tongue when Caleb shook his head, almost imperceptibly, to reign her in, to preserve the group.

Janet Bonnard's talk provoked two other debates which followed expected lines of argument. First, the Farb reenactor vs. Hardcore dispute, in general, and second, the usual question concerning how strict should a Hardcore's adherence to authenticity be? Put another way: how hardcore should a Hardcore be, to be considered an authentic Hardcore?

Celia participated in both these debates, too, with practiced and predictable vigor and scorn, but not to the point of causing the group to irrevocably select sides. But she yielded no ground to those who argued that the group's standards were too high and unnecessary. There was no doubt in anyone's mind who heard her. Celia, beyond any doubt, was a Hardcore.

CHAPTER 22

FTER READING ANNE CARTER LEE'S first letter to her son, Charles, I turned to Elizabeth Van Lew's next letter to learn what happened when she visited Abraham Lincoln.

My dear friend, Philomena,

Did I mention in my previous letters that shortly before the Rebellion ended Mary Bowser, my father's and brother John's former slave, told me — and other bondsmen and bondswomen later confirmed for me on other occasions — that General Lee actually was a light-skin cullud who passed for white? Can you believe that! The nerve! Moreover, General Lee was one of a twin set of cullud brothers born in Virginia at Stratford Hall, but he had been taken from his cullud mammy and raised as their own in the Great House by Light-Horse Harry Lee and his wife Anne Carter Lee. Mary Bowser swore before me on our family bible that this story was true. I have no reason to doubt her as Mary Bowser is a woman of great integrity, and I do not believe she knowingly would lie to me.

When I learned this information I talked to my brother about it. John and I decided I should immediately go to Washington City to tell President Lincoln this information so he could use it for the Union cause.

I made my way from home to Aiken's Landing where I boarded the Flag—of—Truce boat *New York*, and steamed to Fortress Monroe. From there I made my way to Washington City and eventually presented myself at the White House. After an almost six hour wait in line to see Mr. Lincoln, I met with him and a Mr. Stanton and a Mr. Seward, both who Mr. Lincoln called for after I told him my story. Mr. Lincoln asked me to repeat the story for these gentlemen, which I respectfully did.

Mr. Lincoln and these two men consulted together after swearing me to secrecy and telling me to wait in an outer office with a Mr. John Hay who said he was Mr. Lincoln's private secretary.

Mr. Hay was a polite young man. We chatted while I waited to be called back into Mr. Lincoln's office. He told me that his primary job for Mr. Lincoln was to answer letters for him.

After a while, Mr. Lincoln called me back into

his office and said I had done a great service for the country, but that he would not reveal or use the information I'd brought him because the Rebellion was winding down, and the information was too incendiary to spread around at that time. I could understand that and was not bothered by this wise man's decision.

Mr. Stanton made me sign a legal paper saying I would not tell anyone about the information I told to the President until after the Rebellion was long finished. The paper didn't say how long after I should wait, and I wasn't comfortable enough to ask, so I signed the paper anyway, not knowing. I suppose enough time has gone by now so that I am permitted to tell you, and I do not regret doing so in this letter.

I was required to raise my right hand, too, and swear before the Almighty to keep the information secret. Mr. Lincoln said that if I broke my word, the country would suffer. Mr. Stanton said if I told, I would go to prison. I promised not to reveal this information to anyone until long after the war. Mr. Stanton gave me a safe-conduct travel pass to Baltimore, and another to Richmond, so I could go home safely.

I left Washington City by steamboat to go to Baltimore which, as you probably know, remained in the hands of the Union in spite of all the Rebel sympathizers living there. From Washington we sailed up the Potomac River to Chesapeake Bay, and then up the Patapsco River into Port Baltimore. The trip, I am happy to say, was uneventful, and the sea air refreshing.

From Baltimore I hired a carriage that took me to Point of Rocks, Maryland, where I was introduced to a Mr. J. B. Dutton, the local postmaster, I think. Mr. Dutton gave me a pack of letters and asked me to give them to a Mr. French when I arrived back in Richmond, so Mr. French could mail them to people in those states still in Rebellion.

In return for the favor he asked of me concerning the rebel-sympathizers' letters (sympathizers he told me he did not agree with, thereby causing him to have to flee from his home across the river — Waterford, Virginia — over to Point of Rocks), Mr. Dutton, after night fell, rowed me across the Potomac River to Waterford where, the next morning, I boarded a passenger stage to Richmond. I was exhausted when I arrived home later the next day.

Although Mr. Dutton had done me a kind service, and I took the letters and placed them in my valise as Mr. Dutton asked, I chose not to give the enemies' letters to Mr. French when I arrived in Richmond. Instead, I placed them in my desk drawer where they remain unopened to this day.

I felt I had done my duty for my country by bringing General Lee's secret to Mr. Lincoln, so I set it aside in my head and did not think much about it again until recently.

I have more to write, but my present duties as Post Mistress call. I will try to write more to you tomorrow night.

Your friend,
Bet

That, unfortunately, was Elizabeth Van Lew's last letter on the thumb drive.

CHAPTER 23

SINCE I HAD FINISHED READING all of Elizabeth Van Lew's letters, I returned to Isaiah's journal.

Some bad change come over de Massa and Missus when I be 11 or 12 years since being birfed. De Massa began selling furniture and tools and land from our place. I heared later de Massa owed money he could not pay to other white mens. I worried he might decide to put us in his pocket to fix his problems. I was right to worry.

One day de Massa sold three of us slaves to speculators who, everybody said, took dem slaves south to Loosiana to sell dem again. Dat put de fear of de Lawd in me dat de Massa might sell me or sell my mamma. De Massa soon sold off all of de slaves dat worked in de fields and some of de house boys too, but de Massa did not sell me or my mamma, I is happy to say.

After a time, de Massa moved his family and de house slaves he still owned, including me, but not my mamma, to Alexandria, Virginny. He loaned my mamma to some massa at another place and sayed if ever we moved back to our place, my mamma would move back too. For reasons I never knowed, after three years at dat place, we all moved back to our place at Stratford Hall. My mamma moved back too like de Massa sayed. It was good to be home again at our place.

From the contents of the thumb drive, it seems that Isaiah, for some reason, did not write in his journal during the three years he and the Lee family lived in Alexandria. His next entry occurred after the family moved back to Stratford Hall.

After our return to our place, de Massa's new overseer, a kindly man named Clement, rounded up some of us culluds, made us take baths and pick de lice from our heads, and gave us different clothes to wear instead of our usual ones. Der was three mens I didn't know, four womans, me, and my friend, William. We all wondered why we was being treated so special.

After a time, de overseer Clement told us to get in de wagon. Massa Robert came with us up on his horse. We was drove to de town of Richmond in Virginny, and taken to a place de cullud folk called de Devil's Half—Acre.

We was kept at dis place, the Devil's Half—Acre, a

long time until we was moved to an auction place near de river knowed as de James. Dat's when one of de womans, Sally, told us she knowed where we was because she was here before with another massa before our Massa byed her. Dis woman Sally sayed we was at de slave market called Shockoe Bottom. Dat was when I knowed what was going on without nobody telling me. We was going to be sold and put in de Massa's pocket.

I was scared real much. All I could think about was dat some speculator man would buy me and sell me down south so I would never see my mamma again.

After we arrived at Shockoe Bottom, we was treated like hogs at market. We was all put in a room called de pen, mens and womans together, and waited to see what would happen to us. De walls of de pen was more than twice as tall as de mens were when de mens was standing up straight by dem walls. Der was three windows in de pen, but dey was too high to see outside from inside and der was iron bars on de windows.

It was hard to breathe in de pen der was so many slaves in der. I counted seventy-eight mens and boys and twenty-two womans and girls, all in de pen.

De pen smelled from sweat, shit, pee, and something I

was told was called lye dat was brought in and thrown on de floor from a bucket. I didn't ever see dat happen, but I guess from de smell of de pen it did happen.

I needed a short break from this. Isaiah's writings were too intense. I left the journal and went to the office refrigerator to get a beer and some cheese.

CHAPTER 24

Darryl Poole sat across the street from the faculty parking lot at Woodrow Wilson High School and watched the schoolteacher leave the building and enter her Toyota Tercel. He followed her home — a four—mile drive — and watched as she street-parked her vehicle, then entered the front door of the Cairo, a stately building originally constructed as a residential hotel and rental property in 1894, but now operated as a residential condominium. The Cairo was located on Q Street, NW, between 15th and 16th Streets.

According to the dossier prepared for him by Aunt Marge, the forty-three-year-old spinster-teacher owned a one bedroom condominium apartment, and had lived there since the early 1990s when the building was renovated and converted from a rental property to condos.

Based on Aunt Marge's dossier and his observations of the mark, Poole decided he would kill the schoolteacher somewhere within the confines of the Cairo, using her personal habits and, therefore, using her predictability, to reach her.

Poole did not know why the schoolteacher was the object of

the contract, and he didn't care. It wasn't his business to know or to care. His job was to carry out the contract and earn his fee. Nothing else.

He also didn't know who it was who wanted the schoolteacher dead, and was willing to pay to bring that about. As a professional hitter, Poole never met the client or learned the client's identity. That was the role of his handler, who acted as the broker of contracts between the client and Poole, thereby providing them both with some measure of security from discovery through their shared anonymity. The accepted business arrangement was that Aunt Marge would find the job, set the price, compile a dossier on the mark, collect the payment, and pay Poole his fee, less her administrator's cut.

What Poole did know about the schoolteacher was the information contained in the dossier, as well as such additional information as he learned by watching her before he made his move to fulfill the contract. All this was intended to assist him in formulating his plan to reach his target, kill her, and then to make his escape undetected.

CHAPTER 25

I WAS UNCOMFORTABLE WITH WHAT I'D just read in Isaiah's journal and with what I anticipated might come next, so I took my time and finished half my beer before continuing with Isaiah's account of the slave auction.

I settled into my seat in front of the computer and knocked off the screen saver. The journal popped right up.

> After a while, we mens was told to take off all our clothes and stand neked, even though womans and girls was der looking. Den we was made to stand one at a time on a table called de block while traders examined us all over, including our privates. Our arms and legs was touched and squeezed. Our throats, tooths, heads and necks was looked at and poked. Den we each was told to climb back down from de block and walk back and forth. Then some of the mens was taken back to de pen, someone told me later when I axed, because dey'd had too much scars from whipping by dere massas, and could not be selled. Dey was de lucky ones even though dey'd been beaten many times before dat day.

Next de womans and girls was examined while de mens and boys was still der looking on. In addition to dere heads, tooths, throats and necks, de womans and girls was made to lift dere dresses up above dere privates while traders looked at dem with dere faces close to the womans and girls bodies. Dey squeezed da womans and girls ankles, legs, and hind parts. I watched, too, as de white mens touched and squeezed de womans and girls bosoms, and de traders had a big laugh with de other mens der. Some of de womans and girls was told to undo dere dresses and slip dem off dere shoulders down to dere waists, and was given what de traders said was a special examination of de womans and girls bosoms. I looked at first, but was embarrassed for dem womans and girls, so I turned my eyes away after dat first time.

After a while passed, William, me, two girls, one woman, and one man from our place was took back to de pen. I don't know what happened to de others but I later heared dat dey was sold dat day.

After a long time goed by, Massa Robert and dat overseer Clement took us in our wagon from de pen back to our place. I was feelin' good because I weren't selled dat day. Isaiah's next entry reflected the most profound change yet to come over the household.

Shortly after my 14th year from being birfed, de

Massa came back from a trip and died. His oldest son Charles became de new massa at our place.

This was Isaiah's last entry describing the period before the Civil War ended. He had become curiously silent. It was not, however, his last entry in the journal.

CHAPTER 26

C ALEB AND CELIA WERE PUMPED. This weekend was one of those weekends they and their Friday night group lived for, the culmination of all their monthly meetings, lectures, and self-imposed privations, the ever-anticipated yield of their weekend drills in the field.

Caleb and Celia were pumped because the group's members would be assembling in the morning at a four-hundred acre farm in Frederick County, Maryland, and drilling through Sunday night in a full battle dress rehearsal to prepare for the upcoming reenactment of the battle at Antietam, Maryland, the deadly one day engagement that brought Lee's first incursion into the North to a bloody end. This battle was called the battle of Sharpsburg by the South.

Other than full-field dress reenactments, such as the one for Antietam, occasional weekend drills were what most members yearned for. At least the Hardcores did. No one could be sure about the few Farbs still polluting the group.

The weekend drills offered participants all the pleasures of an actual reenactment, but without the loss of control over their own actions that necessarily accompanied an actual battle portrayal with its concomitant integration of disparate reenactor groups, and the complexity of such engagements.

Full dress rehearsal drills, such as the one this weekend, took on all the solemnity and rigor of an organized reenactment which, itself, always strove for strict adherence to the actual military engagement, as portrayed in contemporary newspapers and in history books.

Caleb and Celia, as usual, were the first to arrive at the farm. They put away their gear, then waited to inspect each participant for authenticity as each arrived. Caleb's and Celia's decision with respect to the acceptability of any artifact or like matter concerning authenticity was final among their group. There was no appeal.

Their inspections were rigorous, unforgiving, and sometimes arbitrary. Their goal was to weed out and eliminate anything on the person of a participant that could be viewed as modern or, at least, post mid—1860s. Caleb and Celia checked bedrolls, food, shoes and boots, Union suits — to be sure they were authentically two pieces, not one — shirts, and belt buckles. Celia was more strict and less forgiving than Caleb when it came to confiscating occasional non-conforming goods and items.

Toothpaste and tooth brushes were taboo. So-called *new* food was prohibited. Apples had to be small and gnarled, not modern contrivances such as Fuji or Honeycrisps. Knives and canteens were inspected to determine if they were old or, at the least, were true replicas, not Target-store pristine. Corn cob pipes and chewing tobacco were welcome. Factory-made cigarettes or cigars were not.

People who did not seek authenticity were discouraged from attending the drills and, later, the reenactments. They were as anathema to Caleb and Celia as were the elitists who pretended to care about the Old South, but instead ran private Confederate museums, and belonged to organizations, such as the Golden Knights of the Confederacy, not open to the common foot soldier and his descendants.

"Morning, Sarge," the reenactor said, as he arrived at the farm and walked up to Caleb for inspection. "Reportin' for duty."

"Morning, Private," Caleb said. He eyeballed the private from head to foot, looking for obvious contraband. He made a mental note that the private was as gaunt as before, commendably intent on replicating with his own body the plight of hungry, often starving Confederate soldiers during the war. Losing weight and remaining emaciated for Hardcores endured among the group as an obsession and mark of honor.

"Empty your rucksack, Soldier," Caleb said, "and your grub outfit so I can inspect you and your food." He rifled through the disgorged contents of the private's food kit and rucksack, found nothing objectionable, then cast the private a satisfied nod.

"First drill's in twenty minutes," Celia said, looking over at the young man, as she inspected another arriving soldier. "You'd better put away your gear at the bivouac and step on it, Private."

When the final drill was completed, the men stacked their muskets and assembled around the campfires to cook their meals, consisting of cornbread, a slab of bacon, unsalted peanuts, and burnt coffee. The few women who attended in the guise of field nurses or camp followers joined them. As they ate, everyone joined in an elaborate critique of that day's practice drill.

Like the men and women of the 1860s, the drill participants went to sleep soon after dusk, arranging themselves into two groups — men and women. And, like their models of old, each group arranged themselves like canned sardines into two lines, each physically spooning with the person to his or her front and back, clutching the person in front for the warmth of their generated body heat, awaiting the periodic cry from one of the participants — "spoon right" or "spoon left" — as the group's signal to roll over, as one, in the stated direction.

When the weekend ended, all participants returned home bone-tired and smelling of body odor, bad breath, fake gun powder, and cheap tobacco. Other than the reenactor's high they generally experienced after actual reenactment battles, Caleb and Celia rarely felt as fulfilled as they did on their drive home from weekend drills.

CHAPTER 27

FOUND ISAIAH'S JOURNAL ENTRY DESCRIBING the Richmond slave market so disturbing I decided to set the journal aside for a while. Instead, I turned again to Anne Carter Lee's letters to her eldest son.

June 14, 1829
My dearest Charles,

I regret I was not able to complete my letter to you yesterday, but Dr. Farnsworth's blood-letting left me weak and distracted. I am in similar circumstances today but wish to continue yesterday's missive to the extent I am able.

Since I do not know if we ever will see one another again because I am not able to travel and you have not indicated that you will travel to visit me, I must, as I wrote yesterday, unburden myself concerning a family matter of the utmost gravity. In telling you this, I entrust to you a secret known only to your father, to me, and to several of our former bondsmen and bondswomen. You must go home to your Maker without revealing this secret to anyone except to your eldest son at the time you feel appropriate.

When your father and I married, we were overjoyed when your first brother Algernon Sydney was born. Unfortunately, as you know, he died in his fourteenth month, and I fell into a deep state of melancholy that continues off and on to this day.

Now, Charles, here is our family secret. In the year of our Lord 1806, your father impregnated one of our bondswomen who gave birth to twin sons in January 1807. When, after several weeks, one of the children turned moderately dark, but the other appeared to remain white, your father came to me and suggested we take the white-appearing baby into our home and raise him as if he was our own, as if I myself had given him life. I was horrified at the suggestion and for several weeks refused to even discuss it with your father. Eventually, however, to appease your father, I reluctantly accepted the suggestion and agreed, although I never did become comfortable with the idea. Your father never knew that about me. That child, my dearest Charles, was your younger brother, Robert Edward, and his presence in our family is our family's secret.

Over the next several months and years…

Anne's letter broke off here. It obviously was incomplete. The remaining letters were independent of this one, and I could not find the balance of this letter or any reference to it on the thumb drive or in any of the remaining fourteen letters that Anne had sent her son.

CHAPTER 28

CALEB WORKED HARD AT HIS job. He was a friendly employee, reliable, fairly efficient, and well-liked by the customers who brought their vehicles to him for repair, many of whom took the trouble to comment favorably about him to the shop's foreman. He also was honest in describing the work he did and the time it took him to perform it, never padding his customers' bills.

The work itself was fairly monotonous, even for someone like Caleb whose formal education had ended when he turned sixteen. But this aspect of the job had its benefits, and thus it suited him just fine. The work was moderately repetitive, so Caleb did not have to think hard about what he was doing when repairing a vehicle, leaving him free to daydream about Robert E. Lee and about his reenacting of Lee's roles in reenactors' staged combat.

⸻

"You still a Civil War buff, Son?" the customer said.

Caleb looked up from the engine he was working on and looked at the man who had just spoken. He hadn't seen him for almost a year. Caleb nodded. "Still am," he said. "It's my life."

"Still a serious reenactor? A — what did you call it last time we talked — a Hardcore?"

Caleb nodded again. He wiped his hand on his overalls and turned back to the engine.

"And still a great admirer of General Lee, Son?"

Caleb was tiring of the man's questions. "Uh huh," he said. He kept his head down near the engine as he responded, hoping the man would take the hint and leave.

"You recall that secret about General Lee I told you last year, that he'd been adopted by his parents?" the man said.

Caleb wanted to finish this one-way conversation and get on with his work. But Caleb, assuming the man would not leave before he'd said whatever it was that he wanted to say, put down his tool, stood up straight, and turned to face the man.

"Of course I remember." He stared at the man, and, using his sleeve, wiped the sweat from his forehead.

"There's something else about that adoption I didn't mention last time, but I'll tell you now if you want."

Caleb narrowed his eyes. Was this man mocking him? He didn't like being played with by the shop's customers.

"What else can you tell me about General Lee's adoption that would be more amazing than the fact he was adopted? I still haven't found anything about that in the history books, although I looked it up," Caleb said. "I don't know if I even believe it since I can't find anything out about it."

"Take your smoke break now, Son, and let's walk outside where we don't have to be concerned about eavesdroppers," the man said. "Then I'll tell you another secret about Lee, one that'll knock your socks off."

CHAPTER 29

ANNE CARTER LEE'S LETTER TO Charles had relaxed me to the point that I was ready again to read Isaiah's journal. I turned back to his first post—Civil War entry.

After de surrender by Massa Robert, I heared many bad things said about my brother. Folks sayed he was a trayter to de United States and dat he hated culluds, or why else would he fight to keep slavery.

I never knowed him dat way. I remember Massa Robert was always kind to me, and had good manners with me and our mamma and treated us nice. Until we was about 10 years after being birfed, Massa Robert and me played together. Dat ended when I left work in de fields to work in de Great House.

I don't remember Massa Robert ever saying we was brothers with de same father and mamma, but my mamma said it to me lots of times, so I believed it.

I never saw Massa Robert after de surrender although I thought about him every year in January on our birfday. I seen in de newspaper soon after de surrender dat Massa Robert becomed the presydent of a kollege, whatever dat is, in a place called Lexington, Virginny. Dat was all I knowed about him after de surrender, except when I seen in another newspaper later on dat my twin brother was daid from old age.

From his next journal entries I gathered that life for this freedman, and likely for others, as well, was not what the abolitionists had predicted or promised the antebellum slaves.

After de surrender de culluds kept talking about being freedmens and freedwomans. But dey wasn't free before de surrender and dey wasn't no more free after de surrender den before, except dat dey couldn't be owned and sold no more.

De biggest problem for all de freed culluds was dem Ku Kluxers in dere white sheets and pointy hats who meant no good for all us.

When de culluds was set free many of dem got mighty uppity with de white folks, and even with dem other culluds. You couldn't really blame dem for dat because dey didn't have no better sense and no good example to look at for learning how to act when dey be free.

I always was more scared of dem Ku Kluxers den anything else. Even though de war was fought by de north folk to help free us culluds, de Ku Kluxers never did mean us no good. Dey came around at night, never during de day when we would know who dey was. Dey weared white sheets and dey looked like ghosts.

One night when dey came at midnight, dey said dey was ghost soldiers come back from de daid to get us. Dey didn't scare me dat time even though I was afraid of ghosts because I knowed dere voices and recognized dere horses from daytime. But I didn't say dat to nobody because I was not nobodys fool. But I knowed dem just the same.

After dat I slept on de floor at my house because dem Ku Kluxers shot bullets through our doors and windows in de night. After a while I gots so tired of dem devils dat one day I picked up and left Virginny for good. I walked all de way to Washington City to live.

When I came to Washington City, I found work serving tables in a hotel called Brown's Hotel near de Presydents house. After a few years there, I moved to Fuller's City Hotel on 14th Street for more pay and better treatment as a freedman.

I turned to the final entry in Isaiah's journal.

When my brother Massa Robert died in de Lawd's year 1870, I was very sad. I still was living in Washington City, but working den as a bartender's helper in de Willard Hotel.

When my brother died I was so unhappy I couldn't help myself, so I argued with two white mens who was sitting at de bar and drinking whiskey and saying ugly words about Massa Robert. I was so angry by what dey sayed dat I didn't even try to hide the mad on my face.

I told dem dey should respect de daid and not say no more bad words about Massa Robert. Dem white mens axed why I cared since he hated culluds and fought to keep us slaves. I sayed dat wasn't troo, dat Massa Robert was a good man and dat he was my twin brother who passed for white. After dem mens stopped laffing at me, dey left de bar.

Dat night after work as I walked home de Ku Kluxers jumped me and beat me to within an inch of my life. Before everything spinned around and becomed dark, I heared one of dem Ku Kluxers say dat will teach dat cullud to defame General Lee by saying dat dey was twin brothers, and dat the general was a cullud who passed.

That was Isaiah's final entry in his journal. It left me

troubled. I decided to research him on the Internet to see if I could find out what had become of him after this incident.

It took me a while, but eventually I rooted out the answer.

In 1883, a mob in Leesburg, Virginia, where Isaiah then was living, lynched him. No details were given. I could only assume that he hadn't learned to keep his mouth shut or to keep the mad from his face, and that Leesburg had a lingering chapter of the then-illegal Ku Kluxers, as Isaiah called them.

I closed the folder and locked the thumb drive in my desk drawer. It was time for me to leave to meet Harte for dinner. Time was running out for me to get back to the director to let him know if we would take on the Museum's case or not. Tonight would be decision time for us.

CHAPTER 30

HARTE AND I HAD RESCHEDULED our meeting so we would have dinner at the *Prime Rib*, an upscale steak and rib restaurant/bar on K Street between 20th and 21st. I had been eating and drinking at the *Prime Rib* since I was introduced to it by a friend in 1982.

I arrived first and stood up front by the check-in podium, and chatted with the *maître d'*, John Quade, about the mystery novel he was reading as he awaited the arrival of customers. JQ, as John liked to be called, and I both enjoyed reading mysteries and thrillers, and for the most part liked the same authors — George Pelecanos, James Crumley, Richard Stark, Jim Fusilli, Charlie Stella, Donna Leon, Dana King, and James Lee Burke, among others. Today JQ was reading a Max Allan Collins novel. I had learned over time that JQ was a good judge of mystery writing so I always listened closely when he recommended writers and books for me to read.

Harte arrived about twenty minutes after me.

Once we'd been seated at a table off in a corner by ourselves and had ordered our drinks and meals, we got down to business.

"Walk me through the Richmond meeting," Harte said.

"See if you can use the same words the director did. I want to get a feel for this through his eyes."

I described my meeting, repeating the conversation verbatim as much as I could remember. When I finished, I said, "What about the director's stipulation that when we ID the thieves, we make sure they can't tell anyone what they stole? That's a contract on them, a hit, unless I'm missing something."

"Sounds like it, but maybe, maybe not," Harte said. "In any event, if we take the case we can become passive/aggressive and silently assent to do that if he raises it again. Then when the time comes, we'll ignore it. What's he gonna do, sue us for failure to perform a contract?" He smiled and raised his eyebrows.

That was a little too glib for me. Obviously I wasn't worried about being sued for breach of contract. I was worried about Harte and me being two people who were outside the Museum's inner circle, two people who happened to know the Museum's most sensitive secret. I was worried that Harte and I, like the thieves, might be added to the Museum's hit list once we completed our assignment? I told him this.

Harte shook his head and laughed again. He lifted his glass of *Jack* and took a sip. He sighed and smiled. "Oh, Socrates, you're so young." He shook his head again and clucked his tongue like an old man.

I must have frowned because now he smiled big.

"Come on, Partner," he said, "I'm messing with you. Let's just take things one step at a time. Let's not anticipate problems that might never occur. If we take the case, let's deal with recovering the stolen documents and later worry about hit men, if we even need to."

Harte, as usual, was being cop-hardheaded and cop-practical. Whenever he was on one of our jobs, he was pragmatic, thorough in his investigations, and unrelenting in his pursuit of our targets. Little diverted him from his goal. Humor — at least my brand of humor — never diverted him.

Back when we formed our partnership, Harte hadn't any illusions about my experience, or, rather, my inexperience, as a PI. He had originally seen me as a raw amateur when, five years ago, I investigated the theft of the rare historic fountain pen, the Mandarin Yellow, and he and his partner, Thigpen, had investigated several murders connected with that theft. He also had seen me at work a little less than two years ago, just slightly more experienced than before, when I investigated the crimes at my mother's condominium, the Mount Parnassus.

Because he'd been wounded on the job and forced, first, into a long leave of absence, then, next, forced to take a desk job, and eventually nudged into early retirement, I approached him and proposed that we form a detective agency. He hesitated, but did not turn me down flat. He said he wanted a few days to think it over.

A few days stretched into a few weeks, then into three months, and I hadn't heard back from him. I called him once, but he seemed annoyed that I was pursuing his answer rather than waiting for him to come back to me, so I didn't call him again. Instead, I went about slowly building my PI practice alone.

After about seven months of silence, I marked his failure to get back to me as a strongly implied refusal, and decided we would not be partners. I didn't realize it until later, when

Clotille eventually explained Harte's state of mind to me, but time actually had been on my side.

As Clotille explained it, although Harte had several reservations about working with me because I had never been on the job — had never been a cop — his restlessness and boredom in his forced retirement overcame his doubts, and he decided to give me a try. Clotille also said that her mother had played a big role in his decision because Harte was driving her crazy, hanging around the house all day.

———

We agreed to form an informal partnership and to try it out for six months. That worked out for us, so in our seventh month together we formalized our arrangement, signed a partnership agreement, and rented office space above my old office, at the northeast corner of Connecticut Avenue and Q Street.

Within days of forming our initial, informal arrangement, Harte had taken me out to dinner to explain to me, as he put it, the facts of life for a private investigator.

Perhaps the most practical and obvious matter he emphasized was that as a PI, I had to stay on the right side of the law when conducting an investigation that involved some crime, that I always had to be aware of the vague line that separated our right to conduct a private investigation for a client and the other side of that line that took us into the realm of obstructing justice by interfering with the cops' investigation of that crime.

He also told me to forget about the myths the public entertained concerning private investigations — myths such as the one that held that good detective work proceeded from pure logic and from a receptive, open mind, to lead the investigator to an objective conclusion and to the solving of the crime or puzzle. That wasn't real life, Harte had said. Instead, he told me, as in all human endeavors, PIs worked from partial evidence, conscious and subconscious biases, and that we all necessarily made leaps of logic based on connecting partial dots to arrive at some point we would accept as correct and inevitable.

"Just like in real life," he said.

"You're saying we can't connect all the dots?" I asked.

"I'm saying you need to be aware that we tend to connect whatever few dots we have, then extrapolate from there and guess at a pattern that makes sense to us. That's the way the human brain works," he said. "It demands order."

I must have looked skeptical because he did not let go of this bone.

"Put another way," he said, "we're like the witness to a crime who believes what he thinks he saw, even though his belief is at odds with other eye witnesses, who feel just as strongly about what they think they saw. He thinks he knows what he knows because of what he saw. In fact, he saw what he thinks he saw because of what he already knows."

I must have frowned because he added, "The problem, Socrates, isn't that we don't always have enough dots to connect, but that we want to see order among those dots we do see. Our brains, therefore, to bring order from chaos, favor some dots over others — especially over missing dots — and create the pattern it wants to see, based on what it already knows."

"I don't believe it," I said. "I'm always careful about the evidence I accept and how I use it to locate other evidence."

"Perhaps," Harte said, "but if you think about it, you'll

realize that what I said is why eye witnesses usually suck as witnesses."

I shrugged, and said, "Okay. I take your point." I wanted to end his lesson while I still was semi-conscious.

The practical tips Harte passed on to me from time-to-time have been helpful, but the lesson I learned most, and I learned it on my own, was that the PI's facts of life were constantly shifting as new cases came up. As in most of life, experience was the best teacher.

As we finished our coffee, Harte said, "Let's go back to the office. It's time for me to read the journal and letters so I know better what we're dealing with. Then we should make our decision so you can get back to your contact in Richmond."

Our office was above the restaurant *Circa at Dupont*, where my office had been located before Harte and I formed our partnership. My old office had been on the lower-rent second floor, just above the restaurant. Harte and I opened our office on the higher-rent eighth floor.

Our firm's sign extends out from the wall, cantilevered over the entrance to our office so you can see it when you step off the elevator and look up the hall. The sign has a caricature painting of a plaid hat, with a small protruding bill on its front and back. Below that image is a very large magnifying glass with a small Sherlock Holmes look-alike character peering at you through the magnifying glass, his eyeball disproportionately enlarged as you look back at him through the looking glass, all in basic cartoon fashion.

For obvious reasons, we rented more office space than I had rented when I was working alone. Our agreement was that if Harte and I decided for any reason to end our partnership before the lease term ended, he would continue to pay his share of the rent until the lease ended. I thought that was a generous offer by him. This said indirectly what I would later come to learn — what Harte wouldn't say directly to me — that in the six months we had given our partnership a try he had developed faith in the likelihood our partnership would succeed and we would remain together.

We had a small lobby area with a desk for our receptionist and chairs for clients to sit on while they waited for us, an office for Harte, and one for me, a third, but empty, office for a future hire should we expand, an office for our office manager/bookkeeper, and a utility room for supplies and our photocopy and FAX machines.

As we passed through the reception area on our way to my office to retrieve the thumb drive, Harte instinctively slipped into cop mode. As we walked past his office, without breaking stride or looking down at the door knob, he reached out and tried his office-door handle to check that the door still was locked. It was.

We arrived in front of my office door. I unlocked it, flicked on the overhead lights, and walked around my desk, heading to the top drawer to unlock it and retrieve the thumb drive.

I saw the problem as soon as I made the turn around the corner of my desk. The drawer was open a few inches.

I yanked the drawer all the way open and looked quickly through its contents. I straightened up, looked at Harte, and said, "The thumb drive's gone."

CHAPTER 31

|WAS RATTLED BY THE BREAK—IN. Harte wasn't rattled.
He was furious.

Not that the loss of the thumb drive, itself, would set us back. I still had the duplicate thumb drive I'd made, as well as a copy of the files I placed on my home computer's hard drive. But the loss of the thumb drive flew right in the face of the precautions the director had insisted I take to protect Lee's secret, as well as in the face of the security precautions Harte and I had taken to protect our office from intruders. It also meant that someone in Richmond, perhaps at the Museum, knew that the director had contacted me and had given me the thumb drive. It also seemed that this so-called *someone*, whoever he was, had sent me a message from ninety-plus miles south of Washington, telling me that I could not proceed with the case with impunity, that I was reachable all the way from Richmond.

After Harte and I walked around and checked the entire office for any intruders who might still be present because we'd surprised them when we returned, or for any damage the intruders might have done, we left and headed to *Stan's*. We settled in at a table in a dark, private corner. Surprisingly,

Danika was not behind the stick. I didn't recognize the tender, and I didn't care. Not tonight.

Anyone looking at us would readily see we were pissed off. But it would be hard to tell just by observing us whether we were pissed off at each other or at some circumstance. In fact, we were both unsettled by the fact that the break-in had occurred at all, by its practical consequences and implications, but most of all, we were unnerved by its audacity.

"Any thoughts who might've busted in?" Harte was frowning.

I shook my head. "No one's supposed to know about the case or that I had the thumb drive. This puts everything in a different light."

"Can't fool you, can we?" Harte slowly shook his head in disgust. I couldn't tell if he was disgusted with me or by the situation.

I let his sarcasm pass. I'd learned that sarcasm was how he responded when things did not go his way. It wasn't personal, not directed at me. He was blowing off steam. It had taken me a while to learn this characteristic of his, and some unnecessary, self-inflicted anguish by me to get to that point, but with Clotille's counsel and some patience on my part, learn it I did.

"I don't think the theft was an amateur job, is what I meant," I said. "I think we're dealing with pros who are able to reach out from Richmond and break into an office in DC, an office guarded by a sophisticated security system. Amateurs couldn't pull that off."

"Good," Harte said, as he nodded, seeming to let go of his frustration. "Better, in fact." He seemed a bit sheepish now. I think he realized how he'd just come across to me. "What else does it tell us?" He was turning this in to a learning experience for me.

"That there's an insider at the Museum, someone who knew the director met with me, that he'd given me the thumb drive, and that he wants us to handle the case."

I watched him smile. Evidently his student was learning the business.

"Okay. What's our next step?" he said. His voice had resumed its cop's authority.

"I need to go to Richmond to meet with the director," I said. "I don't look forward to his reaction when I tell him he probably has a mole in his operation, and that the thumb drive's been stolen." I paused briefly, then added, "Want to come with me?"

Harte slowly shook his head, and smiled. "No way. I'll be happy just to hear your report when you return. Now you know why I believe in seniority and the prerogatives of middle age. Travel safely, Partner," he said, as he lifted his glass of *Jack* in a toast.

CHAPTER 32

D ARRYL POOLE'S MANY YEARS AS a contract killer had convinced him that people are most vulnerable and least likely to put up resistance when they have been abruptly awakened from deep sleep, particularly if they have been awakened in the early morning hours around 3:00 a.m., the time of morning F. Scott Fitzgerald had called "the real dark night of the soul." This was especially true if the first thing they saw when they opened their eyes was a Ruger Mark II or its equivalent pointed at their face.

Poole's experience also taught him that people were vulnerable when they were caught naked in the bathtub or shower. When the job permitted, Poole preferred to hit his mark in one of those compromising postures. But, like most work, Poole's job did not always facilitate such advantageous working conditions.

Poole, as he had every night for the past nine days, sat in the dark across the street from the schoolteacher's condominium apartment and looked up at her living room windows, studying the pattern of her evenings. He now knew when the schoolteacher habitually went to bed and when she got up in the morning to go to work. He knew when she went to the gym to work out and when she attended Pilates class. He also knew that she eschewed the use of the Cairo's elevators, and almost always used the building's interior stairway to descend from or to ascend to her sixth floor condo apartment.

Poole decided he would use the schoolteacher's fitness habit against her and would kill her in the isolated stairwell.

Over the next three evenings Poole engaged in stealth entries into the Cairo. He spent his time in the stairwell sitting on the concrete steps between the sixth floor landing and the seventh floor, out of sight of anyone who might appear on the sixth floor landing. He listened to the footsteps of the schoolteacher as she returned home each evening, absorbing their consistent and distinct rhythm and tone. He learned to distinguish the sound of the schoolteacher's footfalls from those of her stair—climbing neighbors.

Poole sat on the chilly, concrete steps and looked at his watch. It was 7:10 p.m. The schoolteacher typically returned home from her Pilates class between 8:00 and 8:20. He would take her tonight from behind as she reached out to insert her key into the doorway leading from the interior landing to the residential hallway.

Poole's predatory senses shifted into high vigilance when he heard the stairwell door on the ground floor open and close. He glanced at his watch, then listened as the schoolteacher steadily climbed the stairs. She hummed an old Aretha

Franklin tune, *I Knew You Were Waiting For Me*, as she ascended to her fate.

Poole silently side-stepped down the stairway toward the sixth floor landing, using the cinderblock partition wall to shield him from sight. He carefully leaned forward, furtively peeping around the edge of the wall, focusing on the schoolteacher's back as she selected a key from the key ring in her hand, and then reached toward the locked door.

In one swift, soundless movement, Poole stepped over behind the woman and cupped his left hand under her chin. He yanked her back toward him, throwing her off-balance. Then he plunged the blade of a nine-inch stiletto into the base at the back of her neck, taking care not to jab his left hand when the stiletto's blade popped through the schoolteacher's throat just below her chin.

Poole briefly held the woman upright with his cupped hand until he was sure she was dead. Then he dropped her on the landing in front of the sixth floor door. He removed one ring from her finger, pocketed her wristwatch, and took her wallet. Then he quietly made his way down the stairs to the ground floor and exited through the lobby, being mindful that the bill of his ball cap was pulled down over his face, even as he turned his head away from the two security cameras surveilling the building's lobby.

CHAPTER 33

H ARTE AND I LEFT *STAN'S*. Harte returned to the office. He said he wanted to look around one more time to see if he could develop a lead on who broke in, and how they'd done it. Especially, how. He said he couldn't imagine that anyone could have by-passed our new, cutting-edge alarm system.

When I asked if he wanted me to go back to the office with him to help, he looked at me as if to say, "What makes you think you'd be anything but in the way?" Harte, too, was learning how to deal with our relationship because he didn't actually say it this time. But I took his hint from his silent scowl.

"I'm going home then," I said.

Harte nodded. He looked impatient, shifting his weight from one foot to the other as we talked.

"I'll call you when I'm back from Richmond," I said. "Wish me luck."

I arrived home and walked into my bedroom to a nice surprise. There was an avocado-color cashmere sweater, a dark skirt, and a bra draped over the foot-railing of my bed.

An open bottle of Pellegrino water sat on the night table. A gym bag huddled on the floor near the closet door. I smelled White Linen perfume.

Clotille had come over. I could hear water running. She was in the shower.

I had given Clotille a key to my apartment a few months before. It was convenient for us, but I still wasn't used to it. I didn't mind coming home and being surprised to find her there, as happened on occasion. In fact, I can't remember any time this occurred that I hadn't been happy she was there. It was just that I hadn't yet learned to let go of my habit of solitude. I hadn't gotten used to opening my door and finding anything awaiting me other than silence, a week's worth of dust, and, occasionally, a blinking red light on my answering machine.

While Clotille showered, I changed from my suit to sweat pants and a tee shirt. Then I took two aspirin to quiet the headache that continued to ebb and flow, depending on whether or not I thought about the call I would make tomorrow morning to the director. I poured a Scotch for myself, went into the bathroom to let Clotille know I was home, and then sat in the living room nursing my drink while I waited for her to finish up and join me.

She soon entered the living room wearing a white-terrycloth robe she kept on a hook behind the bathroom door. Her face glowed from having recently been scrubbed. Her bright-red hair, still damp and toweled wild, hung down in uncontrived chaos. She looked model-beautiful to me, with her gorgeous hair, pale skin, freckles bridging her nose from cheek to cheek, and her large emerald green eyes that always seemed to speak surprise.

She came over to the couch, leaned down, and kissed me on the mouth. Her taste was an odd mixture of vodka, lemon, and Crest toothpaste. She walked away from me, over to the dry sink, and built herself another vodka and tonic. When she returned, she sat down on the couch next to me and curled-up her legs under her. She took a long pull from her drink, looked at me briefly, smiled, then said, "You look like shit, Socrates. Tell me what's going on, you."

Clotille had already left when I woke the next morning. She, unlike me, had an office to report to, with a boss who did not offer her the flexibility with her working-hours I gave myself as a partner in a two-man business. By now she would have headed home, showered, and dressed in clothes she hadn't worn to work the day before.

I poured myself orange juice, drank coffee, waited until 10:00 a.m., then called the director to set up a meeting with him for later that day or the next. His choice.

Although the director pressed me to tell him why I needed to meet, correctly perceiving that my call this soon after our previous meeting must mean bad news, I refused to tell him anything over the phone other than the fact we had not yet made a decision if we would handle the case. I could sense the wariness in his voice when he responded to my request to get together.

"Is it bad news? If it is, I need to know now, Suh."

I didn't want to have this conversation over the telephone. What I had to say to him, much as I dreaded being with him under the circumstances, required a face-to-face meeting.

He finally relented and agreed to meet with me at 3:00

p.m. that same afternoon. I left Washington at 12:15 to drive to Richmond.

Rain fell hard as I drove. It soaked the highway between DC and Richmond, and blurred my windshield. I needed to replace my wipers even though they still were fairly new. *Not a very good sign for a new vehicle.* I thought.

I parked at the curb in front of the Museum. The rain had soaked into the brick front of the building, and had turned the murky brick, already infused with a century or more of soot, into an ominous shade of blood red.

As I walked up to the building, I realized I hadn't noticed before how monolithic it seemed. The building reminded me of television documentaries I'd seen as a child showing the architecture in Moscow under Stalin — looming, windowless buildings designed as if they'd been constructed to withstand a siege by the peasants. *That probably was their original design plan*, I thought, as I smiled at the image I'd called forth.

I had learned in my first meeting with the director that the Museum had not taken its security seriously until the recent theft. That now had changed. According to what he'd told me this morning when we spoke to schedule this meeting, the security staff had installed cameras in and around the building — several of which I was able to spot as I stood at the Museum's front door. He had also said that each evening, at closing, the Museum now released four Doberman guard dogs so they could have free run of the facility. *Now that was security I could respect.*

As before, the director came out to the vestibule to escort me back to his office. He didn't say anything. He seemed to be smiling — I wasn't sure — but then I decided that his expression was nothing more than the baring of unfriendly teeth. The unspoken tension between us was palpable.

I looked around as we entered his office, having neglected last time to pay attention to the surroundings. I was surprised how austere his decor was, entirely empty of artifacts, having bare walls or little else to suggest it was part of a museum. The office was stark, almost monastic.

After we seated ourselves, the director, skipping the usual opening pleasantries one would normally engage in when one party had driven more than two hours to attend a meeting with the other, got right to the point.

"What's going on, Suh?" he said. "Why couldn't you tell me over the telephone. Why did you make me wait?"

I told him about the theft of the thumb drive. I watched the alcohol-pink in his cheeks bleed to scarlet.

"This is a disaster," he said. He cupped his forehead in his palms for a moment, then sat up straight, stiffened, and frowned at me.

"How could you be so careless, Mr. Cheng? I told you the secret must be maintained at all costs. Did you think I was kidding, Suh?"

No, I didn't think he'd been kidding.

I held my anger in check and elected not to respond. I respected his distress and sarcasm even if I didn't think it was justifiably directed at me. After a brief pause, I added the news that I believed he had a mole in his operation, someone who knew that the Museum had tried to engage my services, and knew, too, that he'd given me the thumb drive.

"Impossible, Suh. You are mistaken. Our employees and trustees all are beyond reproach."

"How then do you explain that the only thing taken from our office was the thumb drive?"

He didn't respond. Instead, he placed his elbows on his desk and dropped his head into his open palms. He remained that way for almost half a minute, his head drooping and his eyes closed. I waited for him to make the next move.

He slowly raised his head and stared at me. His voice, when he finally spoke again, was a melancholic monotone.

"What do we do now?" he said. "This will finish me. My career is over." He sighed loudly.

"I can resign from the case if you want." I said this even though we had never formally taken on the case.

"What good will that do? It won't change anything if the secret is out."

"No, it won't," I said. "Or, I can continue with the case if you want, as if this hadn't happened, and try to recover the stolen documents and the thumb drive, hopefully in time to preserve the Museum's secret."

He did not respond to my suggestion. Instead, he turned away from me, picked up the handset of his desktop telephone and punched in a two-number extension.

After a few seconds passed, he said into the handset, "Come to my office immediately." He ended the call and did not mention the name of the person he'd just summoned to our presence.

CHAPTER 34

THE DIRECTOR TURNED BACK TO me. I expected him to fill me in on whom he'd called, while we waited for that person to arrive, but he said nothing. He acted as if it didn't matter that I didn't know, and that I should be content to await that person's appearance. He was right, of course, though not necessarily well-mannered. I would know soon enough when the mysterious person arrived.

A single, sharp rap on the office door announced the arrival of that person.

"Enter," the director said.

I made a quarter turn in my chair so I could face the person who walked in. A man in his forties entered the office, looked briefly at the director, then glanced over at me, but said, and otherwise did nothing, to acknowledge my presence. He lowered himself into the chair to my left.

"Meet Winston Starr," the director said to me.

Starr and I eyed one another with a shared blend of curiosity and misgiving. We nodded our greetings, but did not offer to shake hands.

"Winston," the director said, "is one of the trustees of the Museum, and one of the people who knows General Lee's secret. He also is a recognized authority on the General.

"Winston, of course, also knows of the theft of the journal and letters," he added. "I should tell you, Suh, that Winston was adamantly opposed to bringing in anyone from outside the Museum or outside the Golden Knights to recover the stolen documents."

Great. Once the director tells him the thumb drive's been stolen, I can sit here and listen to Winston tell the director, "I told you so."

When the director finished telling Starr the bad news, including the likelihood that there might be a traitor in their midst, Starr turned to face me. He still did not appear to be welcoming.

"The important thing, Mr. Cheng, Suh," he said, speaking very slowly and deliberately, as if lecturing a child he could barely tolerate, "is to recover the journal and letters, and preserve General Lee's secret, if that still is possible. We shouldn't play *gotcha* with one another, even though it appears you two," he said, as he nodded first at me and then at the director, "have royally screwed up, if you will forgive my candor." He smiled at me as he asked for my indulgence.

I couldn't argue with any of what Starr said, except maybe with the concept of *royally*, but I didn't want to split hairs with him, so I let the dig pass. I briefly glanced over at the director. His face was beet-red.

I looked back at Starr, and locked my eyes on his. I wouldn't yield anything to him at this point.

"I agree," I finally said. "Keeping Lee's secret is paramount." I turned to face the director. "Now what? Do you still want me to undertake this investigation or should I walk away? It's up to you."

The director inserted his finger between his neck and

shirt collar, and pulled his collar away from his skin. He and Starr looked at one another. I watched something unspoken pass between them. The director turned back to face me.

"We want you to continue, Mr. Cheng, but it now is even more pressing that you promptly recover everything. Every day the artifacts and thumb drive are missing is a day it is more likely the General's secret will be revealed." He glanced again at Starr.

Because he kept surreptitiously glancing at Starr, even as he spoke to me, I had the feeling the director was holding something back. His overall body language, too, was a pretty easy tell, as he angled away from me while he spoke to me.

"Is there something else you want to say to me," I asked, "something you should say to me, something you're not telling me?"

The director didn't answer, but his eyes again briefly shifted to Starr's eyes. As I looked over at Starr, I saw him slightly shake his head no.

The director looked back at me, and said, "You know everything you need to know, Mr. Cheng."

Based on what I'd just seen pass between him and Starr, and the arrogance of that statement, I refused to accept this. I couldn't let it pass.

"No, no, no," I said, "you're holding something back. Either tell me now or find yourself another PI." I was pissed. *Royally*, to borrow a quote Starr, but I didn't tell that to them.

"We're supposed to be on the same side here, *Suh*," I parroted, using my best Ralph Harte-type sarcasm, as I stared hard into the director's eyes.

He sighed, long and plaintively. He sounded wounded.

He looked at Starr again, shrugged slightly, then turned back to me.

"I was hoping I would not have to reveal this to you, Mr. Cheng. Trust me, you should let this point go. There's nothing else you need to know." He looked at Starr again and nodded. Starr turned his head and focused his gaze on me, but remained silent.

I continued to stare at the director, but said nothing. I was waiting him out and would not let this go.

He finally looked back at me. When I still said nothing, he took a deep breath, sighed, then said, "Well then, Suh, since you insist, I'll tell you. It's your funeral, one way or the other, so I suppose telling you won't hurt."

CHAPTER 35

YOU COULD HAVE REACHED OUT and touched the tension in the air. Starr crossed his legs and uncrossed them several times. He didn't look at me at all. He stared at the director as if he were trying to will him to get on with it, and get it over with, to tell me whatever it was they had been reluctant to share with me.

The director cleared his throat twice.

A chill coursed through my veins, and I suddenly shivered. *Maybe I didn't want to know what he was about to say.*

As he began his story, the director took on the look of a man walking with tenuous determination into an ice-cold surf.

"There's another secret involving General Lee," the director said, "indirectly, that is, but it is one that will put you in significant, additional danger merely by knowing it. Are you sure you want me to proceed?"

Hell, no, I don't, I thought, *but what choice do I have if I'm to work this case?*

Then what he'd just said registered with me. *Significant additional danger? I didn't realize I was in any danger at this point.*

"Go on," I said. My stomach tightened.

"How much, Mr. Cheng, do you know about the Golden Knights of the Confederacy?"

"Just what I learned from some online research I did recently." I described what I'd learned. My disgust with the organization and its beliefs probably was apparent in my tone, although neither I, the director, nor Starr commented on it.

"Yes," he said, "that's the information we've deliberately put out for public consumption even though some people might not find the information flattering to us. But there also is something the public doesn't know."

"Such as?" I said, feeling the need to say something neutral to help relieve the tension in the room, as well as defuse my growing anxiety. I drummed my fingers on the arm of my chair.

"Such as This. There is a small group of compulsively devoted people within the Golden Knights, a secret society within a larger private organization, if you will, who have taken it upon themselves, in the interest of General Lee's legacy, to protect the General's secret at all costs."

I raised my eyebrows. "At all costs? Meaning—"

"Meaning just what it sounds like it means, Mr. Cheng. Meaning these people will kill, and, perhaps, already have killed, to protect the General's secret. At least that's the tale told about them. I, myself, Suh, don't know for sure, but I respect the rumor."

"Is it just a rumor then?" I said.

"Well," the director said, "I used that term loosely. I believe it's true, although I cannot verify it." He looked over at Starr, clearly seeking his support.

"The same for me," Starr said, looking me in the eyes for the first time. "I also believe it."

This was not what I wanted to hear. It changed everything for me. I stood up and briefly paced. Then I moved behind my chair, put my hands on the top of its back, as if I were gripping a railing, and looked at the director. I considered my response for several seconds, while Starr and the director silently looked on.

If what the director just told me was true, then dropping the case wouldn't protect me. Nor would it help me if I merely recovered the former slave's journal, the letters, and the thumb drive. To protect me from this secret group, this cabal — as I now thought of this so-called group — I had to get out in front of this and control events so I would be safe — safe even though I knew the General's secret and knew that the cabal existed.

This meant I would have to figure out how to do just that, and for the moment I had no clue. What I could not do, I realized, was just drop the case and walk away, not if I wanted to be safe.

PART TWO

CHAPTER 36

I F I HAD ANY UNCERTAINTY whether a group of crazies within the Golden Knights, sworn to protect Lee's secret at all costs, existed or not, the thought quickly passed. All I had to do was recall my own experience five years previously when I encountered the criminal Chinese triad known as *Jiao tu san ku* — the *Cunning Rabbit With Three Warrens Society* — an outlaw organization operating out of Shanghai by Big-Eared Tu, and in the United States by Washington's Li Bing-fa. This Chinese secret society had its fingers in everything in the Washington metropolitan area, both legitimate and criminal, and reputedly committed murder from time-to-time to protect its legitimate and illegitimate enterprises. My connection with this triad had grown out of my long-time relationship with Li Bing—fa's daughter, Jade Li.

The news that there was a clandestine group — I thought of them as a secret cabal — within the Golden Knights dedicated to protecting General Lee's secret, ruled out any possibility I could now just walk away from the case — even though Harte and I hadn't formally taken it on — and merely by keeping a low profile and not divulging Lee's secret, could remain safe.

I had no choice now. Keeping the secret and maintaining

a low profile were just my entry fee to staying out of harm's way. To insure that I would actually be safe, Harte and I would have to accept the case, track down the thieves, return the stolen documents and thumb drive, and root out and expose the cabal and its members, all before they silenced me.

The first thing I did after I returned to DC from Richmond was to call the director and tell him I would take the case as a new project for our firm. He seemed surprised, at least that's how I read his initial silence. Then he said, "I assumed, Mr. Cheng, you had taken on the responsibility of our urgent matter since you didn't say otherwise when you were here."

I let that mischaracterization of our prior conversations pass without comment. What was the point of stirring that hornets' nest again?

I next weighed talking with Harte about the secret cabal, but decided against it for now. He would have lots of questions, cop-type questions, I would not be able to answer yet, and that response would merely frustrate him. I would bring Harte into this loop when I had a better grasp of what I was dealing with and, hopefully, some idea how to deal with it. For now, his cynicism, resulting from his years as an MPD street cop and homicide detective, would be an unwelcome distraction for me.

I also considered talking to my mother about this, but dismissed the idea. While her advice might ultimately be good, it also would be wrapped in folds of motherly worry and maternal apprehension for my safety. No need to put her — or me — through that.

That left Clotille. But what would I achieve by confiding in her and possibly putting her at risk by doing so? I didn't want to place her in danger because she knew the secret or because she was mistakenly thought to know the secret, even if she did not.

Yet the more I considered this, the more I thought I could talk to Clotille in sufficiently general terms to keep her from knowing the secret, and could also keep the cabal from believing she knew the secret, if the cabal was watching me, since it would be natural for me to spend time with my girlfriend, conversing about various matters over drinks or meals. Given natural circumstances, the cabal would have no reason to think our conversations related to the Museum's case. And, in fact, the conversations mostly would not.

Even under this circumscribed approach, Clotille would make a good sounding board for me. She might become emotional when she realized the potential danger I now was in, but in the past she had shown herself to be rational, principled, and pragmatic, just like her father, but without his experiential street-cop cynicism.

———————•••———————

We met for dinner in front of the *Russian House*, a Continental restaurant and lounge featuring food supposedly reminiscent of the food served in Tsarist Russia. It is located where Connecticut Avenue, Florida, and 21st Street intersect, just north of Dupont Circle.

We settled at a table near the front window, looked over the drink menu purporting to describe the largest selection of vodka in the Washington area, and ordered drinks. Clotille ordered a Regalia Silver vodka martini. I ordered a glass of Putinka Classic, straight up.

"This sure is different," Clotille said, as she glanced around. "I've never had Russian food, me."

I smiled. "Well, it's not tortillas, but I know you like to try new foods, so here we are. It's new to me, too, except from word of mouth."

I thought about how I would approach my talk with Clotille. I wanted to give her as much information as she would need to advise me, but, as before when I talked with her about the case, I would only speak in general terms so I wouldn't frighten her any more than was unavoidable. And, of course, I remained mindful of the confidentiality agreement I'd signed.

After we ordered our second round of drinks — each trying a different vodka this time, mine again straight up and Clotille's in a different-type martini — and once we'd taken small talk as far as we reasonably could without obvious contrivance, I said, "We need to talk about something."

I watched Clotille's eyebrows knit together and her forehead scrunch up.

"Did I do something wrong, me?" she said. "Please say it if I did. I don't mean to upset you, Socrates, you know that."

I held up both palms in a gesture of surrender. "Whoa," I said. "You didn't do anything wrong. I have a work-related problem, the Richmond case we talked about, and I'd like your advice because of some new developments. That's all."

You would think by now that I would have learned how to phrase matters when I introduced them to Clotille so I wouldn't upset her, and then have to backtrack. Sometimes I amazed myself at how slowly I learned certain aspects of inter-personal relationships, especially when it came to Clotille.

I could see her silently utter a sigh of relief. She noticeably relaxed her shoulders, and nodded that I should go ahead.

Although it involved some repetition with respect to what I'd told her before, I set out the Museum's case from the time of my first meeting with the director, through my most recent meeting with him and Winston Starr. I used broad, descriptive nouns to identify the players in the scenario. I described Robert E. Lee as a historic military figure. I referred to Anne Carter Lee as a historic early American southern woman. I called Light-Horse Harry Lee the military figure's famous father. And I referred to Isaiah as a former slave connected with the father and son. I used similar obfuscation when I talked about Elizabeth Van Lew.

I watched Clotille's cheeks change to deepening shades of crimson, step by step, as she listened to me. I didn't know if this was the result of her frustration because I wouldn't fully disclose names to her or because she was worried for me as the result of the story I told her. Probably both.

I ended my story without mentioning the existence of the cabal.

When I finished, I said, "So that's the situation, Clotille, that's my problem. What do you think?" I stared hard at her as I waited for her response. I watched her eyebrows arch slightly, no more than a millimeter or so, but enough to tell me that her response would likely be full of endless possibilities.

Clotille shifted her position in her seat and crossed her legs. She looked at me, paused, then looked at her martini. She picked up the glass, held it by the stem, and slowly revolved it between her thumb and forefinger. She slowly brought the glass to her lips and sipped her drink.

When she'd replaced the glass on the table, she said, "I think y'all need to trust me better, Socrates. You need to tell me what we're dealing with, us. Stop being so general and vague if you really want me to understand and really want my advice. Otherwise, stop paying me lip service. It's insulting."

I thought it might come down to this. "It's not a matter of trust," I said. "I signed a confidentiality agreement." *Pretty weak excuse*, I thought, *given what I've already revealed to her.*

"Y'all are talkin' nonsense, Socrates, and you know it. You have violated that paper already by telling me what you just said, so don't you go giving me that confidentiality bull stuff. I'm not some dumb Cajun hillbilly just 'cause I talk like one."

She was right, of course, but only in part. I didn't underestimate Clotille's intelligence or shrewdness merely because she spoke like the indigenous Cajun she was. I was trying to protect her from the cabal by keeping her somewhat in the dark. It was a noble idea, in theory, but dumb in practice. I couldn't have it both ways. Either I told her or I did not. There couldn't be any half measures since the cabal would treat even the appearance of disclosure as if it were full disclosure.

When I thought about this I realized I was attempting to construct a wall around Clotille, a wall built on a foundation of false security lodged strictly in my mind. If the cabal became aware of Clotille, then, from its point of view, she might, or she likely would, have knowledge of Lee's secret merely because of her close association with me. That would be the cabal's perception, and in this case, as in most of life, perception was tantamount to reality. That, in itself, I realized would put Clotille at risk. There was no credible reason for me to believe the cabal would view our talks any other way, even though I'd naively thought otherwise before. Given that, why not tell it all to her?

As for the confidentiality agreement, circumstances concerning the case had changed. Because the director had withheld critical information from me when I signed the document — namely that there was a group of people who might try to kill me just because I knew or might appear to know Lee's secret — I didn't feel I had signed the document with full knowledge of the risks involved. Put another way, as far as I was concerned, the director's failure to make full disclosure to me negated my agreement not to disclose information, since I hadn't entered into the confidentiality obligation with informed consent.

"Okay," I said, "you're right. I'll tell you."

I proceeded to identify Robert E. Lee, Anne Carter Lee, Elizabeth Van Lew, Light-Horse Harry Lee, and Isaiah, as the players in the Museum's virtual docudrama. I then placed each person within the context of the story. I also told Clotille about the Golden Knights of the Confederacy and about the cabal. That last bit of information certainly arrested her attention.

CHAPTER 37

Darryl Poole looked at the readout on his disposable cellphone, recognized the caller, and answered the call. It was Aunt Marge.

"Hello," he said. "Always good to hear from you." He did not state her name over the phone, following their established protocol never to use names.

"Your auntie has an errand for you, Young Man," the woman's soothing voice on the other end said. "Come visit me this afternoon. We'll have tea and cake, and I'll tell you all about it."

Three hours later Poole sat with his handler in her Richmond kitchen sipping tea and eating a slice of homemade gingerbread cake with chocolate icing.

"Before you say no," Aunt Marge said, "hear me out." She patted Poole fondly on his shoulder, then took a seat across the table from him. "It's another Washington-based job, but I figured since you took the last one, you'd be amenable to considering another. If you don't want it, that's fine, but keep an open mind until I finish." She smiled, lifted her tea cup, and sipped the tea, all the while looking over the lip of the cup into his eyes, trying to read and access his feelings.

Poole thought about this and nodded. He did not want

to seem either ungrateful or uninterested because then Marge might begin giving his assignments to other hitters she housed in her stable. But he also didn't want to make it a practice of taking assignments in his backyard. There was no long-term good percentage in doing that. He would have to walk a delicate and perilous course to avoid offending Marge, yet still avoid accepting more home games.

He looked up at Marge, who silently stared at him, waiting for his assent. Her fish-cold eyes remained locked on his.

It'll probably be easier to deal with this job and any downside blowback than to find a new handler to work with, he decided.

He nodded. "Okay. Tell me about it." He looked down at his slice of cake and cut off a small piece with his fork, so he wouldn't have to look into Marge's eyes and be required to hide his anger at being put in this untenable situation.

"Good," Marge said, as she pushed a manila file folder across the table to him. "Once again the assignment doesn't involve a politician or highly visible mark. Just a local who pissed off someone. The job's low profile and minimal risk," she added.

Poole glanced quickly through the file until he was satisfied he understood the assignment it described. He stood up, took his empty cup and plate to the sink, and rinsed them, then turned back to his handler.

"Okay, Aunt Marge, I'll let you know when it's completed. Thanks for thinking of me."

Marge smiled and offered him another slice of cake.

CHAPTER 38

I WAS IN MY OFFICE, LEANING back in my chair with my feet crossed at the ankles and up on the corner of my desk. I was reviewing our partnership's income and cash flow ledgers in anticipation of meeting later in the day with our office administrator, who also acted as our bookkeeper and receptionist. This kind of work bored me to tears, but it had to be done, and Harte had already demonstrated that he had no patience or aptitude for it.

Harte walked in without knocking and closed the door behind him.

That wasn't usual. We operated with an open-door policy except when clients' confidences required us to do otherwise. I looked up, a frown on my face.

"Have a minute?" he said.

"Sure. What's up?" *Did Harte somehow know I hadn't told him about the cabal?*

He settled into a chair in front of my desk, took a toothpick from his pocket, and proceeded to mine the left side of his upper gum. He appeared troubled by something.

I'd noticed in the short time we'd been together as partners that Harte's personality changed when we were discussing investigations. Not that he was jovial at other times. He wasn't. Such humor as he could dredge up on those other occasions totally disappeared when we turned to business.

When we talked about investigations, Harte reflected certain traits I could only assume he acquired while on the job dealing with street crime, traits such as a deep sense of skepticism about whatever we were discussing, an inner toughness I did not see at other times, and a resolute and unyielding insularity.

"Catch me up on Richmond," he said, "your most recent meeting with the director, when you gave him the news flash about the thumb drive. Are we still in the hunt?" His serious tone of voice belied any possibility he was merely curious.

"It seems so," I said. I then told him about the meeting, including my impression of Winston Starr, and about the director's disclosure of the cabal.

"Is Starr going to be a problem?"

I shrugged. I found it curious he seemed to find Starr more of a potential problem than the cabal.

"I don't see it," I said. "Maybe if he had been involved earlier, but what choice do they have now except to keep us looking for the documents and the thumb drive?"

He nodded, and looked off in the distance as if troubled by a thought, then looked back at me and locked his eyes on mine.

"We need to keep Clotille out of this," he said. "Don't go mixing your social relationship with my daughter with your need to be open with her or to have a sounding board. Use me for that. The stakes are too high. If that secret group you just mentioned even thinks she might know Lee's secret, they could move against her."

He looked hard at me, waiting for me to agree to keep

Clotille far from the case. He was a father protecting his progeny, warning off a potential threat.

I don't play poker because my face is an open book. Harte immediately read my body language and facial expression, and picked up on my discomfort.

"What?" he said, his eyes narrowing suspiciously. "Don't tell me you already told—"

I nodded. "Afraid so." I wanted to crawl under my desk because I knew Harte was right about what he'd said, and I knew him well enough to know his reaction would be explosive and full-borne paternal.

"Damn it, Cheng. What kind of fool are you? Do you have any idea what you've done? I thought you said you loved her and—"

I thought about Clotille and how strong willed she was. And I thought about Harte, and how difficult and frustrating it must be to parent a daughter so constituted.

I shook my head. "Come on, Harte, you know your daughter better than anyone. Do you really think I could keep this from her? She knows every nuance of my moods, my facial expressions. The question is, how do we keep her safe, not should I have told her."

Harte stood up and paced. It was as if he was alone in the room. Then, after almost a minute, still not once having glanced directly at me, he sat down in his chair again. He slumped as if the air had abruptly been released from his balloon body.

I watched as he slowly re-inflated. He looked directly at me again. The only difference I could see now from a few minutes ago was that his face and neck retained the ruddy shade they'd acquired a few minutes before. He did not at all look understanding or forgiving.

He nodded rapidly a few times as if confirming his agreement with something he'd just thought of. I had no idea where we were going with this.

"Okay, then," he said. "We'll work the case together, sharing aspects of it as needed, but I expect you to keep Clotille out of it from now on. Understand?" His face did not brook any opposition from me.

"I'll try, Harte, but you do know your daughter. Don't you think that's wishful thinking?"

He slowly shook his head. His eyes narrowed. "Do it, Cheng. It wasn't a suggestion or request."

CHAPTER 39

CALEB, HIS GIRLFRIEND CELIA, JANET Bonnard, and three other reenactors sat around Caleb's and Celia's kitchen table drinking beer and smoking weed. It didn't take long for the group to begin and finish their internecine quarrels, then move on to a mutually accepted target of their contempt — the élitists at the Golden Knights' museum, and other pretenders, many of whom liked to refer to themselves as Civil War buffs. This was a general subject of contempt everyone in the group could unite against, the glue that held their fragile convocation together each month.

"I see the Golden Knights have publicly attacked reen-actors again, this time in their members' newsletter," Caleb said.

"How'd y'all get a copy of the newsletter?" a group member asked. "Aren't they restricted to Golden Knights' members? You're not a secret member are ya, Caleb?" He chuckled and looked around. His mirth fell flat on hostile ears. No one else enjoyed his joke.

"They are restricted," Caleb said, and left his answer cryptically truncated. "I have one. That's all you need to know."

"It's a crime how those assholes talk about us," another member replied.

"What'd they say?" Janet Bonnard asked.

Celia jumped in to answer the question. "They said reenactors, and particularly Hardcores, are preposterous wannabes who act out illusions and don't pay attention to true Southern lineage and history." She looked at everyone, one person at a time, gauging their reactions for future reference.

"They also said — not directly of course, but I can read between the lines — that we would have been the dregs of old southern society if we'd lived in the 1850s or '60s, good only as cannon fodder to protect the genteel folk and their antebellum genteel way of life."

She fluttered her eyelashes and mimed a curtsy, placing her palm over her heart. She sighed theatrically and smiled.

This disclosure caused the expected undercurrent of mumbling and cursing among the group's members.

CHAPTER 40

BECAUSE OF THE INTENSITY OF the Museum's case and the time I spent running back and forth between DC and Richmond, I again hadn't visited my mother for more than a week, so I dropped by her condo to see her. She was in the kitchen when I arrived, but she wasn't cooking or baking. She was sitting at the table with her splayed hands on either side of the *Washington Post,* which was spread out in front of her. She looked up as I walked in, but didn't smile. That, too, was unusual. Something was wrong.

"*Yasou? — How are you?*" she said, as I approached the table. There was none of her usual warmth in her greeting.

"Where have you been, Socrates? I haven't heard from you in days. Not for a week. I've been worried. I almost called Clotille to ask her, but I didn't want that she should worry."

I made an excusing gesture with my hands, and blushed. "Sorry, Ma, no excuse. Been busy with the new case, the Richmond one we talked about."

"*Ach*! It's always work with you. Your usual excuse." She still did not smile. "That's what you do best. You wake up and you work. Then you go to sleep. You don't have time anymore for your mother since you became a detective."

"I liked it better when you sold pens, even if you didn't

make a good living. At least then you closed your store at 5:00 o'clock and had time to visit me."

I didn't bother to point out that when I operated my vintage, collectible fountain pen store she used to nag me to find another line of work because the store's hours kept me from visiting her as frequently as she would have liked. *There was no winning on this subject with this woman.*

She stood up and shuffled toward the oven, taking the coffee pot from the burner, then turning back to me.

"Sit," she said. "I just put on a fresh pot. At least have coffee with me while you're still here, before you run off to who knows where."

That was not a request. I knew better than to think or act as if it might be.

I sat, as instructed, and waited. She brought me a coffee cup and a glass of water, then poured coffee for me and freshened her half empty cup already sitting on the table.

I looked closely at her as she poured the coffee. I tried not to be obvious. She looked old, something I constantly tried to deny, but could no longer ignore. I knew from conversations we'd had that she had recently started falling asleep at night with the television left on. She had never been that way before. She did this, she said, for the white noise, because she preferred the sounds of old movies and repeated news casts to her own thoughts. I wasn't sure I believed her explanation.

"So, Socrates, tell me about this detective work that keeps my only boy from visiting his mother."

"Can't," I said. "No more than I've already told you. It's confidential." That was not what she wanted to hear. In my mother's world, there was nothing too secret for a son to tell his mother.

I didn't want to say to her that I didn't want to expose her to possible danger by telling her about the case, because then she would have nagged me to drop the case so she wouldn't have to worry about me.

She wasn't happy with my response, but, uncharacteristically, she did not press me to disclose more. We chatted for a while about other things, then I said, "I have to run now, Ma. I'll come by soon to see you again. I promise."

She nodded with a mother's seasoned recognition that her son was appeasing her and giving her the old brush off.

She stood and adjusted the string on her apron, then pointed at me with one finger. "Take me out to dinner soon," she said, "with Clotille. Then I won't have to wait days to see you."

I slowly shook my head, smiled, and kissed her cheek. "It's a date," I said. "I'll check to see when Clotille can make it, and will call you. I promise."

"*Yia sou — Goodbye*," she said. "*S'agapo — I love you.*" She offered up a smile that shaved years off her face.

"Me, too," I said. "*Tha ta poume — We'll talk later.*"

As I left the kitchen, I noticed that my mother's gradual elimination in her home of my father's Taoist origins continued unabated. This had started when she first moved to the Mount Parnassus. All the wall hangings from his scroll collection that had been out and visible here, after he died three years ago, now were gone. I also didn't see any of the scholar's studio artifacts my father had taken great pride in owning — the watercolor brushes, the ink pots, and other scholar's pieces he'd displayed in their old home and that my mother brought with her to the Mount Parnassus after my father died.

Although I know my mother loved my father and that she was still, since his death, evolving back to her Greek roots, the changes that eradicated my father's connection with his Chinese antecedents saddened me more than I ever would have expected.

I stepped off the elevator at the lobby level and started for the front entrance door when I heard a familiar voice coming from behind me, on my left.

"Well, well, well. Look who the cat dragged in."

I could hear the sneer in her voice.

The sound of Toula Xandereas' voice caused my breath to catch. I reacted as if I'd heard fingernails scratching along a chalk board. I turned and saw her standing a few feet away, her feet spread apart, her hands on her hips. She was smiling as if she'd just uncovered a sordid secret or as if she was a cat that had finally cornered a mouse it had pursued for weeks.

I hadn't seen Toula since I completed investigating crimes a few years ago at the Mount Parnassus. During that time of my life, Toula and I had engaged in a short, intense, unhealthy and, ultimately, caustic sexual relationship that I wanted to put out of my memory for all time. I always dreaded the possibility that I might run into her when I visited my mother, but had managed to avoid doing so until today.

Toula hadn't physically changed much since I last saw her. She wore her thirty-nine or so years well. As always, my gaze involuntarily zeroed in and locked onto the black eye patch she wore over her left eye socket. As before, doing this made me self-conscious.

"Nice to see you," I said. "How've you been?" I struggled to keep my tone bland.

"Like you really care."

I offered her a Parisian shrug of one shoulder, and said, "I asked, didn't I?" I paused, shrugged both shoulders this time, as if puzzled by her attitude, then said softly, "Suit yourself."

She hasn't changed. Why buy into this crap? Time to hit the road. I turned to walk away. I wasn't about to be sucked into her toxic mind games again.

"Long as you're here, want to hook-up with me?" she said. "It's been a long time for us and my dance card's empty right now. Besides, my mother's out for a few more hours. The condo's empty."

There's no such thing as being beyond someone else's hopes, even when the futility of it should have been anticipated or is obvious, I thought. I turned back to face her, and shook my head. "Not interested. Those days are long gone for us and permanently done." *Thank God.*

"Ah," she said, smiling her feral smile, "that must mean you're still involved with your funny-talking Cajun."

I didn't take the bait. "Bye, Toula," I said, and started to turn away again to leave.

"Look at me, Socrates."

I stopped and turned back to face her. "What?" I no longer cared that my impatience with her showed.

"The offer'll stay open. And you'll be back because you can't stay away from me. Just call when you change your mind," she said.

I watched her slowly close her one visible eye like the fade-out at the end of a movie. I turned away and left. I could hear her cackling as I stepped outside.

CHAPTER 41

I RETURNED TO RICHMOND THE NEXT morning, but was not thrilled to be there so soon again. The director had called me at 6:30 a.m., awakened me without an apology, and ordered me to meet with him at 10:00. That's right, he *ordered me*. I tried to deal with the matter over the phone, but his eminence wouldn't have it. He insisted we had to meet in person. This probably was payback for when I refused to tell him over the phone about the theft of the thumb drive. I didn't like his payback, but I respected it.

When the director and I entered his office, he got right down to business, with no introductory pleasantries.

"You have no idea how much trouble you've caused me by not following my directions." he said. "I thought I made myself clear."

"You did," I said. "Perfectly clear. So how'd I cause you trouble? What instructions didn't I follow?" I reminded myself this foppish man was a paying client, and that I needed to check my impatience and hold my tongue.

"What progress have you made, Mr. Cheng? I insist on a full and honest report from you right now."

That pissed me off. The implication of his statement went beyond the boundaries of typical client restlessness because of lack of information and moved into the realm of questioning my integrity. I didn't like the suggestion that my previous report might not have been full and honest. *The hell with accepting payback*, I decided. *I would dish it right back to him.*

"If that's what you wanted, I could have reported to you over the phone," I said. "I didn't need to drive two hours just for that."

"We're paying for your driving time, Suh." He paused, then said, "Your report?" he said. His eyes were unflinching.

I knew a losing hand when I played one so I reluctantly dropped my objection.

"There's not much to report," I said.

"That won't do, Suh. We hired you to find the documents. Now the thumb drive, too. I told you how urgent—"

That did it. I'd had it with this poseur, with his supercilious, condescending bullying. "Then fire me," I said, speaking as quietly and as unemotionally as I could. I was out of patience with this man, who hadn't been candid with me when he should have been.

"If you'd been honest with me in the first place about the cabal, I probably wouldn't have taken your case. As a matter of fact, I have no problem closing the file on this right now. I'll send you my final bill when I get back to DC." I stood up to leave.

I watched the director's face morph through several shades of ruby-red until he appeared apoplectic. He sucked in a deep breath and slowly shook his head. His deep blush gradually diminished until he returned to his usual blotchy, ruddy shade. He stuttered when he tried to speak. I enjoyed watching him dissemble.

"Don't be so hasty, Mr. Cheng," he said. "Please, Suh, sit

back down." He gestured with his hand toward the chair I'd just left. "I didn't mean to gore your ox. I'm under pressure from the trustees to resolve this and make it all go away before outsiders learn what's going on. Please don't take my criticism personally," he said. "The truth be told," he said, "just between us gentlemen, I'm afraid, Suh, my job might be at stake. That's the source of my impatience." He reached up and fingered his bow tie.

I nodded and returned to my seat. "I'm not sure, in any event, I want to continue," I said, "given what I now know about the risk to me and people I care about." I paused, then added, "You should have been candid with me in the first place."

"The risk is exaggerated, Suh. No one actually knows if the secret group you forced me to tell you about is real or is a myth intended to discourage people from snooping. I, myself, do not take it seriously. I've never had reason to."

"Oh? You say you have people who are sworn to protect Lee's secret at any cost, and now I know that secret. Not only that, you were suggesting I kill the thieves when I recover the documents just in case they'd learned the secret. I'd say that's all pretty serious."

He raised his eyebrows. "No, Suh, it is not as dangerous as you portray it," he said.

"Why's that?" I asked.

"Because we have a controlled environment, Mr. Cheng, and you are now within that environment. That's why."

Whatever the hell that's supposed to mean, I thought.

───────── ·••· ─────────

Before I left, I stopped back downstairs at the archives storage room to look around again, hoping I'd see something this time I hadn't noticed before.

I did, but not because I missed them before.

I saw bars on the windows that hadn't been there the last time I inspected the crime scene. And I noticed two cameras located, respectively, at two corners of the ceiling. *Locking the barn door after the horse, and so forth,* I thought.

Nothing else had changed that I could see, so I left the Museum to head back to DC.

CHAPTER 42

Lthough I agreed I would continue with the case, I left the director on a sour note and with my own stew of mixed feelings.

I had to acknowledge — although I did not mention it to the director — that I really had no choice but to see this through to its end because of the continuing risk of harm to me if I just walked away. Since a secret group existed — notwithstanding the director's statement to the contrary — dedicated to protecting Lee's secret, it was likely, if just left alone by me, that eventually, as an outsider who knew the truth, I would become its target. This was likely in spite of the director's statement that I now was part of the protected inner circle. Our loyalties to one another were thinly based and, I had no doubt, would be comfortably cast aside by the director as soon as he deemed it convenient to do so. The only way I could think to avoid harm was to flush out the cabal, as part of my investigation, and to expose its activities.

I climbed into my vehicle, keyed the ignition, and was rewarded with silence. My recently purchased Lincoln wouldn't start. I tried again, but with the same result. I turned on the radio and tried the key again, but just far enough to engage the battery. The radio sprang to life so I knew the problem wasn't the battery.

I called AAA and arranged for a tow truck. My vehicle was taken to the nearest Lincoln dealer. I sat in the waiting room for an hour as the dealer's mechanic examined the vehicle. They finally reported that the fuel pump had died and needed to be replaced. I was fine with that since the vehicle was under warranty. Then the mechanic told me that the pump would have to be ordered since they had none in stock. It would be available and could be installed late the next day. I told the dealer to hold off ordering while I made a call. I didn't want to take the train back to Washington and then have to return to Richmond tomorrow if I could avoid it. I also did not want to spend the night in a hotel in Richmond if I could avoid that.

I called the very last person I wanted to ask for help — the director. I explained the situation to him and asked if he had any suggestions. To his credit, he was gracious, and offered to do what he could for me. He said he would get back to me within the hour.

He called back twenty minutes later. He said he'd learned from a Museum employee, who had made a call at his request, that a local auto repair shop had several reconditioned fuel pumps available that would fit my new vehicle, and that it could be installed today. I thanked the director, called AAA again, and arranged to have my vehicle towed from the dealer's lot to Blankenship's Auto Repair. As I stood outside the dealership and waited for AAA to arrive, the cloudy Tuesday began to sprinkle a light rain.

I wasn't up to sitting in a molded-plastic chair in Blankenship's customers' waiting area so I wandered into the work area to watch my SUV as the mechanic serviced it.

I walked over and nodded to the mechanic, who was standing by the fender wiping his hands on a grease-coated rag. He stared at me with a look of wary curiosity. When I came closer, I could smell cigarette smoke, stale beer, motor oil, sweat, and abject defeat leaching from his clothes and body. As he reached out to retrieve a tool from his work bench, I looked him over. His haggard face and hunched posture exuded the look of someone who knew he'd made a mess of everything that once had guided the arc of his life.

I spoke before he could chase me away.

"Just killing time," I said, as I approached the vehicle, "because the waiting room chairs were killing my back. Hope you don't mind if I watch. I have no clue what you're doing so I'm not here to judge or criticize."

"No problem," he said, "unless the foreman sees you. If he does, I'll have to lie and say you came to ask me a question. Otherwise I'll be canned for letting you back here. Insurance problem, I guess."

"That's fine. I'll cover for you if it comes up."

I watched him continue to set up, then I said, when I thought my interruption wouldn't interfere with his work, "I'm getting a Coke from the machine out front. Can I get you one or something else?"

He shook his head. "I'm good."

When I returned, I noted his name — Caleb — on the oval name tag sewn on his work shirt above the pocket. Not a name you see farther north, at least not in my experience.

"I noticed your name," I said, pointing to the name tag. "I hadn't heard it before. Is it a family name?"

"Yes, Sir," he said. "It goes back to the Civil War on my mother's side. Her peoples' last name was Caleb, and somehow it became my first name."

"Your family fight in the Civil War?" I asked.

"They did," Caleb said. "For the South. Yours?"

I chuckled. "Afraid not. My father's family was still in China when the Civil War was fought; my mother's ancestors were still in Greece. My family didn't come to America until just after World War One."

Caleb nodded, but said nothing.

I sensed tension between us now, although I couldn't begin to suggest its origin. I decided to make other, harmless conversation to try to relax the situation. Failing that, I would say goodbye and wait out front for him to finish my vehicle.

"Are you interested in the Civil War?" I asked.

Caleb turned his head toward me, and said, "Uh huh. You?"

"Only to the extent it affects my work," I said. "Do you study the Civil War like some people do?"

He nodded and grunted. "I'm a reenactor," he said. "Know what that is?"

When I admitted I did not know except in the most general terms, he said, "I'm due for a cigarette break in a few minutes. Walk out back with me and I'll explain, if you're interested, that is."

We walked around behind the one-story concrete slab building. I saw a few rusting vehicle skeletons, some trash bins, and some burned out metal barrels scattered around the yard. The nearby weeds were two or three feet high and unruly. We stood and faced one another on a cleared gravel patch close to the building. The gravel was littered with crushed cigarette butts in varying stages of decay.

Caleb smoked two cigarettes while I stood nearby in the sprinkling rain. He walked me through the concepts of reenactors and reenactments, taking care to be sure I understood what a Hardcore reenactor was and what a Farb was, and especially that I knew that he and his girlfriend were bona fides Hardcores.

"Most people don't get it, but the difference is all in the attitude," he said, "not in the amount of your experience. You can be on your way to becoming a Hardcore and never be a Farb the first day you reenact, if you're thinking right."

I said, "I see," although I wasn't sure I did.

"Think that would interest you?" he said. His tone belied any expectation I would say yes. He took a deep hit from his cigarette, then stared briefly at the butt he held in his fingers, as if surprised to see it there. He abruptly snapped out of it and took another pull on the cigarette while he waited for me to answer.

"Sounds interesting," I said, "but I don't think I'd be up to it. At best I'd be what you called a Farb, if even that good. I'll leave the Civil War reenactments to you and others. Right now I have my hands full trying to help one of your local museums that has Civil War roots."

That statement caught Caleb's attention. I watched him stiffen.

"What do you mean," he said, "if you don't mind me asking?"

"I probably didn't tell you, I'm a private investigator. I'm doing some work for the folks at the museum run by the Golden Knights of the Confederacy." I saw him flinch as I mentioned the Golden Knights.

"Do you know them?" I said.

"I know them," he said. "We all know them. Hate to say this, Mister, since we've been having a nice conversation and all, but you're hooked up with some pansy-ass, élitist snobs who would just as soon as seen my kinfolk be used for target practice as give me the time of day."

"I met them," I said. "I know what you mean. Frankly, I don't like them one bit. But in this economy, a job's a job."

CHAPTER 43

TWO DAYS AFTER MY MEETINGS with the director, and later that morning with Caleb, I was at home listening to a remastered recording of the 1957 Thelonius Monk and John Coltrane concert at Carnegie Hall, when my cellphone rang. The CallerID readout showed Caller Unknown/Private Line.

I usually avoided answering unidentified calls and let them go to voicemail to screen later. For some reason I answered this one.

"Mr. Cheng? Is that you?" a voice I found vaguely familiar asked.

"Who's calling?" I said.

There was a pause, which raised my curiosity, but then the voice said, "This is Winston Starr, Suh. We met at the Museum in the director's office."

I raised my eyebrows. "I remember you well, Mr. Starr." *Indeed I do.* "How can I help you?"

He paused. "I can help you, Suh. I have some information you should know."

"What's that?"

"The director is dead. Murdered in his bedroom. I thought you might want to know."

He thought I might want to know? That news stopped me cold.

If the cabal was responsible, then so much for the notion that it was nothing more than a rumor or, at best, not a real threat. And I guess the director had been wrong when he said the risk wasn't as great as I thought it was since, like him, I now was a member of the Museum's inner circle.

I was able to elicit most of the relevant facts from Starr although it was like pulling teeth. The bottom line: He said the police had described the killing as a home burglary gone bad, perhaps a home invasion.

If the cops were correct in their conclusion, then I'd just over-reacted because it would mean the cabal had not killed the director. *But were the cops correct?*

Starr insisted that I come to Richmond to talk. I insisted we talk right then on the phone, and afterward I would decide if a face-to-face meeting in Richmond was called for.

When he finished summing up what had happened, I said, "Assuming the cops were wrong and the director's death was not the result of a burglary or home invasion, why would anyone — including the secret group within the Golden Knights — kill the director now? He's known Lee's secret all along."

"That's the correct question, Suh, and it is why I firmly believe the police have it wrong. The answer to your question, I believe, is that the director was murdered because he revealed the secret to an outsider. Revealed it to you."

That roiled my stomach. Talk about reinforcing my fears.

I thought about this after we broke off the call. If this was the reason for the director's death, then the risk to me and to people associated with me — to Harte, Clotille and my mother — had just significantly ratcheted up.

I called Harte to tell him what I'd learned, but he didn't answer his office phone. Our receptionist said he hadn't been in all day and hadn't checked in with her. That was unusual. I tried his cellphone, but after a few rings my call went to his voicemail. Then I remembered he'd mentioned he would be out of the office again today to finish painting his living room. Second coat. I assumed he wasn't picking up his calls.

I went into the kitchen, pulled a beer from the refrigerator, and settled into a chair in the living room to think over what I had learned from Starr. I also wanted to consider what my next step should be.

I was getting nowhere fast figuring this out when my cellphone rang again. Once again, the CallerID did not disclose the caller.

"Hello. This is Socrates Cheng," I said. I expected Starr to be on the line again.

"Mr. Cheng," a voice I wasn't familiar with said, "this is Detective Sam Halpern from the Richmond Police Department. I'd like to meet with you as soon as possible."

That got my attention. "Why?" I asked. *Cops do not make random calls to set up innocent meetings.*

"We can talk about it when you get here," he said.

"You want to talk to me about the recent murder of the director of the Museum of the Golden Knights of the Confederacy, don't you?" I said.

"Yes, Sir, that's right. We do. How soon can you be in

Richmond? The sooner we hear your side of the story, the better for you."

My defenses shifted into high gear. *My side of the story? Was I a suspect? It sounded like it. Should I refuse to go to Richmond and first see how things played out?*

I didn't have any answers. Halpern's phone call had caught me off guard. I decided to buy time so I could regroup and talk over my options with Harte, use his cop experience to guide me.

"I was told, Detective, you think the killing was the result of a home burglary or a home invasion gone bad. Is that right?"

"That's one possibility," Halpern said, "but not our only one. It'd be best for everyone concerned if we meet and clear the air. The sooner the better."

"Sorry, Detective," I said, "but I won't be coming to Richmond, not yet anyhow. I had nothing at all to do with the killing. I just learned about it in a telephone call."

"That's not the best way to proceed, Mr. Cheng. If you have nothing to hide—"

"Perhaps it's not," I interrupted, "but it will have to do for now. Besides, you have no jurisdiction over me. You can't make me meet with you."

That last impulsive statement probably wasn't the smartest thing to say, but it was too late now. My brash statement validated what Harte said I too often engaged in, the exercise commonly known as *open mouth and insert foot.*

There was a short pause before the detective spoke again. "You're right, Mr. Cheng, we have no jurisdiction over you, not yet anyway. But that can change as we develop more evidence. You're a lawyer. You should know your attitude doesn't look good for you." He paused, probably waiting for me to change my mind, but I said nothing.

"I'm talking about an interview," Halpern said, "a fact gathering discussion, not an interrogation. If you're not involved you should be anxious to cooperate with us so we can eliminate you as a possible suspect or person of interest. Right now you're making me wonder why you'd act this way."

"Nice try, Detective," I said, "but I know the drill. You can wonder all you want, but it won't make me come to Richmond." *At least not yet it won't.* "That's my final word on it."

"Have it your way, Mr. Cheng, for now. We'll be in touch."

CHAPTER 44

W HEN DETECTIVE HALPERN AND I ended our call, I wanted to talk to Harte, so I immediately phoned him. This time he picked up.

He listened to what I had to say about the detective's and Starr's calls, then said, "Give me an hour to clean myself up, get out of my painting clothes."

Ninety minutes later Harte and I met for lunch at *Stan's*.

"Tell me specifically what they had to say."

I described my conversations.

Harte listened without commenting, although his occasional frowns spoke silent volumes of criticism. When I finished, he said, "Looks like you were right about those crazies guarding Lee's secret."

"Small comfort," I said.

"You want me to work the case with you? You seemed put off when I suggested it before."

"What I'd like is for you to have my back and maybe run down some leads while I get a better fix on the people involved in the cabal."

Harte raised his eyebrows, but didn't object. After a few

seconds he said, "Okay. It's your case, so your call. Let me know if there's something specific I can do for you."

"I suppose now I have to figure out the best way to proceed," I said. "At the least, it's time to circle the wagons and give a heads-up to Clotille and my mother."

I watched Harte's face change. I could see him resist the temptation to retort, as I reminded him that his daughter might be in danger. His face darkened and his forehead wrinkled. His eyes narrowed. I was glad he decided to restrain himself from saying, "I told you so."

"I'm having dinner with Clotille tonight," he said. "I'll catch her up."

I didn't argue even though I would have liked to be the one to bring Clotille up to speed.

CHAPTER 45

Harte and Clotille had developed a tradition of having lunch or dinner together once each week. They'd been doing this for most of Clotille's adult life. Sometimes Rosie joined them, but usually not. This was time, all three agreed, that Harte and his daughter could best use for ongoing father-daughter bonding. Clotille and Rosie were close to one another, too, and did many things together without Harte's participation.

Tonight, at Harte's suggestion, they went into Chinatown to the Golden Dragon Restaurant, located at the corner of 7th and H Streets. The restaurant was owned by Li Bing-fa, who also used the office space in the back as the site of his various business and criminal triad operations.

Harte and Clotille settled into a booth, ordered drinks and food, then toasted one another when their drinks arrived.

"To your health, darling Daughter," Harte said.

Clotille smiled. "And to you, too, Dad."

Harte smiled, then suddenly frowned.

"*Uh, Oh. Here it comes, whatever it is,*" Clotille thought. "What's on your mind, you?" she said. "You're wearing your worried-father face."

Harte nodded and smiled a crooked smile. "You, of course. You and Socrates, to be more specific."

What else is new? Clotille drew in a deep breath, then let it slowly leak out. "Okay, what now?" she said.

"I'd like you to spend less time with him for a while, until the Richmond case we're working is closed out."

"No way," she said, shaking her head. "I'm not worried about those crazies you two are dealing with, them. Not me." She looked hard at Harte and shook her head even more emphatically than before. Her deep green eyes became slits.

"Your association with Socrates puts you at risk, Clotille. If even a little of what we think we know about these people is true, everyone Socrates touches could be in danger."

Clotille shrugged. "That's the price of me having a dad and boyfriend who are PIs. I'll just have to be extra careful, me, until you two solve the case."

She reached across the table and lightly patted the back of her father's hand, as she smiled at him. "Y'all better hurry up and do it," she said, "solve the case, that is." She winked and smiled now.

Harte did not smile back, but he dropped the subject. He knew from hard-won experience just how much he could push his daughter before she responded by pushing back and deliberately doing the opposite of what he wanted.

CHAPTER 46

I BEGAN TO WONDER IF I'D made a tactical error by refusing to go to Richmond to meet with the detective who had called me. I probably seemed guilty to him as a result, or, at the least, had turned myself into a person of interest, if I didn't already occupy that convenient, if ambiguous, status.

I decided I probably had screwed up, but couldn't do anything about it for the time being. If I now rescinded my refusal and volunteered to meet with him, my prompt about-face might itself raise questions about my motives for doing so. This was an instance where, to use one of Harte's favorite clichés about me, I'd clearly shot myself in the foot.

I shelved these thoughts and considered how I should now go about working the case I'd originally set out to clear. The only way I could think to protect myself from the Richmond police would be to identify the burglar or burglars, recover the stolen documents, then have the police make an arrest. Hopefully, this scenario also would lead to the director's killer, if the two crimes were related. That would leave only the Museum's secret cabal to deal with. All this, of course, while overcoming any obstacles that might be put in my path by Winston Starr, because I was not a Museum insider.

I was thinking this through as I folded the laundry I'd

just finished washing and drying, when my cellphone rang. I looked at the CallerID readout, and was surprised by the identity of the caller.

"Hello, Detective Thigpen," I said. "I'm surprised to hear from you, of all people."

"Not as surprised as I am to be calling you, Cheng."

His voice hadn't lost any of its arrogance over the years. But I couldn't help smiling. Thigpen — Harte's partner when Harte was still on the street with the MPD — had been the bane of my existence when we first met, although he had slightly mellowed as I worked the crimes that occurred at my mother's condominium building. By the end of that emotional and complicated investigation, Thigpen actually had been civil to me. But I still was wary of his reason for having called me now, and was not comfortable hearing his voice.

"Why are you calling?" I said. I tried to keep all emotion out of my voice, and not reveal my apprehension and felt need for caution that I experienced just by talking to him. I'd never forgotten how badly he'd treated me when we first met during my pursuit of the missing Mandarin Yellow fountain pen.

"Why am I calling? I'll tell you why, Cheng. Because once again, true to yourself, you pissed off some cops. Don't you ever learn?"

"What're you talking about, Detective? I haven't had any contact with the MPD for a long time," I said. I didn't have a clue what Thigpen was annoyed about.

"The Richmond PD, you moron, not the MPD," he said. "They called the 2D. Want us to convince you to cooperate with them and go to Richmond for a sit down. Captain kicked it over to me because he knows we're old buddies." I could picture him biting down on his cold cigar after he finished saying that — the cigar I never saw him without, but also never saw lit.

I shook my head as if he could see my reaction to his sarcasm.

After a few seconds of silence, he said, "They're willing to come to the 2D station house to meet if you insist, but they do want to meet, Cheng."

"I don't know," I said. I paused to consider the request. What did I have to lose by meeting at the local DC house? It solved the problem of me now wanting to contact the Richmond cops to tell them I'd changed my mind, and now would meet with them, but still I was skeptical of their motives. So I said, "I need to think about this."

"Don't think too long, Cheng," Thigpen said. "Your refusal don't look good. Get back to me. The sooner the better. Better for you," he added. Thigpen ended the call, without saying goodbye, before I could reply.

Almost an hour later my cellphone rang again. This time Harte was calling.

This cannot be a coincidence. It pissed me off that Thigpen and Harte were tag-teaming me.

"Did Thigpen put you up to calling me?" I asked.

"Well, hello to you, too, Partner. Nice to talk to you," Harte said. His sarcasm was palpable. "No," he said, after a pause. "I called Thigpen on an unrelated matter, and he told me he'd talked to you, and why. I offered to call and talk to you about it. As you might have guessed, he didn't care one way or the other."

"Okay," I said, "I'll accept that, but I'm still not inclined to meet, although I admit I do have mixed feelings."

"You need to meet with them, Socrates. You have nothing to hide," Harte said. "Do it at the 2D like Thigpen suggested. Have your lawyer there, too, if that will make you more comfortable."

I thought about that again. It made sense and, in general, was good advice. But my memories of cops mistreating me in the past were difficult to ignore. The thought of voluntarily subjecting myself to their cynicism and sarcasm, to their previously expressed cultural and racial biases, stressed me.

Unfortunately, I didn't see I had any other choice. After a few seconds I said, "Okay. I'll make the call and set it up."

Thirty minutes later, after I had called and spoken to one of my former law partners — the partner who practiced criminal defense law — to get his advice, I called the Richmond cops to set up a meeting at the 2D, this to occur in two days.

CHAPTER 47

A s I ENDED THE CALL to the Richmond detective, my cellphone rang. Once again the caller's identity was blocked. I couldn't avoid taking such calls at the moment, not while I had an investigation to conduct, so I answered.

"Mr. Cheng, please."

"Speaking," I said. I didn't recognize the caller's voice.

"Mr. Cheng, y'all don't know me, Suh, but my name is Hervey Beauregard. I'm one of the trustees of the Museum of the Golden Knights of the Confederacy. I know y'all have been working with our late director on a top priority and confidential matter. I've been designated to step in and take the director's place running the investigation.

"The other trustees and I would like to meet with you so you can bring us up to date on your progress, now that the director no longer will be involved."

No longer will be involved? That's an interesting way to refer to the director's murder. "When?" I said.

"As soon as possible. Tomorrow morning would be best, if that's possible."

I hesitated while I considered this. The trustees were entitled to meet with me and hear what I had to say. After all, they were footing my bill. "Okay," I said. "Tomorrow morning. What time?"

The drive to Richmond was difficult. As soon as I entered my vehicle, the dark sky gave way to thunder, lightning, and pounding rain. It did not let.

A Museum employee I'd never seen before met me at the front door and said to follow him. As he turned away, I shot my cuffs, smoothed my hair on both sides with my palms, and fell into step behind him.

I was ushered into a small conference room. I counted six people in attendance around an oval table. I expected to see Winston Starr there, too, since he was a trustee, but he wasn't present. I didn't recognize any of the people there.

"Thank you for coming on such short notice, Mr. Cheng," a middle aged, over-weight man said as I entered. He was standing by a chair. Everyone else was sitting. He extended what I was about to learn was his politician's hand. His perfunctory handshake was devoid of any interest in me.

I looked closely at the man. He had the florid cheeks and spider-veined nose of a heavy drinker, and wore a foppish bow tie. His teeth were small like kernels of corn, and almost as yellow.

"We spoke on the phone, Suh. I'm Hervey Beauregard. Please have a seat." He tilted his head toward the only empty chair at the table, other than the one he rested his right hand on. His chair, I assumed.

I took the seat and quickly cast my glance around the table, returning an occasional nod as my eye caught the eye of one or more of the trustees.

After Beauregard introduced me, he said, "We would appreciate it if you will tell us the business terms of your engagement by the director. It seems he didn't create any record of hiring you."

Interesting, I thought. "How did you know he hired me, then?"

"Mr. Starr, Winston Starr, told us," Beauregard said. "I believe you met him through the director."

I nodded. I again wondered why Starr wasn't present.

I described the terms of our firm's engagement, including a statement of our hourly billing rate, and the approximate charges we had incurred so far. I pointed out that our first billing statement remained unpaid, and was overdue. I told the trustees why I had been hired and everything else I could think of relating to the case, including telling them about the break-in at our office and the consequent missing thumb drive. Unlike the director, the trustees didn't show any discomfort when I told them about the stolen thumb drive.

"How much progress have you made identifying the thieves and recovering the stolen documents and thumb drive?" Beauregard said.

I never have been good at giving false assurances to people, but I wanted to give the trustees some hope and comfort, so I said, "Not as much progress as I'd like, but I'm pursuing some good leads. It will take more time before I have anything concrete to report."

I looked at Beauregard. His face had darkened. He did not seem mollified.

After a noticeable period of silence, Beauregard said, "Is there anything you haven't told us, Mr. Cheng?"

Given the secrecy the Museum practiced, I resented the

question. I hadn't held anything back, on the theory that the trustees, collectively, now were my employer, and that they therefore had the right to be brought fully up to speed. The problem was I didn't know if I could trust them all or if one or more of the trustees might be affiliated with the cabal. I also wondered if one of them was the mole I had alerted the director about. I made a point of not mentioning the possibility of a double-dealer among them.

"Nothing else," I said. "I've told you everything about my part in the investigation."

"Good," Beauregard said. He looked around the table and said to the trustees, "Does anyone have anything they'd like to ask Mr. Cheng?" No one did.

"Fine," Beauregard said. "Mr. Cheng, we would like you to continue with the case on the same terms as when you worked with the director."

I thought this might be a good time for me to pursue a line of inquiry I wanted to open. I needed to use what little leverage I still had before it evaporated.

"Before I decide if I'll stay with the case and go forward, I want to know more about the secret cabal within the Golden Knights. What can you gentlemen tell me?" I looked from blank face to blank face.

Silence hovered over the room like a damp blanket. None of the trustees looked at me, choosing this moment, instead, to study their fingernails or to gaze at the surface of the table in front of them. It was as if they were afraid I might call on them to answer an oral-exam question if I caught any of them looking at me. I realized that this was a hopeless avenue of pursuit with this crowd, so I dropped it.

After almost a minute of dead-air time, I said, "I'll

need a point person to report to now that the director's not available." I thought that one good euphemism by Beauregard concerning the director's murder deserved another one from me.

"You will report directly to Mr. Starr," Beauregard said. "He will keep the trustees informed of your progress."

I wasn't crazy about that arrangement since Starr had resisted hiring an outsider — namely, me — in the first place, but I didn't see I had any choice. "All right," I said. "Let's give it a try, see how that works out."

CHAPTER 48

POOLE SAT ON HIS FRONT lawn drinking bottled water and cooling down from his run along the George Washington Memorial Parkway, adjacent to the Potomac River.

The run had been good for him. It had given him the chance to think about the contract he'd accepted the day before from Aunt Marge.

As he passed the three mile mark, just before he turned back to head home, he came to the decision that although he would fulfill the new contract and kill the Washington PI, as he had agreed with Marge he would do, he also would later have a heart-to-heart talk with her to convince Marge not to offer him any more assignments in his backyard. He also would have to convince her not to drop him as one of her first-choice contractors. On balance, he decided, the Washington hit would be the easy part. Staying in Aunt Marge's good graces would be tricky. She could be very temperamental.

Having finally formulated his approach to this nascent career struggle, Poole, satisfied he had just made the correct decision, went inside to shower and to begin planning how he would execute the contract against the DC private investigator.

CHAPTER 49

WHEN MY MEETING WITH THE trustees ended, I didn't leave the building right away. I asked for directions to Starr's office, and was led there by a secretary. I wanted to give Starr the news that we'd be working together, just in case he was having a good day I could spoil for him.

I knocked on his door and entered when he instructed me to. I could tell from his face that he was not happy to see me, but he donned the trappings of a gentleman and recovered quickly. He bade me welcome with what seemed to be a faux smile, and asked me to sit down. He did not rise from behind his desk or offer to shake my hand.

"I didn't know you were here," he said.

I told him about the trustees' request for the meeting and that I had been engaged by the trustees to continue my efforts to recover the stolen documents and thumb drive. Neither my news about the trustees' meeting he hadn't attended nor my re-engagement by the trustees seemed to faze him until I told him I was to report directly to him. I watched him briefly frown at this news, then just as quickly resume his easiest smile.

"That's odd," he said, "the other trustees haven't told me. Are you sure?"

Believe me, I am, it wasn't my choice. I nodded. "I'm sure."

I could see the wheels turning in his head. I changed the subject. "So, Mr. Starr, once again, what more can you tell me about the cabal?"

"Nothing." He shifted slightly in his chair.

"Can you call them off since I've agreed to keep General Lee's secret, and they therefore have no reason to think I might reveal it?"

"First off, Suh," he said, "as I understood it from the late director, revealing Lee's secret, in and of itself, is not the only issue with the cabal."

"I thought you told me that this was the reason the cabal murdered the director," I said, "because he revealed Lee's secret to me?"

Ignoring my question, Starr said, "Merely knowing the secret appears to be sufficient to put one in harm's way." He paused, probably to let this sink in. Then he added, "In any event, Mr. Cheng, I cannot call off the cabal since I don't know if it really exists. For all I know, the director made up the idea of the cabal to keep you and the trustees honest."

I didn't believe this for a minute.

The problem with Starr's assertion was that he and the director, based on their body language and their curt statements when the director first told me about the cabal, had seemed to agree that the cabal existed. Those spontaneous tells by them at that time were more persuasive to me now than Starr's current, convenient disclaimer.

CHAPTER 50

T HE NEXT MORNING, BACK IN DC, I met as scheduled at the 2D house on Idaho Avenue, with Richmond detectives Halpern and his partner, Stella. The first thing Halpern did was badge me so I would know this meeting was formal and official, not the casual interview he had alluded to on the telephone. I felt tricked.

Nevertheless, once we settled into the interview room, Halpern described our meeting as an informal chat to eliminate me as a suspect or as a person of interest.

Thigpen, who was in the interview room when I arrived, did not sit in on the interview, although Halpern invited him to do so as a non-participating observer. I assumed Thigpen would watch us from a contiguous room, from behind the two-way mirror hanging on an adjacent wall.

I didn't know how much I would disclose to these cops because I didn't want to become a defendant in a civil lawsuit against me brought by the Museum for breach of my confidentiality agreement. I would have to proceed carefully.

I wasn't particularly concerned that I had disclosed limited information to Harte, to my mother, and to Clotille because I didn't expect that this would ever become known. But any disclosures I might make to the cops could become part of the public record and would be discoverable in litigation if the cops had any reason to tip off the Museum that they'd learned about the theft of the documents and thumb drive.

On the other hand, I didn't want to be subject to an obstruction of justice arrest by the Richmond police, or even arouse suspicion, by my failure to be forthcoming, that I might have had a hand in the director's murder. I would have to walk a tightrope, high above the fray, and do a delicate balancing act during this interview if I was going to walk away unscathed or, at least, not at future risk from either the Richmond cops or the Museum.

"Thank you for meeting with us," Halpern said. "This is my partner, Al Stella." He canted his head toward the other cop, who sat across the table from me. I noted that Halpern had been informal in his introduction, saying Al Stella, not Detective Stella. *On guard, Socrates!* I thought.

I looked at Stella, and nodded.

Halpern continued. "You're a lawyer, Mr. Cheng, so you should know why we want this informal interview and what we hope to accomplish. If not, I can go through it for you."

I nodded again. I felt as if he was patronizing me with sweet talk or maybe setting me up. Act one, perhaps, of the *good cop, bad cop* routine.

"The director of the Museum of the Golden Knights of the Confederacy in Richmond was strangled in his bedroom," Halpern said. "But you already knew that, didn't you?"

Was he being the good cop or the bad cop? I couldn't tell which yet. "I knew he'd been murdered," I said, "but not strangled, not how he was killed or where in his home."

"And how'd you learn he'd been killed?" Halpern said.

"Winston Starr, one of the trustees of the Museum, called and told me."

"Why would he do that?" Halpern asked. He glanced briefly at his partner.

"Because he knows I'd been hired by the director to handle an investigation for the Museum. The director recently introduced us. Starr sat in on part of our second meeting."

"I see," Halpern said. He stood up from his chair, walked away from the table, and faced the wall. After almost a full minute, he turned back and returned to his seat. He glanced over at his partner again.

"Tell us about the case you're working for the Museum," Halpern said.

I dreaded reaching this point, but it was inevitable we'd get there.

"I have a problem, Detective," I said. I looked at him, then at Stella, then back at Halpern.

"When I agreed to take the case for the Museum, the director required me to sign a confidentiality agreement. Even though the director's dead, I'm still bound by my agreement and can be sued by the Museum if I disclose anything about my investigation."

"Bullshit!" Stella said, from his seat across the table. "You can also find your ass in jail for obstruction, you don't cooperate with us." He spoke in an easygoing tone that belied the threat his words served up. He looked hard at me and did not break eye contact.

Obviously he was the bad cop. I nodded because I knew he was right. It would take a court order specifically instructing me to disclose the confidential information to the cops to protect me from a civil lawsuit brought by the Museum, asserting a breach of the agreement by me. Short of that, I would have to act at my peril. I was trapped.

I decided to tell Halpern and Stella what I could about the theft, the documents, and my investigation, using such general terms as I hoped I could get away with to satisfy them.

I started by saying that some historic documents had been stolen from the Museum, that I was trying to find and return them. I assured Halpern and Stella that when I identified the thief or thieves, I would share that information with them.

When I finished and looked from Halpern to Stella, then back at Halpern, to see if my performance had fulfilled their expectations, Halpern said, "That's too general. Be more specific."

I next said that the documents consisted of a nineteenth century journal and some related-period letters. That, too, was not good enough.

I then said that the journal had been written by an ex-slave and that the letters had been sent by Anne Carter Lee and Elizabeth Van Lew. I had to explain to the detectives who these women were. I did not bring up Robert E. Lee's name or how he figured into the stolen trove of documents.

When I finished, Halpern said, "Well, Mr. Cheng, that didn't sound like no big deal. You could've told us that in the first place and saved us all some ill will and grief."

"I suppose," I said. Even though I apparently had satisfied the detectives, I wasn't comfortable even with the small amount of information I had disclosed. I didn't want it to come back later to bite me.

Halpern stood up and stretched. He closed his notebook and returned his ballpoint pen to his jacket pocket.

"Why don't we take a ten-minute break," he said, "and

when we start up again, Mr. Cheng, you can tell us everything you held back."

"But, Detective—"

Halpern held up his palm. "No *but*, Mr. Cheng. You either come clean or we go to the DA and have you indicted for obstruction. Then we'll extradite you from DC to Richmond, where we do have jurisdiction, and where we're in charge of the rules and define the playing field. It's up to you." He cast a sinister smile at me.

"Can we first see if I can get a waiver from the Museum," I said, "since the circumstances are unusual? Maybe it won't be a big deal, so why anticipate a problem?"

"Sure," Halpern said. "You've got ten minutes before we start up again. Make good use of it. And by the way, don't even think about not coming back."

The Museum — specifically, the seven trustees, speaking through Starr — refused to give me the waiver. Starr acted fully sympathetic with my circumstances, but was unyielding. In fact, he was emphatic that I could not give up Lee's name and the secret the documents held about him, reminding me that I would be sued by the Museum if I did so. Indeed, Starr seemed upset that the Richmond cops even now knew that the burglary had occurred.

"You also are not permitted, Mr. Cheng," Starr remind me, "to say anything about the cabal." He stated again that the Museum would sue me for breach of agreement should I make any other disclosures to the police — any at all. I was rapidly finding myself in a *no win* position, pinned between the Richmond cops and the Museum's trustees.

I headed back to the interview room. Halpern and his partner were there waiting for me. As I entered the room, I felt as if I was carrying a load of bricks on my back.

Halpern turned on his portable tape recorder, said introductory words into the microphone indicating who was present, the time, and the date. Then he looked over at me.

"Let's get started, Mr. Cheng," Halpern said. "Tell us what you left out before. Everything."

I spent the next forty minutes taking the detectives through the whole transaction, with two exceptions. I told them there was a former slave's journal and about the existence of the Anne Carter letters, the Van Lew letters, and everything I knew about the cabal, but I did not tell them that it existed specifically to protect a particular secret concerning Robert E. Lee. I said, instead, that the cabal existed to protect Lee's reputation, hoping that my general statement would pass muster with them. I also did not tell them that the stolen documents referred to a secret. I was betting that this information wasn't necessary for them to know in order for them to do their job, yet it would have sealed my fate with the Museum if it were to become known I disclosed it. Much to my surprise, the detectives didn't press me and seemed satisfied by what I told them.

When I finished and had answered Halpern's questions, he turned off the recording device and said, "Okay, Mr. Cheng. Now, that wasn't so hard, was it?" He paused and raised his eyebrows in a smile. "That should do it for today. We'll be in touch."

CHAPTER 51

THE NIGHT AFTER MY MEETING with the Richmond detectives, Harte and I had dinner again at the *Prime Rib*. I wanted to fill him in on the interview with Halpern and Stella, and talk about our next steps in the investigation. When we arrived at the restaurant, we chatted for a few minutes with JQ, then moved to the bar for a few minutes before ordering dinner.

Harte wasn't pleased with my performance with Detectives Halpern and Stella, and made no bones about telling me. Since I hadn't yet told him anything about the meeting, I assumed the Richmond detectives had complained to Thigpen that I still was holding something back — in spite of their seeming satisfaction with the interview when it ended — and that Thigpen, in turn, had passed on their displeasure to Harte.

"You needed to show them you were cooperating," Harte said. "There's no percentage in holding back or seeming to be holding back. It'll come around to bite your ass every time."

I thought I had done well, and that Harte was showing his one-time cop ties by what he said.

"They seemed satisfied," I said, although I no longer was as sure about that as I had been before Harte and I talked.

"They weren't, not according to Thigpen," Harte said.

He fanned out his hands in a *What am I going to do with you?* type gesture.

"All right," he said "Enough of that." He shook his head, clearly frustrated with me. "What's next?"

"Unfortunately, another trip to Richmond. I need a face-to-face with Starr again. He wasn't very forthcoming the other day when I stopped by his office. Among other things, I want to be sure his expectations and objectives in our investigation now are the same as the director's had been. It's possible they're not and that's why he was holding back when I talked to him."

"Want me along when you meet?" Harte said.

I thought about that. Starr probably wouldn't like knowing that Harte was involved in the case, and likely would be displeased if I brought him along, so I said, "Good idea. Come to Richmond with me. We'll brace him together."

Starr approached us just inside the Museum's front entrance. I watched his usually expressionless face slide into a scowl when he noticed Harte.

He walked up to us, but ignored Harte, addressing me as if I had brought along my pet dog on a leash, but was otherwise there alone.

After nodding to me, he tilted his head toward Harte, and said, "Who's this?" He still hadn't acknowledged Harte directly.

I deliberately mimicked Starr, and tilted my head toward Harte, and said, "My partner. He'll sit in with us."

I could tell from his face that Starr wasn't happy about this, but he didn't say anything. He turned away and silently led us back to his new office. I looked over at Harte as we walked behind Starr. I smiled and winked at him. Harte nodded once. He understood the game.

When we were settled, I said, "Congratulations on your new position."

Starr wrinkled his forehead and looked at me with confusion written all over his face. I was pleased with myself for my ambiguous statement.

"New position? What are you—?"

I cut him off. "I assume you're the new director since you're in this office now." Starr had taken over the director's office.

Starr frowned. "Not yet," he said. "Not officially. Not quite yet." He puffed up as he said this.

"Oh," I said. "I didn't mean any offense. I just assumed it since we're in here..." I glanced at Harte and raised my eyebrows. Harte seemed to be fighting a smile.

"Let's get started, Suh," Starr said, as he looked at me, still ignoring Harte. "You wanted this meeting."

I glanced down at my notes, then said, "Since, as you know, I'll be continuing the investigation and reporting directly to you, I want to be sure your objectives and expectations are the same as the director's. You and I need to be on the same page."

"What do you think the director's objectives and expectations were, Mr. Cheng?" Starr said. His tone had turned decidedly defensive.

"That we recover the stolen documents, including the thumb drive, and in doing so attempt to preserve General Lee's secret," I said.

"My objectives are the same, but you will also need to

insure that the thieves do not ever reveal the secret. That's an important part of your assignment," Starr said. "Didn't the director tell you that?"

Harte and I glanced at one another, moving only our eyes, not our heads. Harte shook his head, almost imperceptibly.

He spoke up for the first time since we'd entered Starr's office. "We won't take part in that," he said. He looked hard at Starr.

Starr seemed annoyed that Harte had responded, rather than me. He frowned and looked at me as if I were a ventriloquist who had spoken through Harte by moving his lips.

"Then you're off the case," Starr said, as he straightened up taller in his chair. He frowned again, nodded at Harte for the first time, then shook his head as if glad to be rid of us pests once and for all.

I stood up from my chair. "Fine," I said. "I'll send you our final bill for our services through the end of today, as we wrap up our part in the investigation." Harte stood up, too. We turned to leave.

Starr quickly rose from his seat and held up his palm in a gesture of abject resignation. "Stop, please. Don't be so hasty, Gentlemen." He sighed. "Can't we at least defer the decision on that part of your assignment, Suh?" He looked at me and then at Harte. Harte stared back impassively.

"No," I said, as I turned back to face him. "We can't. That subject's not open for consideration."

Starr's face and shoulders suddenly slumped. His overall bearing wilted. He suddenly seemed rubbery. "All right," he said, speaking softly, his voice barely audible. "Let's drop it."

His voice and bearing now exuded surrender. He was a beaten man.

Harte and I returned to our seats. We didn't comment on Starr's forced capitulation.

Starr slowly sank down into his chair. He stared at me as if he was lost in confusion. I decided to take the reins, press our advantage, and charge forward.

"Tell us about the secret cabal," I said.

I watched Starr stiffen. He briefly looked at Harte, then at me, then looked away. As he answered, he stared down at his desk.

"I don't know anything specific about it. I told you that already."

Yes, he had, but I didn't believe him then and I didn't believe him now.

Harte spoke up. "Humor us. Tell us what you do know even if it's just rumor. Pretend this is our first conversation about the cabal."

Starr told us everything he knew — or, he said it was everything he knew. He didn't change anything the director had already told me so I tended to believe he was telling us the truth when he finally said he had nothing else to add.

"Okay," I said. "We'll take it from here. I'll get back to you as soon as we have something. If anything comes up at this end, call me right away." I finally felt in charge of my own investigation. It felt good.

Starr nodded, seemingly without any enthusiasm. He stood up, then walked us to the Museum's exit.

As Harte and I started through the doorway, Starr said, "Keep me up to date. I don't like surprises."

"Neither do we, Mr. Starr," I said. "Trust me. Neither do we."

CHAPTER 52

ARTE AND I RETURNED TO DC in time for me to meet Clotille for a late lunch. We had scheduled it before I knew Harte and I would be going to Richmond.

After Clotille and I finished eating, we headed our separate ways, Clotille to her office, I to mine.

I finished up what I needed to do at the office and left for home a little after 10:00 p.m. I'd been catching up on other cases, as well as some office administration matters.

On my way home I swung by *KramerBooks & Afterwords*, a combination café and bookstore located on Connecticut Avenue, between Dupont Circle and Q Street. I wanted to pick up a recently published biography of Aaron Burr. I then cut through Dupont Circle, which had its usual springtime evening crowd of young people sitting around the fountain and on park benches, some playing guitars, some playing chess, and some smoking cigarettes or pot. The ambiance was subdued and friendly.

I crossed the Circle and headed west to the P Street exit, passed *Second Story Books* at the corner of 20th and P, and walked along P Street toward 22nd. Just after I turned south on 22nd, and passed the alley between *Books for America* and the PHASE I/DUPONT nightclub, I felt a hand grab my shoulder. I stiffened, experienced a brief, burning panic in my stomach, and yanked my shoulder away, as I spun around toward the person behind me. My long neglected *Kobudo* training reflexively kicked in but, as I prepared to engage in hand-to-hand combat to defend myself, my head took control of my emotions and I stood down. *Kobudo could not defeat a bullet from the Glock G42 pointed at my chest.*

I faced two men, seemingly in their twenties, their faces unmasked, one with a knife, one with the Glock. The assailant with the pistol stood away from me, out of my reach. I glanced around. Twenty-second street, often backed up with automobile traffic, was deserted just when I needed witnesses.

"Look," I said, staring from the face of one of the muggers to the other, "you can have everything on me." I started to reach for my wallet. "I won't give you any trouble."

"Get ya hands up, Motherfucker," the one with the knife said.

I slowly raised my hands and nodded. My eyes darted from one face to the other, and back again, in an endless loop.

The mugger with the Glock stepped toward me and put his hand on my chest. He suddenly shoved me hard, back toward the deep end of the alley. Then, dramatically, with several jerks of his head, he nodded me more deeply in.

"Move it, Asshole. Walk into the alley away from the street. Do it now!"

I cautiously stepped deeper into the alley, away from the view of anyone who might come along the sidewalk or who might drive by on 22nd Street. I didn't have any other choice.

"Give me your wallet," the mugger holding the knife said.

I reached into my sports jacket, as I walked toward the

back of the alley, and pulled out my wallet. I held it up in one hand just above my shoulder, inviting the mugger nearest me to take it.

"Turn around and empty your pockets," he said, as he took my wallet from my hand.

I stopped walking and turned back to face the muggers. I handed over about $150 in cash, held together by a Tiffany antique sterling silver money clip Clotille had given me for my birthday. Giving up that engraved money clip bothered me more than surrendering my wallet, credit cards, cash, iPhone, or my dignity. More than my felt helplessness.

"The watch, too, Fuckhead," the other mugger said, pointing to my wrist. I handed it over.

It suddenly occurred to me that the muggers weren't wearing masks, that they apparently were not concerned that I might be able to identify them if they later were picked up by the police. That did not bode well for my survival when this mugging had run its course.

The mugger with the knife stepped close to me and patted me down while his companion covered me with the Glock. He came across my 1929 Parker Duofold *Big Red* classic fountain pen I carried in my inside jacket pocket, and took it. That, too, rankled. He also took my cellphone. For the first time, I realized both men were wearing latex gloves.

I remained quietly sullen and stared straight ahead, deliberately not making eye contact with them. I didn't want to suggest in any manner that I might challenge them.

"Walk back deeper into the alley and don't turn around for five minutes," one of the muggers said. "Understand?" He pushed me backward, a long step farther into the alley. "Do it now," he shouted, his face just inches from mine. He pushed me again.

I stumbled, but caught my balance. As I started to turn away from the street to walk toward the far end of the alley, I slowly turned and glanced back. The muggers were gone.

I stood still for about half a minute, then cautiously walked back to the street, and looked around. I didn't see the two men, so I walked home, shivering all the way on this tepid night. My shirt was soaked through with sweat.

The first thing I did when I arrived home was change into a fresh shirt, take two aspirin, and pour myself a tall Scotch. Then I went on line with my laptop and brought up the iTunes Home Page. I navigated to the App called *Find My iPhone*, and sent a signal through my iCloud account to my cellphone, locking it so the muggers couldn't use it. I then sent another signal to my phone that wiped the SIM card clean so its data couldn't be captured if the SIM card was removed from the phone. I quickly drank the entire glass of Scotch I'd poured for myself.

Even though it was late in the evening, I thought about calling the police to report the mugging and theft. I decided neither the effort nor the time was worth it since I had not been physically hurt and it was unlikely my pen, watch, money clip, iPhone, or cash would ever be recovered. I let the police report pass. I did, however, call my credit card companies to cancel my cards and to order new ones with new account numbers.

I also did not call my homeowners' insurance company to file a claim because fountain pens and cellphones were specifically excluded from coverage under the standard homeowners' policy I carried. Besides, my deductible was high enough that I would not recover sufficient funds to justify the long-term increase in my annual premium payment that would result from a claim for my watch and money clip.

What I did do was make a list of things to do tomorrow morning: replace my driver's license; buy a new iPhone; make a withdrawal from my bank account and arrange to obtain a new ATM card; select another fountain pen from my collection to use for everyday writing; and, sadly, get with Clotille to tell her about the loss of the money clip.

In the end, I was rattled by the mugging and by its inherent possibility of physical harm, although this fortunately had not occurred. I was angry, too, mostly with the circumstances. I poured another two fingers of Glenlivet, turned on some music, and sat in the dark until about an hour later when I fell asleep in my chair.

CHAPTER 53

THE NEXT DAY CLOTILLE AND I met for a quick lunch at *KramerBooks*. In a sense, I felt as if I was returning to the scene of the crime since I had been there just before I was mugged. I hadn't yet told Clotille about this. I would bring it up over lunch.

We browsed the history section of the book store while we waited for our table. Once we were settled and had ordered, I said, "Something happened to me last night we should talk about."

Clotille's face tightened. She sat up straighter in her seat. Her concern for me was written large in her stiffened-body language as she leaned across the table and took my hand.

"I'm all right, but I was robbed at gunpoint — and knifepoint, too — last night."

Clotille's entire body stiffened. She dropped my hand, then immediately picked it up again. "Oh, my God. Are you hurt, you?" She squeezed my hand so hard I had to peel off her fingers, one by one, to ease the pressure. The only hurt was right now, in my crushed hand.

"I'm fine. I wasn't hurt, just rattled and pissed off." I hesitated, then added, "Well, my pride also was hurt for what that's worth." I looked to see Clotille's reaction, looked for her ostensible support, but she sat there impassively. When she realized I was staring at her, she cast a feeble smile across the table.

I continued, "Most of what they took I've already taken steps to replace. My wallet, iPhone, credit cards, fountain pen. But they took my money clip, too, the one you gave me. I'm sorry about that. I loved it."

"Oh, Socrates, that doesn't matter. It only matters you're okay, you."

I wished I could have been that nonchalant about the loss of the money clip.

Our meals came and we focused our attention on eating. When I looked up at Clotille several times, I could see she was deep in thought as she stared at her platter. Twice she caught me watching her and returned a forced smile. I tried to make small talk, but it didn't take hold.

As we sipped coffee at the end of the meal, I said, "May we talk about the Richmond case your father and I are working on?"

Clotille came back to life. "Not if y'all are going to use it as an excuse for us to stop seeing each other until it's solved, you can't." Her eyes narrowed and stared into mine, challenging me to defy her.

Where did that come from? Then I realized where. It had to have been Harte. He obviously had said something to her.

"No, of course not," I said, "but I'll bet Harte tried that out on you, didn't he?" I smiled and raised my eyebrows.

"Of course he did, him," she said. "Protect poor little ol' Clotille. That's my father's mantra, you know." She didn't smile. She completely missed the humor in her father's predictable, but futile attempts to safeguard her.

"He ran that by me, too," I said, "but it went nowhere. It's time he and I accept the fact that this beautiful, redheaded Cajun woman we both love is not a child, and that she has a mind of her own. A very strong mind."

"I'm glad y'all got that right, you. Maybe you should work on Harte, bring him around," she said. "It's obvious I can't."

She stared at me briefly, then said, "I'm tired of him treating me like a child." She nodded dramatically, as if the movement underscored her sincerity and resolve. She looked hard into my eyes and stared, as if challenging me to argue against her position. I said nothing. I occasionally knew when to keep quiet.

"Enough of that. What about your Richmond case?" she finally said.

"I need to vent my frustration and pick your brain, if you don't mind."

"Vent and pick away, you. I'm all yours for the next twenty minutes," she said, as she turned over her wrist to check her watch. "Then it's back to work for me."

I summarized the case for her, adding a few facts I'd learned since we last talked about it, as well as facts I'd intentionally left out before. Clotille was a good listener. She didn't interrupt once.

When I finished, she said, "What're the problems bothering y'all?"

"Lack of cooperation," I said, "from the very people I'm trying to help, the people who hired me. The passive/aggressive people who insist we speed up the resolution of the case, but aren't forthcoming when I ask them for information. Specifically, I'm talking about Starr and, to a lesser extent, about Beauregard."

"Give me a for instance," Clotille said.

I paused to think of an example. "Take Starr. He didn't want me involved in the first place because I'm an outsider. I get that. But I am involved now, and have been told to report directly to him. Unfortunately, although he's been demanding a quick resolution, he doesn't cooperate with me. For instance, when we asked him about the cabal, he blew us off." I shook my head at the memory. "I hate passive/aggressive people."

"What else?" Clotille asked.

"Beauregard, too. Another passive/aggressive type. I can't get him to even acknowledge the existence of the cabal. He just insists on quick results. He says he wants to help me, but then does nothing."

Clotille looked pensive and thoughtful while I waited for her response. After a minute she said, "If they won't tell you about the cabal, then we have only one choice."

I didn't care for that *we* stuff, but didn't raise the point. I must have looked confused because Clotille reached over and stroked my cheek with the back of her fingers. She smiled, too.

"If the Museum's people won't tell you what you want to know about the cabal, Socrates, then you'll just have to get the cabal itself to come to you," she said, "so you can learn from them folks what you want to know."

Now I knew I looked confused, because I was. "What are you talking about?"

"You'll just have to do something that will draw out the cabal and make them people come to you," she said. "Set out some bait they'll bite at, them, and have your trap set waiting to spring. Like the cliché about Mohammed and the mountain that wouldn't come to him. That's what I mean."

CHAPTER 54

Detective Halpern looked at his partner across his and Stella's face-to-face desks, noted that Stella was staring off into space — a sure sign he was bothered by something — and said, "What's on your mind, Al?"

"That Washington PI. His whole explanation don't smell right to me."

"How so?" Halpern trusted Stella's instincts. They had been partnered for nine years, and in that time Halpern had learned not to second guess Stella's radar when it came to perps, witnesses, or persons of interest. Stella had second sight when it came to subtle body-language reveals.

"His story's too pat, almost rehearsed. More I think about it, the less I believe it."

Halpern nodded. "Okay. What do ya wanna do?"

"I say let's look at him harder. Even if we have to spend some time in DC. The lieutenant will give us some leeway on that if we make a good case to her for doing so. The Chinaman's our best lead right now anyway, unless you have something better you haven't told me about."

"I'm with you on it. But let's not bring the DC cops into it yet. We don't wanna tip him off. His PI partner used to be on the job, so who knows who we can trust at the 2D house if word gets out we're diggin' into the PI."

Stella smiled and gave Halpern a thumbs up.

CHAPTER 55

"HELLO, MA," I SAID INTO my cellphone. "If you haven't already made lunch, don't. I'll take you out." I explained that this was not in lieu of having dinner with me and Clotille, that I hadn't yet worked out a date for the three of us, but that I thought having lunch together in the meantime would be nice.

After my father died, my mother and I instituted the practice of going out to lunch every other week, no matter how busy I was with work. It had helped us move through our grief. We also enjoyed each other's company.

As my PI practice picked up, however, and I found myself eating sit-down lunches less and less frequently, we fell into the habit of not making lunch plans together or, worse, scheduling lunch, but then cancelling — with me cancelling, that is. I was determined to change this starting today.

I drove over and picked her up at her condo. We drove back to my home and parked the vehicle in my garage space beneath my condo building. Then we walked to Jefferson Place, a picturesque street running between, and perpendicular to, Connecticut Avenue and 19th Street, just around the corner from *The Palm Restaurant* and from Theodore Roosevelt's house when he was vice president of the United States. We were headed to *Giovanni's Trattu* to eat Italian.

Once we were seated and had ordered, my mother said, "This is a nice change, Socrates. I'm glad we're having lunch again."

"Me, too, Ma. I feel bad, but I've gotten so busy I hardly ever eat lunch out anymore, let alone on a regular, scheduled basis. My lunches are usually sandwiches in my vehicle while I sit surveillance."

That seemed to fly right by her.

"*Ti néa, Socrates — What's going on with you?* You don't hardly ever stop by to visit me anymore or even drop in unannounced for coffee like you used to. When you came by last week to talk to me about your case, I was in shock just seeing you."

I didn't want to point out that we'd had this same conversation last week. I also didn't have any response to what she said other than, "I'm sorry." What can you say when your mother's right, and you don't want to come clean about the true nature of the problem, do not want to say that you prefer spending your limited free time with your girlfriend, not sipping coffee in your mother's kitchen talking about and rehashing the *same old, same old.*

"*Signomi, Ma — I'm sorry, Ma,*" I said. "That will change. I promise."

"So, Socrates," my mother said, coyly changing the subject to rescue her favorite, her only son, "What's new in the Richmond case that's keeping you so busy you can't visit your mother? I know that's what it is even if you won't say. Will you at least make a bundle of dough from the work?"

"Just our usual hourly rate and our per diem," I said. "I won't be able to retire from it."

My mother finished her coffee and signaled the waiter for another. I continued to work on my first cup.

"So, Socrates, you never said to me, is this case dangerous? Should I light a candle every morning at Saint Sophia for you?"

Before I could respond, she said, "I hope it's not got the Evil Eye behind it." Her eyes narrowed and she shook her head. *"Panayía mazí tou — May the Virgin Mother be with you,"* she said, as she solemnly crossed herself.

"The case has nothing to do with the Evil Eye, Ma," I answered. I waited while she again made the sign of the cross in front of her chest. Then I decided the best response was to lie. "It's not dangerous," I said, "not at all." I uttered these words knowing this was a futile effort on my part. You cannot fool my mother's well-honed instincts. She knew otherwise.

"Socrates," she said, dropping her voice an octave and narrowing her eyes as she stared into mine, "I know from your face you're not telling me everything. Is it dangerous?"

"Not really," I said. I paused, then surrendered. "Oh, a little I suppose. Everything I do in my business is potentially dangerous. It's a matter of perspective," I said. "Harte and I are taking precautions, so we're minimizing the risk."

My mother frowned again. "What's it about? You didn't tell me enough when we talked before."

"The theft of an ex-slave's journal, some stolen letters, and an important secret involving a Civil War cultural icon. There might be some people who have sworn to protect the secret, people who don't want us nosing around."

"Ach! *Kakòmiros — Oh, ill-fated one,"* she said. "It sounds

unsafe. You might as well tell me. I'll find out anyway." She closed her eyes and patted her heart several times.

I sighed. The woman was relentless.

I thought about the fate of the director. I wouldn't come clean with her.

"I'm not in danger, Ma. No more so than with any other case."

She slowly shook her head. "I know you're not telling me the truth, Socrates, or not telling me the whole story. You're holding back something. I can tell. I see that look you always got on your face, ever since you were a little kid, whenever you were fibbing or hiding something from us. Your father and I always knew." She shook her head again and frowned at me, inviting me with her silence and demeanor to come clean.

"There!" she said, pointing her finger at my mouth. I thought she was about to levitate from her small victory. "You got that look again. That's what I mean. You make this little round circle with your lips and look away when you're not telling me the truth. You're doing it now."

This woman was going to be the death of me. No secret was safe around her. I sighed again, and said, "You're wrong this time, Ma. It's just a routine investigation and recover operation. No more risky than the Mandarin Yellow fountain pen case I worked a few years ago. Just loaded with tedium and frustration, if you must know."

My mother frowned and looked skeptically at me. She seemed about to say something, opened her mouth to speak, then seemed to think better of it. She briefly clamped her lips closed, then said, "You shouldn't try to fool your mother,

Socrates." When I didn't respond, she said, "At least promise me you won't do anything stupid."

I reached across the table and squeezed her hand. "I promise," I said, "nothing foolish. You know me." I crossed the fingers of my other hand beneath the table.

"That's why I worry, Socrates, because I do know you."

CHAPTER 56

HARTE CALLED THE NEXT MORNING. He said he was at the doctor's office for his annual physical, and wanted to have lunch near our office afterward, if I would make the time for him. We met at *Panera*, next to the Red Line Metro train entrance at 19th Street and south Dupont Circle. We ordered our food at the counter, then moved to a table. When our food arrived and the server left, Harte said, "Thigpen called again this morning, called about you."

Normally, I wouldn't have thought twice about Harte's statement, but the fact that Harte specifically brought it up — I always assumed he and Thigpen still talked from time-to-time — and the fact that Thigpen had recently acted as a proxy for the Richmond PD, arrested my attention.

This can't be good. "Anything special going on?"

Harte nodded. "The Richmond cops called him to get a message to me, for me to pass on to you."

"What's that?" I said, my distain for their method of reaching me barely masked. In fact, I didn't really want to know because I was afraid what I might find out. But I also knew I had to hear the message, so I asked. I knew, too, I also had to curb my anger I'd reflexively directed against Thigpen, and, indirectly, against Harte, for acting as the conduit to me for the Richmond cops. It wasn't their fault they were being used as messenger boys by the Richmond cops. Or, was it? *They could have refused.*

"After the cops finished with the crime scene at the director's house and took down the crime tape," Harte said, "someone broke into the director's home and trashed it, apparently searching for something. The director's sister — his heir, I assume — called it in this morning."

"Searching for the stolen slave's journal and the women's letters, I bet," I said. *Why'd the cops call Thigpen about this?*

"Maybe," Harte said. "Thigpen was told to find out where you've been these last two days. Sorry, but I had to pass that on."

I shrugged. "No problem. I'll deal with it," I said. "Why do the cops want to know? Do they think I had anything to do with it?"

"There's a problem," Harte said.

I didn't like the sound of that. "How so?"

"When they searched the director's home after the break-in, the Richmond cops found an old fountain pen that appeared to have been dropped by whoever trashed the place."

I didn't like where this was going. "So?"

"So, the pen's a classic Parker *Big Red*, and the only fingerprints on it are yours."

CHAPTER 57

M Y CELLPHONE RANG EARLY THE next morning. It was Harte. He didn't begin the call with the civility we usually showed one another.

"Thigpen just called again," he said. "As a heads-up, a favor to me. Says you didn't call him yet." He paused briefly, his silence reprimanding me.

When I didn't say anything, he continued. "The Richmond cops have pulled a warrant for your arrest for the murder of the director." He paused for my response. When I again didn't say anything, he continued. "I told you that you should've been more cooperative, not pissed 'em off." He paused again for my response. I had none.

"Thigpen wants me to bring you to the 2D house so he can formally place you in custody until Richmond picks you up to take back with them."

"What the—"

"It's either that or MPD comes to get you. Thigpen's doing me, really doing you, a big favor," Harte said. "Don't ignore this. If Thigpen has to come for you, he'll do it. The it'll be cuffs and the perp walk."

I felt my stomach tighten and my back begin to ache. I was trapped, but not in a situation of my own making as far as I was concerned. I didn't think it would have turned out any differently had I cooperated with the Richmond cops more than I had. That excuse was just window dressing for the cops, cosmetics to cover up what really was going on.

One thing was clear to me. This had to be the doing of the Golden Knights and its secret cabal. They were reaching north all the way to DC, flexing their clandestine muscles to mess with me.

If nothing else had done so, this long-distance act by the cabal to have me arrested for a crime I hadn't committed convinced me that the cabal was not, as Starr had intimated, a figment of anyone's imagination. This was sufficient proof to me that it existed, that it was malevolent, and that it was too powerful for me either to ignore or to incite.

I had to regroup and focus my planning.

I realized that if I was going to come out of this mess unscathed, I needed to get to the bottom of the cabal, and figure out a way to neutralize it before it brought me down.

I also knew I could not fight this alone. The Golden Knights of the Confederacy, and its insular little club of Lee protectors, were powerful, more powerful than I was alone. I needed to find an ally that was at least as inviolable and as powerful as they were.

I thought I knew who that ally might be. What I didn't know, because of our history together, was if this potential, but necessary, ally would be willing to help me.

PART THREE

CHAPTER 58

M Y FIRST PRIORITY, EVEN BEFORE I sought help to equalize the fight with the cabal, had to be the Richmond detectives and the arrest warrant issued against me. I did not want this situation to take on a life of its own because I ignored it. There was too much at stake.

The first thing I did after speaking with Harte was to call Bos Smyth, a criminal defense lawyer who practices in DC, Maryland, and Virginia. Bos had been my law partner back when I practiced law, more than five years ago. He also had represented me several years ago when Harte and Thigpen, in their capacities as MPD detectives, searched my home under a court authorized search warrant, and had threatened to arrest me in connection with the theft of the Mandarin Yellow fountain pen and several murders that followed its theft. In turn, I had recommended Bos as defense counsel to Li Bing-fa when Bing-fa's eldest son had been arrested and tried for manslaughter in connection with a crime arising out of the Mandarin Yellow theft. Now I needed Bos's help again.

Harte and I took an Uber ride from our office to the 2D. Harte said he was coming along to offer me moral support. I believed him and appreciated his gesture.

When we arrived, Thigpen came out to the reception area

to meet us. He led us back to an interview room where the Richmond detectives were waiting. Bos Smyth was there, too.

After everyone had engaged in perfunctory greetings, Bos and I stepped into the hallway to confer privately. After about ten minutes, we reentered the interview room and took our seats.

The meeting began with Detectives Halpern and Stella badging me as if we had never met before. Then Stella read me the Miranda warnings. I followed this by signing a form acknowledging he'd done so. With Bos's consent, I agreed to permit them to audiotape our interview.

"Do you know why you're here, Mr. Cheng?"

I glanced at Bos who nodded his agreement that I answer. He and I had decided in the hallway that I would cooperate, but that he would rein me in if I went too far or if it otherwise was time to call a halt to the questioning.

"You think I had something to do with the murder of the director of the Golden Knights' Museum, so I suppose you're here to arrest me," I said.

"Did you?" Stella asked.

"No," I said. "And furthermore, I don't think you think I did it, not unless you're incompetent or haven't really investigated the murder."

No sooner were the words out of my mouth than I wanted to kick myself for that statement. I had agreed with Bos that I would hold my anger in check and not let the situation take control of my mouth and common sense. I knew there was nothing good to be gained by trash-talking the cops, yet here I was picking a fight with my answer to the second question.

I looked at Bos. He looked as if he wanted to reach over and throttle me. I turned to Stella and said, "Sorry. I shouldn't have said that. I was out of order." I quickly rapped my knuckles on the table to break the tension. Then I turned to Detective Stella and said, "I'm finding this whole scene surprisingly stressful, but I won't be rude again, Detectives." I glanced from Stella to Halpern, and nodded to both as I said this.

I watched Halpern's forehead wrinkle and his eyebrows almost connect above his nose. His complexion had changed from sallow, when we began the interview, to ruddy, once I'd mouthed-off.

"We're talking to you as a courtesy, Mr. Cheng," Halpern said, cutting me no slack in spite of my apology, "because your business partner, Mr. Harte, used to be on the job. But don't push it." His tone of voice and his scowl reflected his anger at me for my outburst.

I glanced again at Bos. He nodded. I reminded myself only to answer the questions as asked, not to elaborate on them or misdirect the questioner with my answers. Doing either could eventually open up new lines of inquiry by the cops. Doing either certainly wouldn't endear me to them.

"Okay," I said, "I appreciate that. And I'm truly sorry for what I said before. What do you want to know, Detective?" I looked at Stella as I asked this.

"Can you account for your whereabouts when the murder took place?" Stella then told me the relevant date and time.

"Let's see." I pulled out my iPhone, and tapped the App for my calendar.

I walked the detectives through my schedule on the day and night of the crime. I showed them my calendar so they would see for themselves I was not making up my response. The calendar exonerated me if you took it on faith that I hadn't retrospectively created the entries or ignored them on the night in question.

Halpern looked at the calendar, looked over at his partner, then turned back to me. "Can we hold onto this. I'd like our lab to examine it." He obviously understood the possibility of retrospective fabrication of calendar events.

"Not without a warrant," Bos said. "We showed you this as a courtesy. For information purposes only. You can see Mr. Cheng wasn't anywhere near Richmond when the murder occurred. If you want his cellphone or calendar as evidence, we'll need to go by the book."

Detective Halpern nodded. "If you insist. Give me a minute to copy your calendar into my notebook," he said, as he held up the iPhone and a small spiral-bound pocket notebook.

When he finished, Halpern handed the cellphone back to me. "We'll verify the entries," he said, canting his head toward my hand now holding my iPhone. "Can anyone vouch for you for that night? State you actually attended the calendared events?"

I gave him Clotille's contact information.

Then Halpern paused. He reached into his jacket pocket and pulled out a see—through evidence bag. He placed the bag on the table between us.

"Recognize this, Mr. Cheng?"

I looked at the bag. It contained the fountain pen Harte had mentioned. It seemed to resemble one of the pens I collected as part of my vintage fountain pen collection, one I had several examples of and often used in my day-to-day writing. "It's a fountain pen," I said. "Specifically, it's a classic 1920s Parker Duofold. The model known as the *Big Red Senior*."

"Do you own one?" Halpern said.

"I own several, six, I think, possibly seven, with minor design variations among them. I collect vintage fountain pens. That is, I used to. Don't do it much anymore. This model is a highly collectible vintage pen made by Parker in the mid-1920s. I recently lost one. That is, I had one taken from me — one that resembles the pen in that bag — when I was mugged in DC." I held Halpern's stare.

I didn't like where this might be heading. "How did you get that pen?" I said, nodding my head toward the evidence bag. "If it's mine, it was stolen from me in DC. I don't understand how you would have it in Richmond."

Of course I already knew why the detectives had the pen because Harte had told me. It had been found at the Richmond crime scene. What I didn't understand was how the pen made its way from the DC muggers to Richmond, and from there into a local crime scene.

"Would you be surprised if I told you that this pen," Halpern said, as he tilted his head toward the evidence bag, "was found at the director's home when his home recently was ransacked, and that it has your fingerprints on it? No one else's. Just yours."

I swallowed hard. I had noticed during the mugging that the muggers wore latex gloves. Now I knew why. The mugging on 22nd Street wasn't random and it was no coincidence their fingerprints weren't on the pen.

I decided to take the initiative, to stop being passive in this interview. "It should have my prints on it if this one's mine. Like I said, I used to own a pen similar to that, but it was taken from me when I was mugged. Other things were taken, too." I paused, then added, "I noticed that the muggers wore latex gloves when they held me up."

"I see," Detective Halpern said. His eyes darted over to Stella. Then he looked back at me. "Do you have a copy of the police report you filed? We'd like to see it."

"I didn't report it," I said. "I didn't see the point."

Halpern looked hard at me, and then slightly nodded twice. "Not much faith in the police, have you?" he said. He didn't wait for me to respond. "Do you have an insurance report you can show us?"

I shook my head. "I didn't file one. My pen and some of the other items taken are excluded from the standard homeowner's policy. All reporting them stolen would have done would be to drive up my insurance premiums for years, without me collecting anything back from the insurance company on my claim. I was better off just eating the loss."

Halpern smiled. "How convenient." He nodded again as if confirming a thought.

"We have an arrest warrant for you, Mr. Cheng," Detective Stella said. "But it don't have to go that way if you cooperate with us."

"I thought I was cooperating," I said, "just by being here, and by answering your questions, even offering you my calendar to look at and copy. What else do you want from me?"

I watched as Stella and Halpern exchanged looks. Halpern turned backed toward me and cleared his throat. "Stop interfering with an ongoing investigation. That's what we want from you." He turned toward Detective Stella, and nodded again.

I frowned and looked over at Bos, then turned back to face Detective Halpern.

"Which investigation other than the director's murder?" I said. "Is there more than one going on? I haven't investigated anything in connection with the murder, if that's what you mean. Or do you mean the subsequent ransacking of the director's house? I haven't investigated that either." I quickly looked over at Bos, who raised his eyebrows and slightly shrugged.

"Or do you mean the investigation of the Museum's stolen documents?" I said. "It was my understanding no police report has been filed in connection with the theft, so I couldn't interfere with a crime you're not investigating, could I?" *Had the director misled me about that?* I wondered.

I looked from Halpern to Stella, then at Bos. I was genuinely confused.

"We're not investigating that theft," Halpern said. "Not yet."

I was even more confused now. "Then what—"

"Based on what you told us in your other interview, we think the crimes — the theft from the Museum and the director's homicide — might be related," Halpern said.

"We're considering broadening our investigation to include the document thefts, too," Detective Stella said.

"Then I'm not interfering," I said, "since there's no official inquiry yet into the burglary."

"Wrong," Stella said. His face now was crimson. "You *are* interfering, and you *will* back off. You're on notice now we might investigate the Museum's burglary in the future, so you need to drop that case." Stella looked hard at me. Then he looked over at my attorney, paused briefly, as if soliciting his help, but then, not receiving any comfort from Bos, looked back at me.

"I wouldn't put your theory to the test, Mr. Cheng," he said, as he continued to stare at me with narrowed eyes, daring me, I thought, to challenge him, to take issue with his warning.

This both confused and angered me. Stella was bullying me.

"What the hell does that mean?" I said. I didn't look over at Bos because I knew he wouldn't like my question or my officious tone. But I didn't care right now. I intended to show Stella he couldn't push me around.

"It means," Halpern said, his soft tone taking the tension down a notch, "we can decide either to take you into custody right now for interference, and sort it all out in a few days, while you cool your heels behind bars, or we can put this arrest warrant in suspension mode and you can walk out of here, in which case we will go back to Richmond without you." He looked over at Stella, then back at me.

"But first you have to assure us of certain things," Stella added. He rhythmically tapped the warrant, which sat on the table between us, with his forefinger.

"What things?" I said, my tone softer now. I had made my point.

I watched Bos lean forward and rest his elbows on the table. He seemed ready to pounce if the cops made an unreasonable demand.

"As we said before, get out of the investigation and stay out," Stella said.

I assumed he was referring to my investigation of the stolen documents, not the director's murder, but I wasn't going to let that go so easily. Not without clarification. My butt was on the line if I said nothing and guessed wrong.

"Detectives, you know I haven't been investigating the murder or the vandalism," I said, trying to sound as innocent and confused as I could under the circumstances.

"Right," Halpern said, stretching out the word. His sarcasm was unmistakable.

It was clear to me now. Even though the Richmond cops were not investigating the theft of the documents, the arrest threat was window dressing to put pressure on me to walk away, to coerce me to stop stirring the burglary pot. The question was: who was it who wanted me to stop stirring the pot and how did they have so much influence over the Richmond cops?

"So, what's it gonna be?" Halpern said. He picked up the arrest warrant from the table and slowly waved it back and forth between us. "This, with you in bracelets in the back of our vehicle heading for an arraignment in Richmond, or a handshake now as we end this meeting, and your word to us you're done with the investigation?"

I agreed to drop my investigation.

Bos and I shook hands and said goodbye in the 2D's anteroom. I started the two-mile walk to our office.

———— • •• • ————

Harte had not waited around the 2D after dropping me off so I summarized the meeting for him when I returned to the office. "So," he said, "I know you well enough to know you're not walking away from the investigation. What's your plan?"

I looked at him and thought about our partnership. Harte had come a long way since we first joined together in our PI business. Had the meeting with the Richmond cops occurred early in our business relationship, when we still were working on becoming comfortable with one another, Harte would have expected that I would honor my word to the Richmond police. Now, however, he was almost as hardened and jaded in that regard as I was. He understood why I had given my word to the Richmond cops, and he knew me well enough to expect that I now would proceed with the case with more vigor than ever, if for no other reason than to permanently put the arrest warrant to bed by solving the break-in and recovering the documents and thumb drive, rendering that issue moot as far as the Richmond cops were concerned.

I wasn't sure how I'd proceed, except in one important respect. If I'd ever had any doubts about needing help from some powerful ally, I didn't have any doubts now. I now knew more than ever that I needed assistance from someone or from something as powerful as whoever had reached the Richmond detectives to make them intimidate me by threatening me with arrest.

I also knew where I might find that help. But to achieve this, I would have to convince my old nemesis, Li Bing-fa, to make his criminal organization, the triad known as the *Cunning Rabbit With Three Warrens Society*, available to me. Pulling that off might be the most difficult obstacle of all for me to overcome in this matter.

CHAPTER 59

I stopped by the Mount Parnassus Condominium to visit my mother as I'd promised I would. We settled around the kitchen table with freshly brewed coffee, a water back, and freshly baked *Spanakopita* in front of us. I noticed that as we sat at the table and my mother watched me eat, she continuously fingered her *Kombolòi* — her worry beads — something she rarely did.

"Something bothering you, Ma?" I cast my gaze at her hands.

She immediately covered the worry beads with her other hand so I couldn't see them, and said, "*Ach!* You already know. I worry about you all the time. That's what mothers do. Don't bother yourself about it."

I knew if I pushed, she would never tell me. I had to approach her obliquely if I was going to find out what was on her mind.

"No need to worry, Ma. I'm good."

"Maybe not," she said. She looked down at her cup for a few seconds, then picked it up and sipped coffee. When she returned the cup to its saucer, she said, "You had a visitor here yesterday."

STEVEN M. ROTH

That gave me pause. Who would attempt to visit me by coming to see my mother?

"Who was it?"

She openly worked her beads now. "That Toula woman from apartment 205. You remember her, the crazy woman who caused you problems before?"

I remembered all right, and thought about how Toula had acted true to form when I recently ran into her in the lobby.

Toula's attention to me when we'd had our sexual relationship had been pleasing on several levels, even ego gratifying, maybe even a little thrilling, at first, but eventually the gratification and thrill had come at a corrosive price much too high to pay.

"Not to worry, Ma," I said, "I have no intention of talking to her. I'm done with that woman."

"*Ach*! But I don't think she's done with you. That's what worries me." She looked down at her hands and briefly fingered her beads, then looked up at me again. "She said I should give you a message from her. Do you want me to?"

"I suppose. What'd she say?" The sooner my mother and I put this behind us, the better off we both would be.

"She said to tell you she has information about some guy who was asking around the building about you." She paused and looked down at her beads as she worked them again, then said, "What's that about, Socrates?"

"I don't know, Ma, and I have no intention of talking to her to find out." *Maybe,* I thought.

"Good. Stay away from her. That woman has the Evil Eye. Talking to her won't be anything but trouble for you."

For the benefit of my mother, I solemnly said, "*Panayia mazi tou — May the Virgin Mother be with you.*" I made the

230

sign of the cross as I spoke. Then I turned one palm upward and dry spit into it three times, making the sound, *ptu, ptu, ptu*, to remove any evil spell I might have caused to be cast upon us by having Toula again come into my life.

My mother nodded — affirming that I'd just performed the correct ritual — made the sign of the cross over her heart, and worked her worry beads again.

CHAPTER 60

"ONE FOR LUNCH, SIR?" THE 20s-something Chinese woman asked.

She was attractively dressed in a solid-black A-line skirt that fell just below her knees, and in a red, silk blouse buttoned to her neckline. The blouse had lucky bat symbols embroidered on its collar. The young woman was much shorter than I was even though she was perched on high heels that were three or four inches tall.

It had been a little more than five years since I last stepped into the Golden Dragon Restaurant, and I had no overwhelming desire to do so now because I doubted I would be well-received by its owner, Li Bing-fa.

Since that last visit, I'd worked hard to put the events involving the historic Mandarin Yellow fountain pen, Bing-fa, his dysfunctional family, and Bing-fa's criminal triad behind me. Now I would have to undo all my efforts in that regard and rip away the scabs that had precariously smoothed over our shared and individual anger, distrust, and wounds.

My last meeting with Bing-fa — here at the restaurant five years ago — had not gone well. It had ended on an unpleasant note that culminated in our unstated agreement that we were finished with one another for all time. We had parted with reciprocal feelings of earned enmity.

Now, still uncertain how I felt about Bing-fa after the passage of so much time — as the man himself, rather than as part of the events that had overtaken us — I came back to his restaurant as a supplicant seeking his help.

The restaurant hadn't changed much since I was last there. It still projected the same stereotypical, Chinese-restaurant décor I remembered from past visits — stereotypes reflecting how westerners think Chinese restaurants in urban-area Chinatowns should look.

The young woman who greeted me at the entrance held several large laminated menus against her waist. She greeted me with an attractive smile.

I responded to her programmed inquiry. "No lunch, thank you," I said. I saw a flicker of concern or curiosity fleetingly cross her face, but she recovered quickly.

"How then may I help you?" she asked. Her hosting smile remained. "Are you here to meet a guest?"

"I'd like to speak with Li Bing-fa," I said. "Is he here?" I smiled.

"Is Master Li expecting you?"

Not too likely. "No, he's not," I said, as I again smiled.

The young woman seemed momentarily confused, but quickly recovered.

"I am so sorry, Sir, but Master Li is not here at the moment, and in any case, Master Li never receives visitors without a prior appointment. If you will leave your name and telephone number, perhaps Master Li will agree to meet with you at an appointed time." She pulled the menus in tight against her chest, wrapping both arms around the documents, almost hugging herself. She patronized me with her practiced smile.

I pulled out my business card, gripped it with two hands — with each hand pinching a lower corner — and held it out to her in the accepted fashion. She glanced quickly at the card as I held it out, but did not take it from me.

A little Taoist deception from me now is something Bing-fa will understand. "Please give this to Master Li," I said, reaching out with both hands and again offering my card.

"Tell Master Li that Socrates Cheng is here to meet with him. Tell him, too, I apologize for asking to meet without having a prior appointment, but that the matter we must speak of is both urgent and of the utmost importance to both of us." I bowed slightly to demonstrate my contrived respect for Bing-fa.

The young woman frowned, but this time took my card. "Please wait here," she said, as she turned away from me.

I watched her walk across the dining room to the far side of the restaurant and pass through a doorway covered with hanging beads. Unless he'd moved his office sometime in the past five years, Bing-fa kept his office down the hallway to the right of the beaded doorway.

After a few minutes, an Asian man, who appeared to be in his late twenties or early thirties, came through the same beaded doorway, crossed the restaurant, and walked up to me. He was dressed in the traditional all-weather charcoal gray, double-breasted, light-woolen Chinese-American-type business suit, with over-sized padded shoulders. The suit was much too tight for his very large, muscular body, and clung to his frame like wet tissue. His black hair was cut in a military-style burr cut. His shirt collar barely covered a black and red tattoo of a dragon that was inked on the left side of his thick neck.

"Master Li not here," he said, speaking Pinyin-inspired English. "Master Li not see anyone without appointment first. You make appointment and come back some other time. Maybe Master Li talk to you then. Maybe not."

I assumed this messenger was one of Bing-fa's many loyal minions who belonged to the *Cunning Rabbit* triad, so I was determined to present myself as deferential and agreeable, yet firm. I wasn't, after all, suicidal.

"Thank you," I said, and offered my best Taoist respectful bow of my head and upper body. In further compliance with Chinese tradition and to make it clear I offered no threat to this messenger, I let my arms hang down at my sides, with my palms turned away from him.

I quickly collected my thoughts and said, "In that case, I would like to make an appointment to visit with Master Li five minutes from now."

The messenger frowned, then said, "Master Li busy man. He have restaurant to operate. He need more notice than five minutes for appointment with you."

He doesn't need any time if he wants to see me. Now it was time to play my ace in the hole. *Let's see if this will pry Bing-fa loose.*

"Please return to Master Li and tell him Socrates Cheng would like to meet with him as soon as possible about an urgent matter involving *Jiao tu san ku* — the Cunning Rabbit."

I watched as the color drained from the messenger's face.

If this message didn't earn me an audience with Bing-fa, nothing would.

I continued to stand near the hostess's table and waited about ten minutes, when the woman I'd spoken with earlier approached me again. I smiled as she closed in on me.

"Master Li says to thank you for taking the trouble to call upon him," she said, "but he regrets he is not able to meet with you today. He asks that you return in the morning in two days after today, at 9:00 a.m., at which time Master Li will see you for ten minutes only."

Still the control freak, is he? I bowed my head and agreed to come back at the appointed time and day. My father, if he were alive today, would be proud of me. I had worked the traditional Taoist formula very well.

CHAPTER 61

DECIDED TO RETURN HOME, AFTER my trip to Chinatown, to run some errands. As I walked into my foyer, my eye caught the flashing red light of my VoIP phone-system's answering machine. The rapid blinking indicated I had several messages waiting.

I spent a few minutes looking at my snail mail from yesterday, poured a glass of grapefruit juice, and then sat down by the answering machine. I pushed the Play button.

The first message was from Toula Xandereas.

"Call me, Socrates. I have some information you'll want to know."

I erased the message.

The second through fourth messages also were from Toula, and made the same point, but with her voice becoming more strident and demanding with each call.

I erased those messages, too, then played the last one.

"Listen, you fool, you're blowing me off like before. Well, this time you'd be wise not to. Believe me, I'm not looking to hook-up with you. I couldn't care less about getting you into my bed. I called to tell you someone twice visited the Mount Parnassus and asked about you. Call me if you want to know more. This is my last try to reach you."

I reluctantly returned Toula's calls, but she didn't answer. I left a brief message telling her I had returned her calls.

CHAPTER 62

Hervey Beauregard called soon after I finished listening to Toula's messages and had attempted to return her calls. He again beckoned me to Richmond for yet another meeting with the trustees.

Beauregard insisted I present another status report. I explained that there had been no new developments for me to report on, but he wouldn't let me off the hook. I think he had to "show the flag" either to impress me with his new authority or to impress the other trustees. Perhaps both. In any event it meant more wasted time while I drove to and from Richmond again.

Or did it?

Perhaps the meeting wouldn't be a waste of my time after all if I used the meeting well. I could turn the meeting into a subtle interview of the trustees, throwing provocative questions at them, then evaluating their responses to see what answers the questions yielded, which words they chose to use, their various tones, their body language, and their facial expressions. Hopefully, some useful truths might emerge from this stew of responses.

Once I was in the meeting it became clear to me that the trustees actually were concerned that I didn't seem to be making tangible progress with the investigation. I felt better now about having made the trip again.

I set out for them what I had done since our last meeting and told them where I saw my investigation heading. I also told them about my interview with the Richmond cops, and their insistence I drop the investigation of the burglary. I assured the trustees that I had no intention of bailing. No one, especially Beauregard, to my surprise, raised the fact that I had obviously breached my confidentiality agreement by talking to the police.

The trustees asked many questions, but in the end seemed satisfied. This time the meeting included Winston Starr's presence.

Unfortunately, every time I tried to ask my own questions, Beauregard cut me off, reminding me with the same curt statement that the trustees were my employer and would ask the questions.

To my surprise, notwithstanding Beauregard's recalcitrance, I found that the act of engaging with the trustees in this limited way fired up my enthusiasm for the case. When we finished our meeting, I was anxious to return to Washington and get on with the investigation.

I left the meeting and settled into my vehicle for the drive back to DC. I turned the key, but the vehicle wouldn't start. *This, again? This was becoming tiresome.* I checked to see if the radio and lights worked. They did. As before, the problem was not the battery. I was willing to bet it was the fuel pump again. It had that same distinctive sound as before when I had tried to turn on the engine. I didn't waste any time with it. I immediately called Blankenship's and arranged to be towed there.

I was right. The fuel pump had died again. I counted my blessings that Blankenship's Auto had another pump in stock, this time a new one, not one that had been reconditioned, as before. In fact, I would later learn that Blankenship had several pumps in stock now. I guess I'd made a market in Richmond for this item.

I waited until I saw my vehicle placed up on the rack, then I moved from the customers' waiting area to where I could watch Caleb Livengood as he again set about replacing the pump he had recently installed. *Thank goodness for warranties.*

When Caleb took a break, I followed him out back to talk to him while he smoked.

"Sorry about the pump," he said. "Must have been a lemon. It happens."

I shrugged. "Right, it happens. Glad I wasn't racing in traffic on I-95 when the engine quit on me."

"You still workin' that case you mentioned before?" he asked.

I said I was. "Can't really talk about it though. I signed an agreement not to."

"Whatever," he said. "Is it about the stolen slave journal and some stolen letters?"

That pulled me up short. "Why do you say that?"

"One of my customers told me about it."

"Who's that?" I said.

"Can't say. Like you, I gave my word to keep it under wraps."

Then why did you bring it up? "Why would this person tell you?" I said.

I immediately regretted my words and their negative implication, and rushed to ameliorate my skepticism. "I mean—"

Caleb frowned. His tone became defensive. "Because I'm interested in General Lee and everything about him. That's why. I reenact General Lee at reenactment battles. The reenactments I told you about last time we talked, unless you forgot that."

That was not a good enough reason for someone connected with the Museum, someone obviously within the Museum's inner circle, to have revealed the occurrence of the burglary to him. I didn't buy Caleb's facile explanation although, from his point of view, his explanation probably was sufficient. This didn't seem to me, however, adequate to explain the motives of the Museum's insider who had revealed to an outsider one of the Museum's innermost secrets.

"My contact also told me what the journal and letters said about General Lee's secret," he said, "and that the journal's a forgery. The letters, too."

"Based on what?" I said. I realized then that I'd become protective and defensive about the Museum's secret. "You might want to talk to your source again about that. I don't think you have it right."

But having said that with as much righteous indignation as I could muster, I had to admit to myself I wasn't sure if he was right or not. After all, I, too, once had asked the director if the documents were genuine or faked. I certainly didn't have a monopoly on skepticism in this investigation.

CHAPTER 63

AFTER I RETURNED TO WASHINGTON from Richmond I called Clotille. She had invited me to have dinner with her that evening at her apartment. She promised me a special Cajun meal I hadn't eaten before. I arrived a little after 8:00 p.m. I brought wine and a dozen roses.

The meal was exceptional. It consisted of an appetizer-size serving of Jambalaya-Pastalaya, a main course of red beans and rice, and a side dish of shrimp fettuccine with Boudin sausage. Desert was Tomato and Corn Pie. I ate more of everything than I should have, but did not regret having done so.

After we finished the meal and cleaned up, we moved to the couch in the living room, with a bottle of Courvoisier and two brandy snifters.

"There's something related to the Richmond case I want to tell you," I said. *I finally was learning how to introduce a subject to Clotille in a way that wouldn't seem to her to be a reprimand or a threat to our relationship.*

Clotille stopped pouring our drinks, and put down the bottle. Her face could not mask the apprehension she felt. I also could read it in her body language, her sudden rigidity. Clotille was a born doomsayer. Nothing I could do or say would ever change that. I had to change my approach to dealing with her.

"All right. Tell me, you. Are you in any danger?"

I shook my head. "Remember that crazy woman, Toula, who lives in my mother's building?" I watched Clotille's mouth turn down as I reminded her, by the mere mention of Toula's name, of Toula's existence and the trouble she'd caused us before.

"Of course I do, me. I could never forget her, that slut."

This was strong language for Clotille, and reflected how powerfully negative she still felt about my prior, albeit brief, sexual relationship with Toula, a relationship I ended when I started dating Clotille.

I was sorry to dredge up painful memories for Clotille, but I wanted to be perfectly open with her. This was the way we'd agreed to move forward with our relationship. I intended to keep that promise.

"Toula called me the other day. She stopped by to see my mother, too. She left six or seven messages on my answering machine before I finally called her back."

Clotille leaned forward, picked up the Courvoisier bottle and finished pouring our drinks. "Does she want to become involved with you again?"

"Possibly, but I doubt it. It doesn't matter. I have no interest in going there at all, and won't. You know that. At least I hope you know that. I promise it won't happen." I reached out and squeezed her hand.

"Then why'd she call you, her?" Clotille sipped her drink, and stared hard at me over the rim of her glass.

I had to deal with Clotille's insecurity even if it was unfounded.

"She said someone had come to the condo recently asking about me. Had come there twice, in fact, according to her messages on my machine." *I needed to stop using Toula's name, to make my statements about her more abstract, more impersonal, to use "she" and "her," not Toula's actual name.*

"Who was it that came there?"

"She wouldn't tell me on the phone. Said I had to buy her a drink at *Stan's* to learn anything else from her. So I'm going to meet her, and I wanted you to know because I don't want to keep secrets from you."

I watched Clotille's shoulders slump. This was what I'd feared.

Clotille nodded. She said nothing, but didn't have to. I clearly understood. She looked so sad.

"I need you to trust me on this, Clotille. It's strictly business, nothing else. No matter what she might think or try, you have my word you have nothing to be concerned about." I stared into her eyes and smiled weakly. "I promise."

"I do trust you, Socrates." She reached out and took my hand. "It's that bitch I don't trust. She's dangerous, her."

I couldn't argue with that.

CHAPTER 64

I CALLED TOULA AGAIN WHEN I returned home because there was no message from her on my machine. She picked up on the second ring. Her CallerID must have revealed me as the caller because she answered by saying, "Hello, Socrates. Nice of you to finally return my calls."

She obviously had not heard my voicemail message or, if she had, she had chosen to ignore it. Either was possible with this woman who thrived on control and game-playing.

"Did you get permission from your redheaded hillbilly to meet with me?" she asked.

I shuddered when I heard her voice. Even though I had initiated the call in response to her messages and her subsequent failure to call me back, my previously dormant baggage awakened and took control of me, triggering vexatious memories. I intended to make this as quick and as painless as possible.

"Hello, Toula." I kept my tone flat and neutral. "Your messages said you have something to tell me, that you think we need to meet."

"Be nice, Socrates, if you want my help. I didn't have to call to give you a heads-up, you know."

Some things never change. "Right." I adjusted my tone and

patter to what I assumed Toula was fishing for. "How've you been?" I said. "I'm sorry we haven't talked sooner, but you know how it is." *I would play her game for now.*

Silence followed. After about fifteen seconds, Toula said, "Nice try, but that doesn't cut it, Socrates. I'm not a fool."

"Didn't mean to suggest you were. Sorry you took it that way. So let's get to it. What do you want to tell me?" *Maybe,* I thought, *we can do this without meeting.*

She sighed. Then she said, "Like I said in all those messages you ignored, some guy came to the building, twice, at least, that I know of, maybe more. I ran into him in the mail room. He asked if I know you. I said I did. He had other questions about you I didn't answer, so he left. Later, my mother said he asked her about you the next day when she ran into him in the laundry room."

I didn't like the implications of any of that. "Do you know who he was?"

"Never saw him before."

"What'd he look like?"

"Enough freebies for now, Socrates, enough over the phone, I mean," Toula said. "If you want to know more, including what he looked like, you'll have to buy a girl a drink."

We arrived in front of *Stan's* at the same time, and walked down the stairs and into the bar as if we were a couple. I hoped no one I knew was there today.

Danika was behind the stick, and looked up as we walked in. I swear I saw her chuckle and stealthily shake her head when she registered who we were. Although I continued to look at her for a few seconds, she refused to look me in the eye. Danika probably realized she wouldn't be able to keep a straight face and avoid laughing if our eyes met. I knew I'd blush if she caught my eye, and would need to come back later today, in any event, to explain why I was there with Toula. I couldn't just let the question hang out there unanswered, not at my watering hole. There were too many implications and possibilities for my drinking pals to contemplate. In any event, I was glad Danika played the situation as professionally as she had.

We settled at a small table near the back, away from the bar, where Danika couldn't easily see us. The waitress took our drink orders, then returned with the drinks and two menus.

I didn't plan on hanging around and having a meal with Toula. She didn't know it, but her time to come clean and tell me what she knew was very limited.

"Okay, Toula," I said, once we were alone, "I'm here like you wanted. What more can you tell me about the man asking about me?" I put my elbow down on my menu to make it clear I had no interest in picking it up to read to order dinner.

"Just what I said before. He asked if I knew you, if you come around often to visit your mother."

I didn't like it that this mystery-man had involved my mother in the discussion, whoever he was. "Anything else?"

"I said I never see you around anymore, so I couldn't really say."

"Did he leave a name?"

"No. Never said."

"What'd he look like?"

She paused as if collecting her thoughts. "Like I said

before, Socrates, he was a male, maybe in his late thirties or early forties, I think. You really need to pay attention when I speak to you, Socrates." She lifted her drink and took a sip. "He was fit. In pretty good shape, but fit from running or swimming, not bulked up from lifting. Short hair like someone in the military. Maybe a cop or ex-cop."

"Anything unusual about the way he talked?" I said. "Did he have an accent?"

She slowly shook her head. "Didn't notice one." She paused and stared across the room as if again thinking about my question. "No, I don't think so. No accent. Nothing else unusual either. He was a genuine white-bread WASP male." She smiled her ferine smile, and said, "Let's eat while we're here. Then we can go back to your place."

Clotille had you nailed, Toula, didn't she?

Toula's persistence in trying to have me again hook-up with her pissed me off. "I told you, those days are over for us. Get it through your head once and for all. Just give it a rest." I raised my arm and made a writing motion in the air with my hand, signaling the waitress for our check.

"I appreciate you giving me the heads-up about the man. Don't say anything to my mother. I don't want to worry her."

I paid the check, stood up, waved at Danika as I left, and walked out, intentionally leaving Toula sitting at our table, fuming.

CHAPTER 65

THE TIME HAD COME FOR me to keep my appointment with Bing-fa.

I walked into the Golden Dragon at exactly 9:00, the appointed time. Bing-fa had been a stickler for punctuality when I'd dealt with him before. The restaurant wouldn't open for business for a few more hours, but he would be there as his minions set up for lunch.

The same young woman I talked to before met me again. She led me through the restaurant, across the serving area and through the bead-covered doorway to Bing-fa's private office. He obviously had alerted her to expect me this morning, and had instructed her to take me back to him without first announcing me.

I knocked once and waited until Bing-fa instructed me to enter. I walked into his office with more than a bit of misgiving. I glanced around as I entered. We were alone.

Not much had changed in the five years since I'd last been here. Bing-fa's exquisite, orthodox Confucian taste continued to dominate his office, just as it had dominated his home. His office exuded the ambiance of a traditional scholar's studio, with its *Feng Shui* layout and siting, and with its Taoist principles of design, furnishings, displayed objects, and informed utility.

Bing-fa had furnished his office with a simple Ching Period rosewood desk, two horseshoe-back chairs made from huanghuali wood, two yoke-back chairs — also made from huanghuali wood — and with an antique, five meter high, A-frame wooden cabinet made from mahogany. All the furniture seemed to be museum-display quality.

As I looked at his beautiful rosewood desktop, it seemed to me he hadn't moved or added a single scholar's artifact in all the time that had passed since I visited. All the objects still were arranged in one corner on the desk's top — his ink stones, modern and antique calligraphy horsetail paint brushes, a dozen or so ink sticks, a single brush pot, and three Ming Period ivory brush rests. Nothing else sat on the desk's surface to mar the perfect balance and harmony created by the arrangement of his scholar's artifacts.

I glanced at Bing-fa, who sat behind the desk, as I stepped over to take a seat across from him. He didn't stand to greet me as he always had in the past. *Not a good sign*. He cast his open palm in the direction of a yoke-back chair in front of his desk, and silently nodded me into it.

I pulled back the chair to sit. As I took my seat, I was pleasantly distracted by the chirping of Bing-fa's caged songbirds and his lucky crickets he kept resident in hanging cages in the two far corners of the room.

"Why are you here, Mr. Cheng?" Bing-fa said. He stared hard at me. His eyes gave away nothing. His face remained inscrutable.

You know I'm here to ask you for a favor. I told that to your hireling the other day, I thought.

I slightly bowed my head as a sign of respect, although I felt no respect for this man. There was a time when I would have addressed him as *Shifu*, the reverential title for *Master*. Now it took all the self-discipline I could muster just to call him by his given name.

We both know the ritual, I thought, *so let's just play it out and get it over with so we can turn to the reason I'm here.* "I appreciate your wiliness to see me," I said.

"Why are you here?" he repeated.

He's not following the Taoist script. No point, then, in me sticking to it. "I need your help."

"Why would you ever think I would help you? Your memory must be as fleeting as your integrity."

Okay, Bing-fa, I'll play the game your way. "To save face. To save your face, not mine. To preserve your honor." *The illusory façade of your honor, that is.*

"You have as good a reason to respect my request for help," I said, "as you might now think you have to refuse it. You would be wise to listen to me, however, before you make any decision." *I know you don't like hearing that.*

"I cannot imagine why," he said. He reached across his body and ran his palm over one silk sleeve of his gown, smoothing out wrinkles. He never took his eyes from me as he acted out this deliberately distracting ritual.

"I hope," I said, playing my ace in the hole now, "you will grant my request to repay the honor debt you owe me from five years ago. Then we will have no other outstanding obligations to one another, just a clean slate. We will never have need to communicate again." *That should be as tantalizing a scenario for you, my Oriental friend, as the thought of it is for me.*

"What debt do you think I owe you, Mr. Cheng. As I

recall matters, you destroyed my family, not aided me. I owe you nothing but my contempt."

So you still refuse to accept responsibility for what happened, do you? I thought. "I don't see things the way you do, Bing-fa, but it doesn't matter.

"As far as I'm concerned, there's one issue of honor still reflected on the balance sheet between us that requires you to help me if you want to maintain your honor. It has to do with the aid I rendered Eldest Son in his time of trouble."

I knew this statement would strike home. As I'd learned over the years from my father and, indeed, from Bing-fa, one's face and, therefore, one's honor, real or perceived — so hard to come by, but so easily lost — is everything to the Chinese male.

Now that I'd put it out on the table, Bing-fa could not ignore my request for help even if he disagreed with my interpretation of the underlying facts and their impact upon our previous relationship. Since I believed, or, at least, because I acted as if I believed, that Bing-fa owed me a debt of honor, then no matter what he might have thought of my point of view, the ancient sage Lao Tzu mandated that Bing-fa did owe me a debt that had to be repaid when he was called upon to do so.

CHAPTER 66

B ING-FA LISTENED TO MY EXPLANATION without commenting. I could see distain lodged in his eyes, although his face remained passive and cryptic.

He surprised me by deviating from the prescribed Taoist script.

"I do not recall any favor you rendered to me sufficient to offset the damage you visited upon my family," he said, speaking Mandarin. He reached over and adjusted the left sleeve of his ankle-length silk gown. "Any debt of honor you might believe I owe you was more than cancelled by your treachery."

Bing-fa's self-serving pathos pissed me off. Although five years had passed, I had no doubt he knew exactly what I was talking about. But he had me where he wanted me, although he likely didn't know it yet. I desperately needed his help, so I would play along with his ritual of ignorance.

"You should recall, Bing-fa, that I recommended legal counsel to you when Eldest Son was arrested for—"

"Cease referring to my son as Eldest Son," Bing-fa suddenly blurted out, his voice high pitched and uncharacteristically loud. His obvious anger stopped me short. Although I hadn't intended to, and would not have bothered trying, I had cracked his veneer of stolid Taoism.

"You are not a member of our family. To you he is to be addressed by the less familiar, Li Bing-wu."

"Whatever," I said. I had lost sight, until now, of how much I despised Bing-fa. This was going to be a test of my patience.

I had to keep my eye on my goal. *Wei wu wei.* I reminded myself not to get in my own way.

I took a deep breath to regain my equilibrium and slowly let it out. Then I said, using as soft a tone as I could call forth, "Without my recommendation of Bos Smyth, as defense counsel, to you, your son likely would still be in prison rather than at home living with you. That was the favor I rendered to you."

Bing-fa sat silently. He neither acknowledged the truth of my statement nor disavowed it.

I decided to go for his jugular now. "I'm sure other members of your community would interpret your failure to help me as your refusal to honor your debt, were they to learn of it." *And I would take great pains and pleasure to see that they learned of it.* "Your honor requires that you redeem this favor or lose face." *Such as your honor is these days, but I wasn't going to waste time debating that.*

I waited for him to say something. I had taken this as far as I could without resorting to sarcasm or, worse, resorting to begging for his help, neither of which was likely to achieve my desired end. A full minute passed without either of us saying anything. We sat quietly and stared into one another's eyes.

After the full minute of silence, Bing-fa said, "What help do you seek?" His tone was deceptively neutral, even flat.

It's about time. "I'm being confronted, maybe threatened is the right word, by a dangerous Occidental secret organization located in Richmond, Virginia. It wields great power and influence, even reaching as far out from Richmond as Washington. I need the help of the *Cunning Rabbit* to level the playing field for me."

"That is too vague, Mr. Cheng. What is it you want us to do for you?"

He had me there. The problem was I wasn't sure what I wanted done. But I knew I needed help, and hoped the power and influence of his triad could give me that help. I decided to be general in my request.

"I want the triad to be my eyes and ears in Richmond, my backup and protector, as I work a case located there. I'll probably also need to call upon its influence with the Richmond cops or local politicians."

Bing-fa's face showed the first crack in its impassivity. Now, his face spewed forth pure distain.

"As you *should already know*, Mr. Cheng, the *Cunning Rabbit* is a charitable organization, nothing more. It does not have the influence you choose to imagine."

Bullshit. You really think I believe that? Wei wu wei.

"Perhaps, then, Bing-fa, I made a mistake coming to you, and I should instead seek the help in Shanghai from Big-Eared Tu. As your benefactor, he will be obligated to repay your debt to me, if you refuse to do so."

I'd decided to throw his distain right back at him.

"As we both know, Bing-fa, Tu's power and reach is reputed to be far and dominant, even as far reaching as here in the American home city of the *Cunning Rabbit*, perhaps even as far as Richmond, too. Who knows how far Tu's authority actually extends?" *That should get his attention.*

I could see I'd stung Bing-fa. Big-Eared Tu, although very elderly now and thousands of miles away in China, was Bing-fa's mentor and only significant rival in the triad, at least that was true five years ago. Bing-fa's eyes narrowed and his mouth briefly turned down, but he recovered quickly.

"That's all I ask of you, Bing-fa," I said. "Then your debt to me will have been paid in full, and we will be free of one another forever." *One could only hope,* I thought.

Bing-fa remained silent as he slowly turned his head and looked across the room at his caged crickets. After a few seconds he turned back to face me. He again ran one palm over the sleeve of his gown, smoothing out wrinkles, real or imagined. Then he did the same with his other palm and his other sleeve. When he finished, he folded his hands together, interlacing his fingers, and placed his hands on his lap. He now presented the perfect image of Taoist repose.

"The *Cunning Rabbit*," he said, "operates in Richmond as a community organization, acting through the good offices of the Richmond Oriental School. I will arrange for the headmaster of the school to help you. Then I do not ever want to see you or hear from you again."

I nodded. "That will suit me fine."

CHAPTER 67

LATER THAT DAY I PICKED up Clotille at her office and
we went out to dinner. We settled at a table at *Ris* on
the corner of 23rd and L. After we placed our orders for
drinks and food, Clotille smiled at me and said, "I really love
you, Socrates. You know that don't you?"

Uh, oh. That statement could mean one of two things:
that Clotille wanted to reaffirm for me that she loved me (an
unnecessary effort since I had no doubt she did, although it
was possible she had need to say it for her own benefit) or
that a big *but* was about to follow. I knew which I preferred
and which I dreaded.

"I know that," I said, wary of what might come next.

She said nothing else.

After a few more seconds, I said, "But?"

She frowned. "But what? No *but*, Socrates." She allowed
a big smile to overspread her face. "Can't a girl, me, tell the
man she loves that she loves him? Tired of hearing it, are
you?"

I shook my head and smiled. I reached across the table
and took her hand. "No, not tired at all. Don't ever stop
saying it and don't ever stop loving me. I crave being told I'm
loved by you." I squeezed her hand.

"I love you, too, Clotille," I said, "but I do have something to tell you, so hold onto that thought."

Our drinks arrived. I sipped mine and looked at Clotille. She had furrowed her forehead. My last comment didn't sit well with her.

"What's the problem, you?" she finally said.

"No problem. None at all with you and me. I just want to bring you up to date on something because we don't keep secrets between us."

I watched Clotille's shoulders relax and the color return to her face.

"I had that meeting earlier this week with Toula, the meeting I told you about. Nothing happened, as I said it wouldn't, but, as I told you, she said some man had come to my mother's building twice and asked about me. She couldn't — or wouldn't — tell me anything else other than his general description."

"Do you think it's someone you know?"

I shook my head. "I don't think so. No, I'm sure it's not. Anyone I already knew wouldn't have reason to ask her about me. And they wouldn't have asked about me at my mother's building."

I paused to see if Clotille had anything to say about it. When she stayed silent, I said, "I'm worried because Toula also brought my mother into the conversation, so I can't ignore it now. I need to find out who this person is and what he wants."

CHAPTER 68

IT WAS SATURDAY MORNING. CLOTILLE had spent the night at my condo and had just left to go home. I was puttering around in my den, trying to decide if I would pay bills or go back to sleep for a few more hours, when my cellphone rang. I looked at the CallerID. Harte's name and number showed up.

Harte never calls on a weekend. "Morning, Harte," I said.

"We have a situation."

I felt my stomach tighten. In a voice in which I put all of the tiredness of someone awakened long before he was ready, of someone out of patience with the upcoming day just on principle alone, I said, "Now what?"

"Thigpen just called. The Richmond cops are on the way to the 2D with a warrant for your arrest."

"What?"

"You need to go to the 2D right now. No delay. No bullshit games from you. Bring your lawyer."

"I thought we were clear with them?"

"There's a new development. Winston Starr was found stabbed to death in his apartment. The place was trashed just like that director's place."

I was stunned. Why would anyone kill Starr? Worse, why

would the Richmond cops think I was responsible? It had to be the cabal again.

"Why are the cops doing this to me?" I said. "We settled all this before." I hoped Harte would give me some reason that would make sense to me.

"Like I said, there's a new wrinkle. Just like before when the forensics team worked-up the crime scene, this time they found a sterling silver money clip on the floor near Starr's body, the money clip you said the muggers had taken. It had your initials engraved on it. The cops have already established that only your prints are on it," he said.

"You have to deal with this now and get out front on it. Call your lawyer and get over to the 2D."

CHAPTER 69

"I ASSUME YOU KNOW WHY WE'RE here again, Mr. Cheng?"

We were spread around a bare, metal table in an interview room. Detectives Halpern and Stella were there. Bos Smyth, too. I assumed that Harte, who had driven me over to the 2D, and Thigpen, who had come out to meet us in the lobby, were observing us from the other side of the room's two-way mirror.

I nodded my head. "Winston Starr's murder. I had nothing to do with it."

Smyth put his hand on my forearm and shook his head in a clear message to stop talking unless he signaled me I should speak. I assumed, too, his admonition was also meant to remind me not to lose my temper or be sarcastic if he allowed me to speak.

"You know we found your money clip at the scene. Your prints were on it. Only yours."

"Of course they were. It's mine. But I had nothing to do with Starr's death. I didn't even know about it until Ralph Harte called me a few hours ago."

I looked over at Bos Smith for retroactive acknowledgement that I hadn't spoken out of turn because I hadn't first just checked with him first. Bos, among other things, was a realist. He nodded slightly. I glanced at the mirror and nodded once at Harte, although I could not see him back there behind it.

"I told you before. The money clip was one of the things the muggers stole from me," I said, looking back at Halpern.

"That's quite a coincidence," Detective Stella said. "You claim to be mugged in DC, but your pen turns up at one crime scene in Richmond and your money clip at another. Why is that?"

"It's not a coincidence at all," I said. "It's clear the mugging wasn't a chance encounter, but was set up in DC to set me up in Richmond."

"Why would someone go to all the trouble to do that?" Stella said.

So we would have this conversation, is why. "To intimidate me by framing me. To get me to back off the Museum's case, just like you tried before. I guess it's obvious to you I didn't back off." Neither detective showed any surprise or otherwise responded to this statement, so I assumed they had known all along I hadn't dropped the case.

"Who would want to frame you, Mr. Cheng?" Halpern asked.

I hesitated telling them. I looked at Bos, but found no comfort there. He knew what I was thinking. I looked again at the detectives.

"Mr. Cheng," Detective Stella said, "is there anything you want to tell us about that? Who would send muggers after you all the way to DC? And who would plant your fountain pen and money clip at two crime scenes in Richmond? And why would they even bother? Can you tell us that?"

I took a slow, deep breath and looked at Halpern and

Stella. They stared hard back at me. Then I opened up and told them everything about the Museum's case, from the moment I first received the call from the director up until today. I didn't hold anything back, not even Lee's secret or information about the cabal. I didn't care at this point if the Museum or the Golden Knights sued me for breaching my confidentiality agreement. My freedom was on the line.

When I finished, Halpern and Stella glanced at one another. Halpern turned to face me, and said, "Where were you yesterday and last night?"

Fortunately, once again, Clotille was my alibi. We had been together all night in my condo. As I explained this, I wasn't thrilled that Harte was watching and listening from the other side of the two-way mirror on the wall.

"Okay for now," Halpern said, once I brought Clotille into the mix. "We'll check out your alibi and your story about the Museum's case."

"Any idea who might have killed Starr?" Stella asked "Or why?"

I shook my head.

"All right, Mr. Cheng," Halpern said, "you're free to go for now. Meantime, assuming your alibi holds up, I'd watch my back if I was you. If you're right about what you told us, seems like there are some bad folks out there who might have it in for you."

CHAPTER 70

T HE NEXT MORNING I RETURNED to Richmond to keep an appointment with the headmaster of the Richmond Oriental School. As I drove south away from Washington I couldn't help chuckling at the irony of the way one aspect of this investigation had unfolded: The Richmond cops left Richmond and had come to Washington to see me, and I, in turn, was leaving Washington and driving to Richmond to investigate the burglary. I guess this amounted to my own form of gallows humor.

Before I drove to Richmond, I looked up the Oriental School using both the Google and Bing search engines, as well as Google Earth.

The school presented itself as a non-profit social organization founded in 1975 to educate Chinese immigrants, who settled in or around Richmond, in the ways of the West. Its stated purpose was to advance the social, political, and economic well-being of Chinese-Americans and other Asian-Pacific Americans. The school also offered classes for Westerners interested in the history, culture, and languages of China. Specifically, the school offered language classes to Westerners in the Pinyin and Bopomofo phonetic-language systems, as well as classes in advanced, classic Mandarin dialect.

The school was located in Richmond's historic district. The school's three story, red-brick building sat on a wooded campus located on Libby Avenue, not far from the site of Libby Prison, the notorious Confederate Civil War prison. The setting reminded me of the luxurious green campuses of some of Washington's exclusive private preparatory schools.

I parked in the lot adjacent to the most imposing building I saw, among several imposing structures in sight, because when I made my appointment I was told to enter the largest building I would see, that this would be the administration building housing the office of the school's headmaster.

***

As I looked around the cavernous, darkened lobby, I spotted a sign marked Visitors hanging over an entrance door. I crossed the lobby and stepped through the entryway.

A middle-aged Asian woman sat behind a desk. She looked up and smiled as I walked in.

"Good morning, Sir. Welcome. Can I help you?" She had no noticeable accent.

I smiled and nodded. "Thank you. I have an appointment with Headmaster Zhao. My name is Socrates Cheng. I'm a little early." I bowed my head slightly as a sign of respect.

Two minutes later I settled into a chair across the desk from Headmaster Yaowu Zhao. We immediately engaged in and quickly dispensed with the Taoist ritualistic greetings and small talk required in these formal circumstances.

"The Honorable Master Li told me to expect your visit, Mr. Cheng. Welcome."

"Thank you."

"Master Li said you would solicit our help, although I

cannot imagine what we could do to assist you. We are but a small charitable organization operating as a school and cultural center, aiding our countrymen when they move to Richmond."

I would play the required game and not directly state that I was aware that the school was really a Richmond-based front for a criminal triad based in Washington and Shanghai.

"Perhaps you will not be able to assist me after all," I said, "but Master Li thought otherwise. He led me to believe that the Oriental School wields great respect and authority in the Richmond community, with both Occidentals and Orientals, and that the school has a long and influential reach. I hope Master Li has not been misled in his assessment of the school." *Let's see you worm your way out of that one.*

I watched his eyes smile, although his mouth yielded nothing. Zhao now understood that I understood the rules and that I would play hardball with him, if necessary. This scenario had been necessary. Now we could move on.

I continued my ritualized role by now moving onto the next stage of the prescribed rite, implicitly saving Zhao's face by not dwelling on the fact that I knew his response had been nonsense.

"There is a powerful, secret organization in Richmond operating within the museum run by the Golden Knights of the Confederacy," I said. "I have reason to believe this organization intends to cause me harm. Perhaps, too, to cause harm to people I am close to because of their proximity to me."

Zhao sat impassively, giving nothing away to me.

"This organization has already attempted to injure me by trying to have me arrested for two crimes I didn't commit.

I believe this organization has great influence with the Richmond police and politicians. They, in turn, seem to have influence with the Washington, DC police."

I waited as Zhao let this sink in. He still didn't show any response.

"I would like the Oriental School, even though it is but a simple, charitable, and cultural organization, to use its well-known and much respected influence and good will in Richmond to neutralize the Golden Knights and to rein in the Richmond police when they try to interfere with the investigation I'm pursuing here."

"You overestimate our power, good will, and influence, Mr. Cheng."

"Perhaps," I said, giving a slight shrug, "but not according to Master Li." I watched Zhao frown briefly, then catch himself. He recovered with admirable agility.

He leaned forward and rested his forearms on his desk. He tented his fingers and smiled indifferently. "Tell me more, Mr. Cheng."

Bing-fa's name, it seemed, worked wonders here. I proceeded to tell him everything, mentioning Bing-fa whenever I could seamlessly work in his name.

CHAPTER 71

HEADMASTER ZHAO LISTENED TO ME with what seemed to be silent resolve while I set out my case. Neither his face nor his body language yielded any hint what his response would be. I wished I could have pealed back the layers of his mind to see what he was thinking.

I couldn't tell if Zhao was merely tolerating me and my described needs in order to accommodate Li Bing-fa, or if he actually was interested in what I had to say and, therefore, was interested in helping me. My instincts, because of the power wielded by Bing-fa, told me it likely was the former.

Although I didn't really care which of these two choices it was, I didn't know how much Zhao would be willing to do for me to appease Bing-fa or for how long he would be willing to do it before he put his foot down and said, no more. Accordingly, I decided to triage my needs and to limit my requests to the most important, bare essentials. If he helped me with those matters, and later was willing to do more, I'd again ask for his aid.

"I'm a private investigator," I said. "I'm working on a case involving the museum run by the Golden Knights of the Confederacy."

I watched Zhao's eyes slightly close, then open again.

It was an interesting, but meaningful, reptilian-like tell. I doubted the Golden Knights' membership welcomed or even tolerated immigrant Chinese into the Richmond community, any more than they welcomed any other non-Ante-Bellum-aristocratic-Caucasian individuals into their narrow fold.

"Let me tell you the details of this investigation," I said. I no longer felt bound in any respect by the terms of the confidentiality agreement.

When I finished, Zhao said, "Specifically, Mr. Cheng, what is it you want from us?"

How do I put this and not cause him to lose face by telling him the obvious?

"I would like two things from you. First, I would like you to have your cultural organization investigate the secret cabal working within the Museum, then tell me everything you find out about it and, hopefully, suggest some way to neutralize it."

Zhao remained silent, but nodded.

"Second, I'd like you to convince the Richmond cops to leave me alone. Somebody has turned them on to me, likely the cabal, but not necessarily. I need room to investigate without constantly looking over my shoulder to see if the cops are coming after me."

"That will not be a problem," Zhao said.

Time to insert the closer into our discussion. "If you can do those two things, that will be plenty. Both I and Master Li will be most pleased and grateful to you."

"Consider them both done."

I drove back to Washington feeling a sense of modest accomplishment. If all Zhao could pull-off would be to counterbalance the effect of the Richmond cops, and to educate me sufficiently about the cabal to enable me to deal with it with some hope of success, he will have helped me immensely.

I looked forward to getting home. Clotille and I planned to go out to dinner again, and then spend the night at her apartment. Otherwise, I probably would have checked into a Richmond motel for the night because I had business in Richmond again the next morning, business that wouldn't wait.

CHAPTER 72

I woke early the next morning, drank coffee with Clotille, then left her while I headed home to shower and change before I drove back to Richmond. I was heading for Blankenship's garage.

For once I wasn't heading there because I'd had a problem with my vehicle. My Lincoln MKZ was fine. The replacement fuel pump seemed to be functioning correctly, so far. My mission today was not a vehicle repair. Instead, I wanted to arrive Blankenship's before it became too busy so I could cut Caleb Livengood from the herd of mechanics, isolate him, and ask him some questions as part of my investigation.

It took some persuading, but Caleb agreed to take an early cigarette break and join me behind the main building.

"I appreciate you giving me your time," I said.

"No problem," he said. His tone of voice and his frown gave the lie to his words, but I didn't care. He was there, so we could speak.

He reached into his shirt pocket, extracted a cigarette from the soft pack he was carrying, then put fire to it.

"You told me the slave's journal and letters stolen from the Museum were forgeries. Are you sure?"

"I'm sure I was told that by someone who should know. Can't be more sure than that though. Why?" He took a slow, long pull on his cigarette, held the smoke for a few seconds, then let it stream out his nostrils.

"What makes you think this person was correct, not just blowing smoke?" I said, not intending the obvious pun.

He shrugged. "Maybe they were, I don't know, but we all talked about the documents in my reenactment-group meeting last Friday, and agreed the documents were bullshit. Else why wouldn't any of us ever have heard of them before? Answer me that."

Right. What better test could there be than that? "They're not bullshit," I said. "I read copies of them. I believe they're genuine." *Now there,* I thought, *was a circular, weak argument if ever there was one.*

"So you read 'em. Big fuckin' deal. What's that prove except they seemed real to you. Can you say for sure they weren't fakes? Did you test the ink? The paper?"

He's brighter than I gave him credit for. I thought about that. I had to admit I really couldn't say one way or the other. Not only because I couldn't actually tell by looking at digital, printed copies, but because I didn't have the expertise to determine the authenticity of questioned documents.

My knowledge of documents was pretty rudimentary, limited to what is known as textual investigation and confirmation — determining the authenticity of content and the text itself by comparing an original document to the questioned document, examining words used, phrasing that repeats itself or is anomalous, and other eccentricities we all demonstrate when we write something.

I didn't have the expertise to judge and to authenticate the paper, ink, handwriting, and the other indicia that trained document examiners look at. Nor did I have the expensive scientific forensic equipment some museums have available to them to study ink and paper. And, of course, I didn't have the documents themselves to examine, only digital copies. To render an opinion concerning authenticity based on copies would be a fool's undertaking.

Time to put him on the spot and see if he believes what he said. "Why would someone create forgeries and fabricate a derogatory myth about Lee?"

Caleb shrugged, then sneered. "Maybe to discredit the one person who represented all that was noble and good about the Old South, the one person who cared about the common foot-soldier," he said.

Lee? Cared about the common foot-soldier? Nonsense. Lee let his troops be butchered en masse at so many battles when he should have retreated and fought another day?

"Again, why?" I said.

"I don't know *why*, but that's what someone did," Caleb said. "They won't get away with it, though, not if I have anything to say about it."

With that, he pinched the burning end of his cigarette between his forefinger and thumb, snuffing out the fire, then flicked the dead butt beyond the gravel clearing into the weeds. He turned and walked away. Our meeting was over.

CHAPTER 73

WHEN I ARRIVED HOME FROM my meeting with Caleb, I called Harte and arranged to meet him the next morning for breakfast.

We met around the corner from my condo at the *M Street Bar & Grill* in the St. Gregory Hotel. Harte was there and sipping coffee when I arrived.

Before I could even settle in and order coffee, Harte said, "Good news for you. The Richmond cops dropped you as a person of interest in both killings."

I wondered if that was Zhao's influence. I assumed it was.

I described my brief meeting with Caleb Livengood, and made a point of emphasizing his belief that the stolen documents were forgeries.

"Why would someone fake them and place them in the Museum's basement to be found?" Harte said. "It doesn't make sense."

I shrugged. "It's always money. You seed the archives with some phony, but credible documents, placing them among genuine ones to lay the basis for the discovery of the fakes. This placement of the fakes among genuine documents gives a sense of authenticity to the faked documents. It's an old trick," I said, "called salting."

Harte understood, and nodded.

"Or perhaps to give the fake documents the appearance of authenticity just by reason of where they are found, even if there are no genuine documents with them," I said.

I thought more about Harte's question, then said, "Maybe it's not money with this crowd. Maybe, assuming, of course, they are forgeries, it's just to stir up controversy. It could be any or all of those reasons."

Harte chuckled and shook his head. "Maybe it's just to drive you nuts, is why," he said. "Or maybe, more realistically, to discredit Lee, although I wonder who would care to discredit him other than a few wackos who still are fighting the Civil War in their screwed-up heads."

This is too much speculation, I thought. I changed subjects.

I told Harte about my meeting with Bing-fa and Headmaster Zhao. I didn't mention that I had asked Zhao to intervene with the Richmond police, and that's probably why they dropped me as a person of interest or as a suspect. I wasn't sure how Harte, as an ex-cop, would take that kind of influence-peddling or pressure applied by Zhao against men and women on the job. And I certainly had no desire to find out how he might take it.

CHAPTER 74

H EADMASTER ZHAO CALLED ME THAT afternoon. I was surprised he called me directly and didn't either have one of his minions do it for him or just summon me to Richmond to meet with him, as Bing-fa would have done under similar circumstances.

"Mr. Cheng, this is Yaowu Zhao. I have investigated the two matters you asked me to look into. I am happy to say that the Richmond authorities no longer have any interest in you."

"Thank you. I appreciate that." I shut up now and waited. It was his play.

"As for that other matter, we have determined that the secret society, what you called the *cabal*, operating as part of the Golden Knights of the Confederacy, does not exist. It is a myth spread by someone to intimidate others."

That stopped me cold. "Are you sure? There's plenty of evidence to indicate it does exist, but that it operates clandestinely." *Actually,* I thought, *there was no evidence at all, none at least that I'd seen. Just assertions and inferences made by the director, Starr, and Beauregard.*

"If you will show me that evidence, we will consider it," Zhao said. "The information we uprooted points to a mythical group founded in rumor only. Rumors, to be sure, that have taken on the mantle of truth, but unsubstantiated rumors nevertheless."

That didn't make any sense, but I wasn't in a position to argue with Zhao.

"Thank you, Headmaster Zhao," I said. "I will take it from here." I stood up. "I'm indebted to you for your efforts on my behalf." I paused, then added, "I will gladly inform Master Li that you have been both gracious and very helpful to me." I bowed my head slightly to show him the respect from me he'd earned.

I called Harte, but didn't reach him. Then I remembered he was out on a surveillance assignment. I considered my next move. Then I called Beauregard and set up a meeting in his office for the next morning. I told him I wanted a one-on-one meeting. He could tell the other trustees later that we'd met and what we had met about if he wanted to, but I wanted our meeting to be between us only. After dissembling for a few seconds, he agreed to my terms.

CHAPTER 75

I STILL WASN'T COMFORTABLE WITH CALEB Livengood's assertion that the stolen documents were fakes, so after I finished my call to Beauregard, I called Livengood. I hoped I could get together with him after my meeting with Beauregard the next day and again pursue this issue with him. But that wasn't to be. The foreman at the garage said Livengood was off for the day and also for the weekend to attend a reenactment at some battlefield site.

Caleb's absence didn't help me. I needed answers from him to some basic questions: Why would someone forge the documents? If they were forged, how had they wound up in the Museum's basement? Why did the Museum protect the documents as if they were genuine? I didn't know if Caleb had the answers, although I suspected he did, but I wouldn't know until I asked him.

I also wasn't fully comfortable with Zhao's assertion that the secret cabal didn't exist. What if he was wrong? I had no reason to doubt him, but the director, Starr and Beauregard had all been pretty certain it did exist. At least they had acted as if it existed.

Beauregard closed his office door and took his seat behind his desk. He leaned forward, elbows on the desktop and his fingers tented. He assumed a smug smile.

"So, Mr. Cheng, Suh, what is so important we had to meet this morning and meet alone?"

I took a deep breath and assumed my most convincing posture of righteous indignation. "I'll tell you what's so important, Mr. Beauregard. I don't appreciate being lied to and jerked around by my client."

That didn't faze him. Beauregard remained outwardly composed and self-satisfied.

"Who lied to you, Suh?" His voice betrayed indifference.

"The director, Starr, and you, Suh." I stretched out the last word to telegraph my indignation. *See how you like it dished back at you, Suh. Childish of me, for sure, but it certainly did feel good.*

"I beg your pardon. I have never lied—"

"Let's talk about the Lee documents and the secret cabal," I said.

Beauregard abruptly sat up straight in his chair. He extended both his arms and shot his cuffs. I assumed this ritualistic movement was intended to buy him time before he responded to me.

"What about them?" he finally said, now looking me in my eyes.

Let's see how you handle this question. "Why does the Museum have me chasing forged documents?"

Beauregard squirmed in his chair and used one finger to pull his shirt collar away from his neck.

Nice tell, I thought. I doubted he was aware he'd done this. He clearly was not comfortable.

"What are you talking about?" he said.

"The journal and letters. They're fakes." *He doesn't have to know I'm not yet convinced of this.*

"Not to my knowledge, Suh. With all due respect, you don't know what you're talking about." He shot his cuffs again. I was again distracted by his anomalous affectation.

"Don't you think it's strange the documents were discovered in the Museum's basement, but no one knew about them before that?"

"Yes and no, Suh. Actually, it isn't strange at all once you know the circumstances. They were discovered because the Museum developed a rodent problem in the basement. Before the exterminator could do his work, we had to clear out uncatalogued boxes and useless files. The journal and letters were found in one of the boxes that had been sitting on a shelf unopened for who knows how long."

Plausible, but not necessarily a satisfactory answer. "What about the secret cabal. It doesn't exist, does it?"

Suddenly the room took on a tomb-like hush. Beauregard seemed to have stopped breathing. He opened his mouth as if about to speak, then hesitated and closed his mouth. The moment was charged with dense thoughts. After a full minute passed, he said, "No, Suh, y'all got me there." He offered a weak smile. "It does not."

"I must admit," he said, "it does not exist as far as I'm aware, except in the imagination of the director, who conveniently thought it up. Winston Starr and I were persuaded to go along with his idea. How did you find out?"

"I'm sure the Richmond cops will be interested in knowing they have been chasing a phantom in two murder investigations," I said.

Beauregard slumped back in his seat, suddenly diminished in size. He sighed.

"You can't hide it anymore, Mr. Beauregard. The story of the documents and the cabal is going to come out, one way or another. Maybe at a trial when the people who killed the director and Starr are arrested, maybe some other way, but it is going to come out. You might as well tell me what you know."

He stared into the far corner of the room while I waited. He nodded once, looked up, and fixed his eyes on mine.

"It was the director's idea, Mr. Cheng. Starr and I went along with it. We all wanted to protect the Museum."

"Why?"

"When the journal and letters were discovered in the basement, we thought it odd they'd hadn't been cataloged right away when they were first acquired as part of the Museum's collection. That's our standard practice. And then Starr and I questioned their authenticity because of their content. As General Lee scholars, we both were shocked and dismayed by what we read. Yet the place of their discovery argued for their likely authenticity.

"So, Mr. Starr and I, over the objection of the director, who argued that the subject matter of the documents was too explosive to risk having it discovered during the normal authentication process, ourselves subjected the journal and each letter to the usual, rigorous tests to determine if they were genuine.

"And they turned out to be fakes?" I said.

"No, Suh, not for sure. Our results were inconclusive. But the director then took a firm stand, insisting that we must keep their existence secret and, between ourselves and the other trustees, behave as if the documents were genuine, but also act as if they did not exist.

"Mr. Starr, our primary Robert E. Lee expert, however, pronounced the documents fake even though the tests had been indeterminate. He took this position in spite of the director's orders. The director continued to insist that the documents might be authentic and therefore should be dealt with as if they were genuine for the sake of the Museum.

"I didn't know one way or the other if they were genuine," Beauregard said, "but I tended to side with the director's way of dealing with the issue, trying to maintain an open mind to the extent I was able."

Beauregard paused to stretch his neck and loosen his collar.

"The one thing we all agreed on was to keep the existence of the documents confidential until we knew the truth about them. The exception was that Starr and I felt duty-bound to inform the other trustees. We prevailed on the director to do this, against his strenuous objection, as he continued to think it best to keep those of us who knew Lee's secret to as few in number as possible."

"So," I asked, "this is what led the director to create the myth of the secret cabal?"

Beauregard nodded. "Yes, Suh. That was the reason. Now you know. It was the director's idea to keep the trustees in line by frightening them into maintaining their silence. He thought the existence of a secret, dangerous group would have an *in terrorem* effect on them. Mr. Starr and I agreed to this deception in order to convince the director to go along with us and disclose the discovery to the trustees."

I tapped my finger on the desk. I didn't know if I could

trust Beauregard. He seemed to have only a small reserve of candor, and, so far as I could tell, had used it all up in his early encounters with me.

"So who do you think killed the director and Starr, if there was no secret cabal?" I said.

"I have no idea, Suh."

Well, I had an idea, but I would have to do some sleuthing first to see if it panned out. I thanked Beauregard for his time and said I'd be back in touch when I knew something more.

I left the Museum and drove back to DC.

The hunt was on and, if I was right in my assessment, I was closing in on my quarry, just as he might be closing in on me.

PART FOUR

CHAPTER 76

WHEN HARTE AND I FIRST formed our partnership, he spent months relentlessly drumming his cop's mindset into me, a mindset developed by him over the course of his years as a MPD street cop and detective, a mindset concerning investigations and their outcomes.

His outlook was unhindered by classroom theory, and boiled down to this group of axioms: that there is a periodicity to investigations; that investigations ebb and flow; and, that investigations sometimes reveal what had been hidden, but at other times obscure what should have been obvious. The trick, he said, was to view the investigation as a whole, and not become bogged-down in minutiae.

Harte's other admonition was to stick with it, moving onward, day in and day out, one step at a time, permitting the pieces of the puzzle to reveal themselves, the parts to find their natural connections, – letting things take their natural course without forcing them.

He also drilled into me the importance of not becoming enamored by or fixated on any particular piece of evidence, claiming that otherwise you risk placing yourself in the trap that the investigation will become a quest to prove that particular item of evidence correct, to the detriment of other possible evidence not yet known or, if known, not yet fully appreciated.

I spent the morning at home reading over and updating my notes from the investigation, hoping to see the emergence of a theme that would point me in the right direction.

I read through the files with the hope that the known facts of the theft would, like the fabled Ouija board, somehow magically arrange themselves into a meaningful order, into some sensible concatenation that would yield up its secrets to me. It was this hope that kept me reading the case file over, and over again.

Of course this hope of mine didn't mean that we, as PIs, wouldn't play a role in helping the investigation along. If we did our jobs right, we would act as catalysts, leading the way to a resolution.

Harte had also drummed into me that investigations in the real world, unlike those we see on TV or in the movies, proceed on the assumption that there are no coincidences, that life is not based on the random intersection of chance events, that synchronicity does not play much of a role in solving crimes. Harte, of course, didn't quite express it this way. Instead, he said that real life investigations depend on the cop's or PI's patience, stubborn unyielding persistence, an open mind, and luck — good luck, that is.

I'd since learned on my own that real world investigations by private investigators (as opposed to investigations by the police) consist of ninety percent office work (checking facts, reviewing evidence or thinking through various scenarios) in front of a computer, plus five percent field work, and five percent inspiration. These all were hard truths for me to accept, but accept them I did. And once accepted by me, these truths suited me just fine since I generally am a person more comfortable contemplating action than engaging in action, more comfortable spending time in my head, than in the playing fields of life and action.

I reviewed all the information I'd accumulated so far.

I made a list of everyone involved with the theft of the documents and everyone I'd met who was otherwise connected to the Museum. I wrote under each name one or two sentences describing each person's current status and possible involvement with the theft. To that end, I listed the director, Winston Starr, Hervey Beauregard, the other trustees, the Golden Knights of the Confederacy (as an entity, but not its many members), the cabal (even though I now knew it was a red herring created by the director), Caleb Livengood, and the as yet unidentified mole within the Museum. Then I pared-down the list to eliminate the director and Starr, given their current conditions. Because I trusted Zhao's findings with respect to the cabal — that it did not exist — I treated it, too, as if it were dead, and removed it from the list. That left my inventory populated by the Golden Knights of the Confederacy, Beauregard, the other trustees, the mole, and Caleb Livengood.

I had already researched the Golden Knights, so I didn't see any reason to do it again. That didn't apply to its insiders, however, such as Beauregard and the other trustees who had knowledge of the slave's journal and two groups of letters. I decided, however, to defer my background research into these people until later because I was very curious about Caleb Livengood, and wanted to learn more about him. Specifically, I wondered how an automobile mechanic had actually come to know about the secret documents, and why he thought they were forgeries. The reason he'd fed me about the Museum's employee, who was his customer, being his source didn't seem plausible to me.

I had no intention of disparaging Livengood because he was a blue-collar worker, but it seemed unlikely to me that someone from the Museum, someone he barely knew, would trust him with the Museum's most closely guarded secret. Beyond that, his certainty about the inauthenticity of the documents was curious, to say the least.

I grabbed a beer from the refrigerator, climbed into my reading chair, and closed my eyes while I thought about Livengood and what I knew about him.

He was a walking anomaly. Presumably he had limited education, but he was (according to what he told me) an autodidact who was well-schooled in Civil War history. He also was a dedicated reenactor and a self-proclaimed Robert E. Lee authority. Curiously, if Livengood was to be believed, he also had managed to strike up an acquaintance with someone who was an insider at the Museum, someone who told him about the existence of the Lee documents, that they were contrived forgeries, and had then also told him that the journal and letters had been stolen.

I was skeptical of his whole story, but I had to pursue it as if it were true. I also needed to learn more about the so-called insider. Was he or she the mole?

I booted-up my desktop computer and typed Caleb's name and location into Google's search engine. This returned little

I didn't already know, plus his landline telephone number and his home address. I next tried the Bing search engine. It returned the same results.

I next spent two hours roaming through the databases Harte and I subscribe to as part of our PI business. These were enormous warehouses of personal and public information culled from many disparate sources.

My database search, unlike my Internet search, turned up some things about Livengood I didn't already know: his social security number, his drug possession arrest record (with an actual copy of the police arrest report), information about his stay at a rehab facility, his employment history for the past twelve years, his credit history, and the name of his girlfriend.

I telephoned Caleb at Blankenship's and spoke with him briefly. He didn't want to discuss anything over the phone, repeatedly claiming he had to get back to work. I persuaded him to meet me for dinner in Richmond. He gave me directions to a restaurant he favored, and agreed to meet me there the next night.

When I ended the call, I called Harte and set up dinner with him for tonight. I would bring him up to speed on the case, and with his help would plan a strategy for dealing with Livengood the next night.

CHAPTER 77

HARTE WAS IN AN UNUSUALLY jovial mood when we left our office and headed downstairs to have dinner at *Circa At Dupont*. We chose this restaurant in case we discovered in the course of our talk that we needed something from the office files. The unspoken thought was that if we needed something, the junior partner (me!) would run upstairs and retrieve it.

"You're pretty chipper tonight," I said.

"Cute," Harte answered. He frowned. "I'm always in a good mood, except when you piss me off."

I smiled and let it pass.

We settled into a table for two at the back of the dining area, ordered our drinks and meals, and got down to business.

"I'm liking that Richmond auto mechanic I told you about, as a probable perp for the burglary," I said. "I just don't know yet how he pulled it off or if he did it alone."

I took a sip from my beer. "Probably teamed up with someone inside who's been feeding him information. Maybe the Museum's mole."

Harte nodded, and sipped the shoulders off his draft. "Why him?"

"Other than the director, he's the only one who seems to have intimate knowledge of the documents."

"How can he know anything about them? Didn't the Museum keep their existence secret? That's what you told me."

"Says he had a customer who told him, someone from the Museum."

"That's pretty unlikely. Why would someone tell him, of all people?"

"My thought exactly," I said. "That's one of the things I'm trying to figure out. If you can believe him, he says it's because he's a Civil War buff and a General Lee reenactor. But these seem like weak reasons for someone he didn't already know well to divulge sensitive inside information to him." I shrugged and took a sip of my beer.

Harte said, "Unless the person had his own agenda unrelated to what the Museum would want or unrelated to the mechanic. You don't just give up secrets to your vehicle repair guy without some specific motive."

He looked off in the distance, then refocused on me. "Okay now. Enough speculation. Bring me up to date on your investigation. Facts and evidence. What do we actually know?"

I described my list of people who were involved and their current status in the investigation. As I wrapped it up, I said, "Beauregard's still a big question mark. He'll need more looking at."

"I'll do that for you," Harte said. "My surveillance case has wrapped-up, and I'm light on work right now."

I nodded and brought up Caleb again. "Like I said before, Livengood's a mystery to me. An uneducated garage mechanic, an ex-druggy who has a penchant for the Civil War and Robert E. Lee. That's a strange combination." I paused to think about what I'd just said. "I hope my meet with him tomorrow night will clear up some of my confusion about him."

"Maybe you should have your contact at the Oriental School look into him," Harte said. "He might turn up something you couldn't find, like he did with the cabal."

Good suggestion. I nodded. "Will do."

CHAPTER 78

THE DRIVE FROM WASHINGTON TO Richmond the following night was slow going. A heavy fog had set in.

Although I typically try to arrive early at meetings to get the lay of the land, I was running about fifteen minutes late because of the weather. I hoped Caleb would not use this as an excuse to bolt the meeting. He did not.

We met for dinner at *Mac's BBQ* in the Shockoe section of Richmond, near Tobacco Row. *Mac's*, one of the restaurants grandfathered under the state health code rules prohibiting smoking in public facilities, was dark inside, but not too smokey. A juke box blared a Waylon Jennings tune as I walked in.

I saw Caleb sitting at the bar. He was not alone. He seemed to be in a heated discussion with the woman seated on the stool facing him.

I eyeballed Caleb as I walked over. He must have noticed me approaching because he stopped talking, turned to face me, and looked me up and down, taking my measure, just as I was taking his. We continued to study one another as I approached, each avoiding the other's eyes while we made our assessments. I stopped directly in front of him, and nodded. He nodded back. He spoke first.

"This is my friend, Celia," he said, introducing me to the woman. He must have seen my quizzical look because he added, "We live together. She's a Hardcore, too."

"Nice to meet you, Celia," I said, as I stuck out my hand to shake hers. "I'm Socrates."

"I know," she said. She didn't smile to welcome me. "Caleb told me about you. Cute name. Nice to meet you, too," she said. Her greeting sounded forced and uninterested. "I'm Celia Pomeroy," she added. She dropped my hand, turned toward the bar, and retrieved a burning cigarette from among a pile of butts crammed into an overflowing ashtray sitting on the bar midway between her and Caleb.

She inhaled, then blew out a stream of smoke. She looked in my eyes and, this time, smiled as she shrugged her shoulders. Her smile was pleasant, even inviting, equally present in her eyes and mouth, but I couldn't get past the feeling it was forced.

I looked her over quickly, not wanting to be obvious as I tried to take her measure, based on her appearance. She was dressed in inexpensive casual wear, but also wore an expensive Movado watch on her wrist. She was slim, but not emaciated. Her dark hair was arranged in careful chaos.

Caleb remained silent until we'd all settled at a small table and ordered a pitcher of beer. Then he looked at me, and said, "What do you want from me?"

Caleb's question didn't surprise me. What surprised me was that his tone of voice made his question, and its implied offer to help, seem genuine.

"I don't know what I can tell you I haven't already," he said. "But, hey, a free dinner's a free dinner, too good to pass up." Something crossed his face I hadn't noticed before — a predatory leer that came and went in an instant.

"Tell me again how you learned about the existence of the Lee documents, and how you learned they'd been stolen."

"Like I said before, from a customer who works at the Museum. He told me both times."

"Who was that?" I said, as nonchalantly as I could.

Caleb leaned his chair back on it rear legs. He looked me in the eyes and seemed to silently laugh at some private joke. "Won't say. Promised not to and don't wanna get him in any trouble. I already told you that. Stop trying to trick me into telling you." He smiled and hooked his thumbs into his belt.

"Okay," I said. "I understand. Tell me this, then. How'd you learn the documents were forgeries? Same customer?"

Caleb nodded. "Right."

"Were the documents examined before or after they were stolen?" I asked. I wondered if he would fall for this question.

"Couldn't really say."

"Couldn't say or won't?"

He stiffened. His eyes narrowed. The leer I'd briefly seen before again flashed across his face, then was gone just as quickly. I might have pushed him too hard. When he spoke again, his voice was less easy than it had been a moment before.

"Nice try," he said. Then he shut down. He lit a cigarette and looked briefly at his girlfriend. When he turned back to me his face had hardened.

I have rarely seen a person propel himself so quickly into a silent rage. Sweat beaded on Caleb's forehead. His cheeks turned red and his eyes, already small and dark, appeared to have become even smaller. His hands trembled. Spit collected in the right corner of his mouth. He turned toward his girlfriend again, shook his head slowly, then turned back to me.

"You know," he said, "I don't have to say anything at all to you. I was trying to be nice, but if you are goin' to be pushy or try to trick me—"

I held up both my palms in simulated surrender. "I didn't mean to be pushy, Caleb, or try to trick you. I was just curious, is all. It won't happen again."

I watched him relax his posture. "All right. But don't do it—"

"Sorry," I said, interrupting him again.

I thought I'd bring the tension down a notch or two before I asked him again about the documents.

"Lee seems controversial," I said, "even among professional historians like Southall Freeman and Alan Nolan." Caleb didn't respond. "At least that's how it seemed to me when I read Lee's biographies years ago. I could be wrong though."

Celia chuckled and raised her eyebrows. I wasn't sure what that signified. Caleb continued to eye me with a suspicious frown. I decided to change subjects again, ask something that wasn't controversial.

"How'd you two meet?" I said, "if you don't mind me asking, that is." I looked at Celia, then back at Caleb. I smiled innocently.

"In a drug rehab program," Caleb said.

"I'm sorry," I said. "I shouldn't have asked. I didn't mean to—"

"It changed our lives," Celia interrupted, "so it's good. It's okay you asked. Don't be embarrassed. We're both clean. Have been since the program."

I offered a feeble smile. "I guess getting clean can change your life for the better," I said.

"That, too," Celia said, "but the best part is we met and have stayed clean together. It was me who introduced Caleb to reenacting. He'd never heard of it before."

I looked briefly at Caleb, who said, "That she did, all right." Then I turned again to Celia.

"How'd you get involved with reenacting?"

"Grew up with it. My family's been reenacting long as I can remember. My daddy used to do Stonewall Jackson when he was alive." Celia smiled. "When my daddy was alive, that is, not when General Jackson was alive." She laughed at her own joke.

I couldn't help laughing, too, but at the simple irony of her joke, not its humor.

"Daddy always said that doing a general who died early in the War of Northern Aggression was a blessing, that it took a lot of pressure off him to use up his free time by reenacting. Besides, Stonewall was rumored to be our kin on my mother's side, so he was a natural for my daddy to do.

"Not only that," Celia said, as she chuckled again, "reenacting a famous general was my daddy's way of poking his thumb in the eyes of the élites in our town. It drove them crazy that a small time tobacco farmer, a tenant farmer at that, was indirectly related to an important Confederate general he would do at reenactments."

I laughed again.

We ended dinner and split up early. I was back on the road heading to DC by 6:45. The fog had dissipated and highway visibility was good. The ride home was easy and uneventful.

As I drove, I called Zhao. I left a message on his school voicemail system. I asked him to look into Caleb for me. I said I would call him back in a few days to see what he'd learned.

CHAPTER 79

I DIDN'T HEAR BACK FROM ZHAO the next day, so I waited to give him time to complete my request before calling him again. I tried him two days later. I could tell from his tone of voice he was becoming tired of my requests. I hoped he would remain helpful to me for as long as I needed him. If not, I would have to visit Bing-fa again, this time with my hat in hand, requesting that he put Zhao back on track. That was not something I wanted to do if I could avoid it.

Beauregard called an hour later. He said the trustees were again concerned I was not making noticeable progress on the case. I said they were wrong, that I was making progress, and, in fact, was beginning to understand the profile of the person who had burgled the Museum, although I hadn't put a name yet to the profile. He seemed surprised when I said I would likely wrap-up the case in a week or two.

"Will you be willing to come to Richmond again soon and tell the trustees what you just told me?" he said.

Just what I needed. Another trek to Richmond. "No problem, Mr. Beauregard. When?"

"The sooner, the better, Mr. Cheng. In fact, it would be helpful, Suh, if you will kindly lay out for us what that profile is you discovered, and why you believe it describes the thief."

"I can do that." *I would rather stay in Washington and use Skype to have this meeting. Fat chance of that with these knuckle-draggers.*

We set the meeting for next Friday, three days from today.

The travel back and forth was beginning to wear me down. I'd have to remember that in the future when deciding to take on a case or not.

CHAPTER 80

Darryl Poole completed his meeting with Aunt Marge, left her house, and started the drive home along I-95, back to Arlington.

He thought about their conversation. He was again experiencing mixed feelings about having accepted the contract for the PI who lived in the Washington-Metropolitan area. But Marge, when she first offered the job to him more than a week ago, had assured him that this would be the last such contract she would present to him, that she understood his concern, and would respect his sense of disquiet about taking on Metro-DC assignments. Poole, in turn, had agreed to perform this last such contract as an act of good faith.

Anyway, he reasoned, he couldn't pull out now. Especially now that he saw the dossier Marge had prepared on the mark. The job would be fairly cut and dry.

Aunt Marge's dossier indicated that the target was a DC-based private investigator, currently working a case centered in Richmond. Poole decided there was minimal risk to this assignment. He would kill the mark somewhere not far from Richmond. And he knew just how he would do it.

Now all he had to do was watch the mark for a few days until he knew his target's habits.

CHAPTER 81

I DROVE TO RICHMOND FRIDAY MORNING for my meeting with Beauregard and the other trustees.

Beauregard met me at the entrance door and led me back to the conference room.

The other trustees, as usual, were scattered around the conference table. No one greeted me as I entered the room and settled into the only vacant seat. I used the silence to study the men before me.

I spent thirty minutes reporting to the trustees and answering their questions. Although they had been stand-offish and reserved at the beginning of the meeting, by the time I finished my report and my prediction of wrapping up the case in the next week or so, they'd warmed to me. After we scheduled a follow-up meeting for next Friday, I left the Museum and prepared to start my drive back to Washington.

Once again, my vehicle wouldn't start. I recognized the plaintive sound it made as I turned the key, so I immediately gave in to the inevitable and called Blankenship's. I could imagine Caleb Livengood laughing at my predicament as he awaited the arrival, once again, of my new Lincoln.

I spent the next hour at the auto shop. The analysis of the problem was that something in the vehicle's electrical system had been causing each fuel pump to short out. Caleb said the shop would run computer generated diagnostics to see if he could identify the source of the problem. This, he said, would take anywhere from thirty minutes to five hours, depending on how soon the problem revealed itself, then some additional time to fix the problem and install another reconditioned fuel pump.

"You're lucky," he said. "We have only two pumps left in stock. If you keep this up you're goin' to have a problem pretty soon." He laughed at his own joke.

I resigned myself to a long, wasted day in Richmond, called Uber, and visited several museums, until Caleb, after five hours had passed, called me on my cellphone to say the problem had been identified and fixed, that he had installed a replacement fuel pump in my Lincoln. I could come by the shop and pick up my vehicle.

CHAPTER 82

Darryl Poole's plan of attack, if executed successfully, would give him control of Socrates' vehicle while Socrates was driving. Poole had twice before successfully used this method to kill targets.

The first thing Poole did was watch Socrates for a few days. This gave him a general sense of his lifestyle and driving habits. Then, when he had the opportunity — it was at 4:00 a.m. — Poole entered the condo's parking garage where Socrates housed his vehicle and installed a GPS tracking device under the right, rear fender of the Lincoln. He also installed two wafer-thin video cams, one in the grillwork at the front of the vehicle, so Poole would have a driver's-eye view of the road ahead, and another on the rear interior ceiling. The latter cam had a wide-angle lens so Poole would be able to see the entire interior of the vehicle as he remotely controlled it in Socrates' place. Each device was the size of a dime and tinted with protective coloring to match its surroundings. The disc cams were undiscoverable unless you were looking for them and knew what to look for.

⚫━━━━◆◆◆◆━━━━⚫

The following Friday, after having shadowed Socrates part way to Richmond, Poole sat at a rest stop along I-95, approximately twenty miles north of Richmond. He had been there for more than one hour waiting for Socrates to finish his business and drive back to Washington. He kept his eyes on the portable GPS reader installed on his dashboard. It would indicate when Socrates had re-entered I-95 to drive home.

At 6:30 p.m., Poole's GPS reader indicated that Socrates was on his way out of Richmond, heading north on I-95. Poole took his last bite from the sandwich he'd brought with him, used the rest stop's men's room, and settled back in his vehicle to wait. He booted up his laptop and waited while it ran through its slow, laborious start-up program, before becoming functional.

Socrates was now approximately six miles outside Richmond heading toward Washington.

Poole turned back to his laptop and opened the software program he'd written to enable him to gain control of the computer systems found in most modern automobiles and SUVs. He checked the screen to make sure his computer and Socrates' vehicle still were paired; he logged onto Socrates' vehicle's central computer; and then sat back and bided his time as he watched Socrates come to him.

CHAPTER 83

WAS DRIVING ON I-95 HEADING home. The posted speed limit was 55 mph near the city, but at some point would become 65 mph as I got farther away. My vehicle's cruise control was set at 60 mph. I was thinking about the investigation and my next step when I heard the four door-locks click, unlocking the doors. I hadn't touched the driver's lock control. That spooked me. *An interesting glitch. I'll have the dealer look into it. Better than the fuel pump failing again though.*

I again became lost in thoughts about the investigation until a few minutes later when my seat belt clicked to indicate it had unlatched itself. I hadn't touched it. *Could this be related to the electrical problem Livengood said he just fixed?*

I had barely considered this possibility when I felt myself pushed back against the seat as the vehicle suddenly accelerated, ignoring the cruise control setting. My foot had not been on the gas pedal. I gently touched the brake to disengage the cruise control and to gradually slow the vehicle, but my effort had no effect on the vehicle's increasing speed.

I watched the speedometer climb from 60 to 70 to 80 mph, then move toward 90. My spine stiffened and I began to sweat. My hands gripped the steering wheel with such force my knuckles whitened.

I again lightly touched the brake pedal, intending to gradually slow down. Nothing happened. Although the brake pedal did not collapse uselessly to the floor, as it would have if it lacked brake fluid — a possibility I briefly considered — the braking system did not resist the vehicle's increasing acceleration.

I tried with one hand to relock my seatbelt, but the mechanism wouldn't remain engaged. The two halves clicked when I pushed them together, as if locked, but then fell apart onto my lap when I let go of them.

I pushed down the driver's side door-lock button, using my elbow. The lock promptly popped up again, unlocking the door.

I looked at the speedometer. I was hurtling along at 95 mph, and still picking up speed.

I gripped the steering wheel with both hands. My shoulders and neck ached. I looked for a place to safely steer the vehicle off the highway. I didn't see any. I wove in and out of traffic, blasting my horn until it suddenly went silent, even as I continued to press it.

No brakes? No horn? No seat belt? Unlocked doors? The vehicle steadily accelerating. *What the hell was going on here?*

CHAPTER 84

POOLE CONTINUED TO SIT IN his vehicle at the rest stop, watching his computer's monitor as it displayed Socrates' vehicle, now only ten miles away and rapidly closing with him.

On the left half of Poole's laptop monitor, using the hood's grill web cam he'd installed, Poole viewed the road ahead in real time, bouncing about and swaying from side-to-side, just as Socrates saw it. On the right half of the screen, using the interior web cam he'd installed in Socrates' vehicle, Poole watched Socrates as his head swiveled from left to right and back again.

It's time to put an end to this, Poole thought, *time to take charge and lock the steering wheel.*

CHAPTER 85

MY SHIRT WAS SOAKED THROUGH. My hands had fused with the steering wheel. My knuckles were pasty white. Pain sparked up my arms like shooting electrical charges, settling into my elbows and shoulders.

I whipped my head from side to side looking for a place to steer the vehicle away from traffic. Horn blasts greeted my efforts as I recklessly wove in and out of lanes, flying by other vehicles. I couldn't alert them to my approach and proximity using my horn.

I bounced along the highway, without brakes to slow the vehicle or to stop it, without a seatbelt to restrain me, in a vehicle that had become an alien missile, having a mind of its own. Stomach bile sluiced in my mouth, and I reflexively swallowed it back to its origins, only to immediately bring it up again.

I robotically pumped my useless brakes, hoping for the impossible to suddenly occur.

Road signs flashed by, but I barely saw them as I focused my efforts and waning strength on avoiding the vehicles ahead of me. My horn remained silent, ignoring my stabs which, in spite of my expectations, I continued to press. *The triumph of hope over experience.*

My arms ached; my neck and back throbbed.

"Shit, shit, shit!" I heard a scream erupt near me, and realized I was the screamer.

For the first time since my vehicle wrested control of itself from me and took on a life of its own, the highway before me was clear of other vehicles as far as I could see. Now was the time for me to act or I might not have another chance. *Would I have a chance anyway, acting upon a vehicle that yielded up no response to my attempts to take back control?*

I turned the ignition key to the off position to kill the engine, but only managed to provoke an angry, ear-splitting screech from the ignition system. I pulled on the emergency brake, but without any effect other than to produce the smell of burning rubber.

My vehicle raced toward the entrance to a rest stop and, on its own, abruptly left the highway, steering itself onto the exit path, my wheels throwing up a dust storm of gravel and stones as the vehicle briefly crunched the ground between I-95 and the access road. I entered the long driveway-like route leading to the parking area. The speed limit was posted at 35 mph. I was doing 103. Maple trees rocketed by on my right side.

I did the only thing I could think of. I shifted the automatic gear stick from its setting in Drive to Park. The sound of the shrieking gears ripping apart was deafening.

Poole watched Socrates' vehicle erratically meander across the screen of his laptop monitor. Then he typed a command into the computer and locked Socrates' steering mechanism, removing Socrates' last hope of control over the vehicle.

CHAPTER 86

AWOKE IN A HOSPITAL BED with an IV line running into my left arm. I had no idea how long I'd been there. I wasn't even sure where I was at first — Washington or Richmond — although I could tell from my surroundings I was in a hospital. The last thing I remembered was cannonballing along the access lane leading from I-95 toward a rest stop, experiencing abject terror as my gears stripped and my steering wheel first became self-steering, then locked altogether.

I touched my forehead. It was bandaged. My left wrist was splinted and taped. I moved my legs. My right knee hurt. I felt a sharp pain in my ribs. I touched my rib cage and found that it, too, was bandaged. The tops of both my hands were black and blue, as was the part of my right arm I could see. Later, when I was given a hand mirror, I saw that my face was a patchwork of black and blue, red, some green, and many yellowing bruises, in varying stages of repairing themselves.

I reached for a glass of water sitting on the rolling cart next to my bed, but this movement triggered so much pain in my ribs that I abruptly pulled back. My movement must have tripped an alarm because a few seconds later the door to my room opened and a nurse walked in.

She smiled, as she said, "Welcome to Bon Secours, Mr. Cheng. How are we doing today?"

We? I don't know how you're doing, but I know I'm not doing very well. "I don't know. Where am I?" I was in that murky state somewhere between sleeping and waking, definitely drugged.

"Y'all are a patient at Bon Secours St. Francis Medical Center. A hospital. You were in a vehicle accident. A bad one, I'm told."

I'd never heard of this hospital in DC. "In Richmond?"

"Where else? Yes, in Richmond, Mr. Cheng."

"How long?" I said.

"Four days, including today."

I groaned in despair. "I have people I have to let know I'm here. They'll be worried I'm missing, that something's happened to me. Can you give me my cellphone? It should be in my sports jacket inside pocket." I looked around, but didn't see my clothing. "Do you have my sports jacket?"

"People already know. We took care of that for you. You've already had visitors. You just weren't awake to know it."

That surprised me. "Who? How'd they find out I'm here?"

"You had an emergency contact list in your wallet. The hospital social-work staff contacted the people you had noted."

That meant my mother and Clotille. Probably Harte, too. I couldn't remember if he was on my list. I sighed and nodded. "Thanks."

"A pretty young woman with beautiful red hair, and your mother, and the Richmond police, too, visited."

The Richmond cops? "What's my condition? My injuries?"

"The doctor'll be in soon to see you. He's on rounds right

now. Y'all can ask him yourself when he's finished and stops by. Right now I need to know how much pain you're feeling. On a scale of 1 through 10, where 1 is no pain and 10 is excruciating. How much?"

I had no idea how to measure my pain, but I wanted the nurse to feel I was cooperative so I said, "4, I guess." She smiled. Apparently I had hit upon a right number.

The doctor stood at the foot of my bed with a clipboard in his hands.

"You have a serious concussion, Mr. Cheng, and three fractured ribs. You also had a torn meniscus in your right knee which we've repaired, some minor burns, many abrasions, and a fractured left wrist which we've set."

His name tag read, Dr. Leary.

"You're a lucky man," he said, "from what I've been told about the condition of your vehicle. A very lucky man, indeed, though not the first I've heard about who survived an accident that should of killed him. You should light a candle next time you're in church and say a prayer of thanks to the airbag god. I understand you weren't using your seatbelt." He shook his head in a *tsk, tsk, task* motion, silently reprimanding me. "You should know better."

I do know better and, in spite of my survival, I don't feel very lucky. "I guess so," I said.

The doctor listened to my heart with his stethoscope, then my lungs. He took my blood pressure and measured my pulse. He poked around my skull, too, and admired the nine stitches holding part of my head together. Then he examined my burns and other injuries. He wrote something on my chart.

"Yes, Suh, you are a very lucky man, indeed," he said. He checked his watch and made another notation on my chart.

"We ran tests to make sure you have no internal injuries. If the results come back negative today, you can leave here tomorrow. We don't want to fix you up here in the hospital only to have you bleed out internally in a few days and die at home." He chuckled.

That's really funny. Hospital humor, I assumed.

"You'll need rehab to get your right leg functioning normally again. One of your visitors said she'll make arrangements for you to have a physical therapist come to your home."

We were interrupted by a knock at my door. I looked up as the doctor nodded to two strangers who entered the room as he eased himself out.

———— ·•· ————

Two young men in navy-blue suits entered my room before I could ask them in. Their body language exuded all the indicia of federal agents — dark suits, burr haircuts, eyebrows almost knitted together to reflect the seriousness of their careers and mission, and ramrod stiff postures.

"Can I help you?" I said. I was propped up in a sitting position, with two pillows behind my back and neck.

One of the men reached into his jacket pocket and removed his billfold. He flipped it open to badge me as he approached my bed. I couldn't make out what his ID said from that distance, but it looked official and I could tell it was Federal from the American Eagle logo.

"Mr. Cheng, I'm Special Agent Lewis, Federal Bureau of Investigation. This is my partner, Special Agent Bourse." He canted his head toward the other man. "We'd like to talk with you. It should only take a few minutes."

I said nothing, but I did nod.

"We understand you were in an automobile accident, and that you said something when you were brought into the ER about your vehicle having a life of its own. Do you remember that? We'd like to know what you meant."

"It wasn't an accident I was in, was it?" I said. "Someone or something did this to me." I looked from one agent to the other, but saw no reaction. "I don't remember saying anything like what you said about the vehicle having a life of its own, but maybe I did. I just don't know."

"Tell us what happened."

I described the events from the time the doors unlocked themselves and my seatbelt unlocked itself until I was barreling along the rest area's access road and the steering wheel suddenly took control of itself before it froze.

"Why's the FBI interested? You guys don't do local vehicle wrecks," I said.

"We're with the counter-terrorism unit of the Bureau," Lewis said. "Other people have reported similar experiences. It's our job to catch whoever is hacking into vehicle computer systems before they do the same thing to many other vehicles at the same time, before they cause mass, simultaneous crashes."

The other agent, who had been silent and stayed back near the doorway, spoke for the first time. "Do you have any idea who might have done this to you or why?"

This was the first time I'd ever heard of auto or vehicle

computer terrorism spoken about, although I had read a brief article about it in *Autoweek* magazine while I sat in the waiting room the first time I had my Lincoln towed to the dealer in Richmond. The article stated that modern vehicles are rolling computers, with millions of lines of computer code controlling all of their vital systems, and that such systems are vulnerable to hacking. I hadn't given the article much thought at the time. My focus had been on getting my new vehicle diagnosed, fixed, and running again.

I shook my head no to both questions, but I was beginning to form a picture of who might have done this to me. If I was right, the *why* someone had done this would inevitably follow. But I wasn't about to tell this to the two Feds.

Bourse asked a few more questions, made some notes in his notebook, and reached out to hand me his card. As I took it, he said, "Call if you think of anything relevant you haven't told us."

I was discharged the next day. Harte had arrived with my mother in tow right before the docs cut me free. He was going to drive me to DC. Harte said Clotille had arranged to have a physical therapist visit me at home.

The Richmond cops visited me while Harte and my mother were there. We had the same conversation I'd had with the Feds, with the same meaningless result.

Harte drove us back to DC. When I asked why Clotille wasn't with him and my mother, he said she was busy moving some of her things into my condo, and rearranging things there so she could stay over and look after me while I convalesced. That was fine with me.

CHAPTER 87

*T*WENTY-FOUR DAYS LATER.

I was glad I was taking my physical therapy at home and had not moved into a rehab facility, even though such a move would have been temporary. I was happy, too, that Clotille was there at home for me. I was operating at about forty percent of my physical capacity and sixty percent of my normal cognitive capacity. I assumed the latter resulted from the general anesthesia I received when they repaired my torn meniscus, from my concussion, and (since my discharge from the hospital) from the pain meds the doctors had prescribed for me and insisted I take in connection with my PT sessions.

I slept most of the first week I was home, waking for meals and PT. On the third week, after Clotille finally agreed to return to work and had left me for the day, I went into my den and retrieved the Museum Case Book from my desk. I returned to my bedroom, climbed back into bed, and began to turn the pages, reading as I went along, hoping something I would see would light a fire under me and cause me to see connections and to recognize patterns among the facts I hadn't seen before. I hoped that the time I'd spent away from the case would enable me to see it with a fresh and clearer vision.

The Museum Case Book, an evolving depiction of my investigation, was our equivalent of a homicide detective's Murder Book.

The detective's Murder Book, according to Harte, was the case bible for a homicide detective.

Although a working copy still was kept in a three-ring binder, as before, to satisfy those holdouts who refused to use computers more than necessary, these days the master Murder Book was also placed online, with additions and amendments made to it for all participants to see using their mobile devices or desktops, as new information or reports became available. Detectives no longer had to wait to see the whole picture as a piece of evidence or a report slowly circulated from person to person.

The Murder Book was a key part of the investigation, almost as important as any single piece of evidence as an investigatory tool. An official Murder Book contained everything about a homicide that the investigating detectives could put together, both official and unofficial. The goal was to have everything thought pertinent to the case available in one place. Thus the Murder Book incorporated information about every suspect, every person of interest, every person interviewed by the cops, every piece of physical evidence, all the field and lab reports, and information on every witness and the victim, including transcripts of interviews, autopsy reports, and all forensic results. It also contained all crime scene photographs.

Our Museum Case Book was modeled after the police Murder Book, but without the homicide aspect since our investigation involved a burglary, but not the murders that might have been related to the theft. Our binder was a civilian's compendium of every move made by me or Harte in connection with our investigation, every interview, and every piece of evidence discovered. It contained summaries of our theories of the case and lists of open questions.

I sat up in bed and slowly turned pages. I thought about each item before moving on to the next.

I read summaries of my meetings with the director, Starr, Beauregard, and the trustees. I looked at my research into the Golden Knights, and the non-existent cabal. I studied my notes involving Caleb Livengood.

Nothing new revealed itself to me. No *Ah, ha!* moment gripped my thoughts.

———— ·•·•—— ————

Harte told me that the case had been dormant while I was in the hospital, except for daily calls from Beauregard wanting to know our progress. The man wouldn't accept that I couldn't work the investigation while still hospitalized.

I studied the Museum Case Book.

I thought about the stolen documents.

I edited and revisited my thoughts about the investigation, making extensive new and revised notes on a yellow pad and in my head.

I wondered if Harte would ever become comfortable enough with computers so we could put our case books online and give up the three-ring binder format? I doubted it.

I also thought about my vehicle's crash. According to the FBI, it definitely was not an accident. The vehicle did not mechanically or otherwise malfunction on its own. Someone had intentionally wrested control of the vehicle away from me with the obvious intent of killing me. *But who would want to kill me and*, I wondered, *who would have the ability to remotely take control of my Lincoln?*

After two hours of paging through the Museum Case Book, with some intermittent dosing off by me, things became clearer. I was grateful that I was an obsessive note taker. The answer, it seemed, was in my case notes. I just hadn't paid sufficient attention to them before. Now, I was pretty certain I knew who was involved with my vehicle crash and who was responsible for the other crimes. I knew *who*. I just didn't know yet the *why* or the *how*. That information would come next.

CHAPTER 88

S EVEN MORE WEEKS PASSED BEFORE my DC doctor declared me fit to return to work on a restricted basis. Until today I'd taken physical therapy every day at home. To my surprise, although I suffered agonizing pain during the PT sessions, I looked forward to the sessions because I saw measureable progress each time. I used a cane for now to support myself when I walked.

It took me a few days back in the office to regain my bearings. I spent all my time at my desk rereading case files, searching computer databases, and working the telephone. Once I was satisfied I had sufficiently caught up with the other cases I'd been handling before the vehicle wreck, and finished my review of office administrative matters, I turned back to the Museum's theft case.

The first thing I did was again slowly read through the Museum Case Book, focusing especially on my notes, although I probably could have recited the entire collection from memory, I had read the case binder so many times while convalescing.

It didn't take me long to realize, but longer to accept, that my cognitive functions still were not where they had been before the crash. I now was operating at about eighty to ninety percent of my full-reasoning capability. Mostly, my short term memory still was erratic, sometimes sharp, sometime fair, sometimes missing. It was a stark reminder for me, and a recollection I didn't relish experiencing, of my father's slow, but inexorable descent into crippling dementia over the course of the two years before his death. It frightened me to experience this even though I knew my current decline would end with the passage of sufficient time, and I would eventually rebound with my faculties fully restored. My father didn't have that knowledge, luxury or resolution.

I closed the Museum Case Book and called Detective Halpern. He had called me that morning before I arrived at the office, and had left a message for me to call him.

CHAPTER 89

Detective Halpern showed me into the interview room at the 2D. Stella was already there. Halpern seemed genuinely solicitous of my comfort as he set me up at the table and fetched a Coke for me. I appreciated that he and Stella had taken the trouble to come to Washington to see me, as an accommodation to my injuries. Thigpen, too, had put himself out. He had made an interview room available to the Richmond detectives.

"Sorry about your accident," Halpern said. "Heard your speedometer froze at 102 mph when you sideswiped some trees, before coming to a rough stop."

"Smart of you to strip the gears to slow down your vehicle," Stella said. "Lucky for you a bystander saw it happen and pulled you from your vehicle." He glanced at Halpern, then back at me.

"What possessed you to race like that on an off-ramp?" Halpern said.

"I didn't have control of my vehicle. Someone else did. Controlled it remotely."

I told the skeptical detectives how my vehicle had come under the control of some outside force, probably a hacker according to the FBI. I watched as Halpern and

Stella occasionally stole furtive glances at one another. It was apparent neither detective was able to willingly suspend disbelief in this instance and accept my account at face value.

"Feel free to talk to the FBI, you don't believe me," I said. "I'll give you the phone number of the Special Agent in charge."

"That won't be necessary," Stella said.

"Why'd you ask me to meet with you?" I asked.

"We've hit a dead end in the Museum murders. Since you seemed to think when we met before that the murders were related to your case, we thought we'd lay out for you what we have on the homicides and listen to what you have on the theft case, see if doing this lights a spark for either of us. Any problem for you with that?"

"I'm good with it," I said. "I have some ideas you might find interesting." I reached into my briefcase and pulled out the Museum Case Book. I set it on the table between us. I watched as Halpern and Stella again stole glances at one another, as if to say, *Who does he think he is having that binder? A homicide cop?*

Before the detectives looked at the Museum Case Book, we talked, spending the next half-hour bringing each other up to speed. Then we took a short break while Halpern went to their vehicle to retrieve the official Murder Book for me.

The rule they imposed with respect to my access to this official compendium was: look only; ask questions if I wanted; no photocopies; and, no notes. I imposed a reciprocal rule on them with respect to our Murder Case Book just to show them they couldn't push me around.

As Halpern and Stella turned the pages of the Museum Case Book, I looked through the Murder Book.

The detectives didn't show much interest in our binder, and were perfunctory in their page turning. When they finished, Stella said, "So, where are we after almost two hours of flipping pages and talking?" He didn't look at his partner as he said this. He looked directly at me as if it was my fault they didn't find our binder interesting or enlightening.

"I have one more thing to add," I said. "Something not yet reflected in the Museum Case Book." I paused to collect my thoughts, then said, "I think I know who stole the documents and, by extension, probably killed the director and Starr. I know *who*, I just haven't gotten to the *why* or *how* yet."

CHAPTER 90

H ALPERN SCOWLED AT ME. "WHY didn't you just say so before, save us all a shit-load of time here today pissing into the wind?"

The time had been well spent from my point of view. It showed me the cops didn't have anything that would help me that I didn't already know about or hadn't theorized myself.

"I wanted to know what you had before I accused anyone," I said. "I didn't want to jump the gun if I was going to find out from you I might be wrong."

"Okay, so now you know what we have. Who is it?"

"Livengood. Caleb Livengood."

"Who?" Stella said. He turned and looked at his partner, then back at me.

Halpern shrugged, and looked at me. "Who?"

"The auto mechanic. You just read about him in the Museum Case Book," I said. *If you actually bothered to read anything in there.*

Halpern sighed loudly.

Stella tossed his pen onto the table. He sneered at me as he pushed his chair away from the table. "What a crock," he said.

"Okay, I'll bite, Cheng," Halpern said, "but quit the word

games you're playing'. Start at the beginning. Tell us why you like this guy. Start with the homicides."

I spent the next thirty minutes laying out my thinking, reporting all of my conversations with Caleb, describing him as a Hardcore reenactor and a Robert E. Lee fanatic.

I described his interest in the stolen documents, how he purported to know about their existence, and also knew that they'd been stolen from the Museum even though the Museum had kept both these matters secret. I also said that he'd revealed to me his belief the documents were forgeries, thereby cementing his intimate acquaintance with them.

"What's more," I said, "he was in a perfect position to mess with my vehicle the times he replaced my fuel pumps."

When I finished, neither Halpern nor Stella leaped up and shouted, *Eureka!* They didn't seem convinced that Livengood was good for the homicides or the theft — not based on the evidence and logic I offered them. I hadn't shown them a motive for the theft or homicides, the means for either, or, in the case of the homicides, the opportunity — the three classic requirements for cops investigating felonies.

"Anything else about this Livengood we should know?" Stella said.

"He has a girlfriend, also a Hardcore, a serious reenactor." I told them Celia's name.

"Anything more we should know?" Halpern said.

I shook my head.

"We'll check out this Livengood person."

———— •••• ————

Detective Stella called the next morning.

"You were wrong, Cheng. Livengood alibied out. He

was working when you wrecked your vehicle, and has alibis for when the homicides occurred. He was away on that reenactment thing each time. He's covered by witnesses."

"What about the theft?" I said.

"Don't know, Cheng. Didn't bother asking. That's not our case unless a complaint gets filed."

I was disappointed, and not satisfied. Something was missing. I just didn't see what it was yet.

CHAPTER 91

T HE RICHMOND COPS' CURT DISMISSAL of Livengood as good for the crimes didn't dissuade me.

When Blankenship's opened the next morning, I was there waiting for Livengood. I walked up to him as he set out his tools by a work bay.

"Morning, Caleb. We need to talk."

He eyed me warily, then looked away. "What about?" he said. He didn't stop arranging his tools as he asked, and faced away from me the whole time, as if trying to avoid eye contact.

"The Museum's documents — the stolen ones — and other things."

"I don't have to talk to you. I don't know nothing about them except from my customer, what I already told you."

"Let's talk anyway. You'll be better off dealing with me rather than the cops. If there's no problem, maybe I can establish that with them for you."

We stepped out back so Caleb could take his smoke break. He glared at me with sullen eyes, then looked around as if to confirm we were alone. He pulled a cigarette from behind his ear, lit it, and blew a stream of smoke toward me. His face had taken on the look of someone who would bring trouble as yet unseen.

"Say what you want, then I'm out of here," he said. "Follow me back inside, I'll call the cops. You won't have to."

I pulled my thoughts together. "I figured out you were involved in the documents' theft. Maybe with the murders, too." I paused to let him digest this.

"That's bullshit." His face and neck reddened. "I had nothin' to do with any of it." He shook his head and stomped his foot. He hawked up a wad of phlegm and spit it to the ground by his boot. "We're done here."

He dropped his cigarette onto the gravel and crushed the stub under the toe of his work boot. He squinted at me.

"You can get yourself hurt making accusations at people like that."

"We can talk," I said, "or I can take what I have to the cops. It's your call. It's all the same to me."

He looked at the ground for almost a full minute as if contemplating his boot, and said nothing.

When he languidly raised his head again and looked at me, his eyes blazed with fury. "Not here," he said. "Meet me back at *Mac's* at six tonight. Come alone."

CHAPTER 92

I HAD SEVERAL HOURS TO KILL until it would be time to meet Livengood again, so I spent the balance of the day visiting the American Civil War Center at Historic Tredegar, the Black History Museum and Cultural Center of Virginia on Clay Street, and the Museum and White House of the Confederacy, also on Clay Street. These visits not only passed time until Caleb and I would meet, they gave me the quiet time I needed to think about the case, my investigation, and Livengood's role in all of it. As the afternoon passed, I found myself engaged in an interior monologue, confronting Livengood. *Dress rehearsal for our upcoming meeting at Mac's.*

As I left the Museum of the Confederacy, I looked at my watch. It was close to 5:45. Time to head to *Mac's*.

As I often did, I thought again about Harte's advice to me concerning how to conduct an investigation. He had emphasized that we needed to take whatever available information we knew, but look for the holes in it. Applying that to Livengood's case, that meant I needed to examine his role within the overall framework of what I'd learned from my investigation: Caleb had known about the slave's journal and the two groups of letters, even though the Museum had tried to keep their existence secret. He also knew the documents had been stolen. Then, later, he claimed to know that the documents were forgeries. All this, according to him, learned because he was a self-described General Lee authority and a Lee reenactor. *Pretty self-serving and implausible.*

I also considered the fact that someone had tried to kill me by taking control of my vehicle's computer and electronic system. Assuming the FBI was right about this, was it a coincidence that Caleb had swapped out my several defective fuel pumps and had access to my vehicle's computer system on more than one occasion?

CHAPTER 93

MAC'S HAPPY HOUR WAS A barrelhouse affair, not populated by men in three piece suits and women in business-dress casual, comparing today's DOW averages and the mercurial value of their 401(k)s. *Mac's* bar area was dense with smoke, rowdy talk, and raucous laughter. The juke whined a Hank Williams ballad lauding the virtues of some honky-tonk woman gone wrong. There were no iPods or iPads in sight. No one I could see was carefully studying his smart phone or playing with phone Apps.

As they used to say on the radio, the joint was jumping.

I glanced around trying to spot Caleb. I saw him at the bar facing me, a longneck Bud in one hand, looking through the haze of smoke into my eyes. He clearly saw me, but didn't acknowledge my presence. As I approached, he raised a cigarette to his lips and took a long drag. His eyes never left mine.

He was bracketed by an empty stool on each side. A glass of carmen-color whiskey sat on the mahogany in front of the left empty stool, as if someone had placed it there and vacated the seat. The right stool did not have a drink in front of it. I assumed that would be my place.

As I came close, Caleb dropped his cigarette to the floor

and jumped a second one from the soft pack he was holding. He placed the new cigarette in the corner of his mouth, flicked open a Zippo lighter, and fired up the butt. He took a long, slow drag, held the smoke in his lungs, then blew a stream directly at me. He never took his eyes off mine as he covered me in smoke.

When I came within range, I reached out, took the cigarette from his lips, and dropped it to the floor. I looked into Caleb's eyes, and never blinked. Without looking down, I ground out Caleb's cigarette under my shoe.

"Whoa," he said, his voice truculent. "What are you doing?" He started to rise from his bar stool.

I looked down at the remnants of the cigarette, then looked back at Caleb, and raised my eyebrows. I slightly shrugged. I raised my palm to face him, and said, "Sit." It clearly wasn't a request on my part.

Caleb scowled, but sat down again. "Those are expensive—"

"Give up the habit. Save your money," I said. I held his stare.

"That's bullshit. Like you give a damn if I smoke?"

"I don't. I couldn't care less that *you* smoke. I do give a damn if you cause me to smoke by polluting the air around me. Keep the cigarettes in your pocket until I leave."

I watched Caleb take a slow, deep breath as he looked away from me and around the room, as if trying to see if anyone else was watching or listening to us. Then he relaxed his posture, turned back to face me, and said, "This time only. Not again."

He didn't sound or look as tough as he tried to come off.

We settled into a booth. When we walked from the bar, Caleb carried a new bottle of Bud and the glass of whiskey that had been sitting next to him. I noticed lipstick on the glass as he set it down.

Celia's drink? I nodded toward the glass and said sarcastically, disingenuously, "A whiskey back for you?"

Caleb looked confused.

"Yours?" I said, helping him out, nodding toward the glass.

He shook his head.

"Who's joining us?" I said. *As if I didn't know.*

"Celia."

I looked around, but didn't see her.

I was tired and would have a long drive back to DC, so I said, "Let's get started. You can catch up your friend after I leave."

Caleb looked away, peering into the crowd, probably to see if his girlfriend was in hailing distance. He frowned as he turned back to me. "Why'd you want to meet?" he said.

"To go over some things again so I can get them straight in my head."

Caleb shrugged, picked up his long neck, and took a deep pull on his beer. "Suit yourself."

"Tell me again how you learned about the stolen documents?" I said. "Be specific this time."

"Damn it," he said, "that again? I told you already. Don't you listen? I said I learned it from a customer."

Time for the moment of truth. "I don't believe you. Doesn't make sense a casual customer would tell you about that. What would his reason be?"

"I don't give a rat's ass you believe me or don't."

"Why, then? Tell me that? You must have wondered why yourself."

A sly sneer crept across his face. "Maybe 'cause of my interest in Lee, is why."

"That doesn't make sense," I said.

"Maybe he wanted me to know the lie the Museum's élites were spreading about Lee, seeing as how I'm a Lee reenactor."

This is going to be like pulling teeth. "Why would it matter to him if you knew about the lie?"

"I dunno. Maybe it just did." Caleb said. "He didn't tell me why. You'll have to ask him yourself."

"I will. Who was he?"

A slow grin overspread Caleb's face. "Nice try. You won't learn that from me. I have standards, you know. I gave my word."

This was going nowhere. "Why'd you tamper with my vehicle's computer system?"

I watched his face grow dark and his eyes become slits.

"That's bullshit. I don't know what you're talkin' about. You can't pin that—"

"Maybe, maybe not. But it doesn't look good for you, Caleb. You had access to my vehicle's computer system several times. Only you."

"That doesn't mean crap. I didn't do anything to your vehicle except fix the fuel pump and run diagnostics on it. I don't give a shit you believe me or not." He reached into his pocket, took a cigarette from the soft pack, then looked at me and hesitated. He frowned, then put the cigarette behind his ear.

Good boy, I thought. I didn't say anything.

"We're done here," Caleb said. He looked at his watch. "I have to meet someone."

I pointed to the glass and said, "Guess your girlfriend's not going to put in another appearance tonight."

But I was wrong.

I felt a tap on my shoulder, and turned to face Celia who stood slightly behind me in the aisle. She had come up on my left as silently as an assassin.

Caleb nodded at her and stood up. He reached behind his ear and grabbed the cigarette. As I stood to leave, he lit it and blew smoke across the table in my direction.

CHAPTER 94

I LEFT *MAC'S* AND STARTED MY trip home. In spite of myself I couldn't help feeling skittish about the drive, remembering how control of my vehicle had been wrested from me the last time I made this trip. I knew my reaction was irrational since I was now driving a vehicle I'd rented at the last minute, a vehicle no one nefarious could have had access to. But I couldn't help myself. I had a long way to go to get past that experience.

I drove with my windows open and the air conditioning blasting. I wanted to purge myself of the impregnated stink from Caleb's cigarettes.

As I drove I dialed Zhao. To my surprise, he answered his phone. I asked him to perform one more assignment for me in addition to the one I'd asked about before. He didn't seem thrilled, but I reminded him how much his help would please Master Li. He agreed to perform this last task.

Zhao and I spoke again that evening. He'd done exactly what I needed. I thanked him and said I did not think I would need to bother him again. I also said I would let Master Li know that he'd been very helpful to me. I intended to follow through with that although I did not look forward to contacting Bing-fa again. Zhao's voice had warmed by the time we said goodbye.

I awoke early the next morning and headed for Rock Creek Park. When I left my condo to begin my walk, the clouds had been comforting MGM-like cotton balls — Hollywood-studio clouds — but as I progressed into my walk they darkened. When I left the park and headed home, rain began to fall, cutting off natural light, shrinking and tightening the visible world around me.

As the morning progressed, so did the rainfall, so I was glad to stay home. I turned on my iPod, and broadcast music through my docking-station speakers. I set to work in my study using the information Zhao had passed along to me.

After an hour, I had a pretty good fix on who had sufficient motive to steal the documents from the Museum and, likely, to have committed or orchestrated the murders of the director and Starr. I tied up a few loose ends, called Harte, and ran my conclusions by him. I got his agreement that my conclusions made sense, given the evidence available to us. Then I placed a call to Caleb at his job.

I was surprised that Caleb agreed to meet with me again, although I had already figured out how I could probably force the issue, if necessary. I think the turning point was when I told him I knew who had stolen the Museum's documents and had murdered the director and Starr. I said that I would lay it out for him when we met. He grumbled and feigned disinterest, but agreed to meet once again at *Mac's*.

I placed two more calls. One to tell Harte I would be going to Richmond to meet with Livengood. The other to Detective Halpern.

CHAPTER 95

I WAS BACK IN RICHMOND AGAIN. If I didn't wrap up this case soon, I would have to rent an apartment here. The travel back and forth was wearing me down. But, hopefully, things finally were winding up. Tonight would be critical to resolving the case.

I looked over at the bar as I entered *Mac's*. Caleb was sitting there with Celia. A bottle of Bud stood on the mahogany between them. Celia had a glass of whiskey in her hand. They faced each other, but turned to face me as I walked over to them.

Our greetings were, at best, perfunctory; at worst, slightly hostile. I didn't care.

"We should go somewhere else so we can talk without having to yell over the noise," I said. "I don't want anyone listening to what I have to say." It *was* too noisy here for me to pull off what I wanted to do. It also was too smokey for my taste, but I wasn't about to feed Caleb that thought so he could use it against me.

We left *Mac's,* taking two cars. I followed them to a Cajun restaurant, located on 1st Street, called *Mama J's*.

At our request we were seated at a table at the back of the small dining room, away from the nearest occupied table. We'd be able to talk without being overheard.

I looked around. The walls were dark red; the wood was stained dark, too, exuding warmth. Celia commented that the food here was good home-cooked Cajun fare. She had no idea I would be able to judge that for myself since I frequently ate homemade Cajun meals cooked for me by Clotille. I didn't share that information with them.

As we drank our first round together and looked over the menus, the dining room began to fill. Soon we would not be able to talk with much privacy. I also was aware that Caleb was staring at me with sullen eyes. Each time I looked at him, he turned away. I could take the hint. It was time to get to my agenda.

CHAPTER 96

"I KNOW WHO ARRANGED THE THEFT of the Museum's documents," I said.

"You don't know shit," Caleb responded. "You just like to act like you know what's goin' on." He turned and looked at Celia, then turned back to me. His eyes had become slits. He reached into his shirt pocket and retrieved a loose cigarette. As he pulled his Zippo from his pants pocket I shook my head and pointed to the No Smoking sign on the wall. Caleb glowered at me, but tucked the smoke behind his ear.

"Just as important," I said, "I also know why the documents were stolen."

I looked first at Caleb, then at Celia. Caleb's fury was visibly bubbling over, although he remained quiet for the moment. He flexed his right hand, first making a fist, then undoing it, over and over.

Celia saw me looking at Caleb's hand. She seemed amused. She turned to face me, and locked her eyes on mine.

"Tell us what you think you know," she said. Her voice was calm, almost flat, betraying no emotion. "We're curious." She placed her hand on Caleb's knee, as if to calm him.

I nodded. "First off, I know about you, Celia. A lot about you."

That did not sit well with her. Her face darkened. She sat upright, and looked quickly at Caleb, then back at me. "Such as?" she said. Her eyes had turned feral.

"Where to begin?" I said, as if thinking out loud. I wanted to approach this lightly, but not flippantly or in an accusatory way. I wanted Celia to cooperate with me, to fill in the missing blanks I could not yet fill in, not resist me as she surely otherwise might. Most of all, I didn't want her to become hostile. I might not ever have another chance to perform this theater with Caleb and her.

"For starters, I had both of you investigated. You're an interesting couple. Much more interesting than you appear on the surface or led me to believe when we first met."

CHAPTER 97

"ALWAYS GLAD TO BE THOUGHT of as interesting," Celia said, "but what's that have to do with what you think you know about the Museum's theft?"

"And about the two murders," I added.

"And that, too," she said, with a slight shrug, as if dismissing the murders as mere inconveniences.

"Get on with it," Caleb said. "You're pissing me off with your insinuations." He put his beer to his lips and took a long, slow pull.

I looked at Caleb, shook my head once, and turned back to Celia.

"For openers, it seems everything you told me about how you two met and how you introduced Caleb to reenacting was true."

"We already know that," Celia said.

"It's what you didn't tell me that's interesting," I said.

"Like what?"

"Like the fact that your family, Celia, has been involved with the South's lost cause since the Civil War. That your ancestors were grunts in the Confederate army. That two of your ancestors were summarily shot by the Confederate military for cowardliness and desertion."

I could see her spine stiffen as she frowned.

"Except for Stonewall Jackson, her relative on her mother's side," Caleb said. "We told you about him. He's her ancestor, and he died a hero."

"Yeah, you told me, Caleb, but that was bullshit," I said. I turned to look Celia in her eyes. "You're no more related to Stonewall Jackson than I am. Your ancestors were all Confederate cannon fodder in the War, nothing more, nothing less. Nothing to be proud of from your point of view, I suppose. Tenant farmers supporting the aristocratic landlords in the great Confederate cause."

Celia swallowed the balance of her *Jack*, then caught the waitress' eye as she held up her glass to order another.

"We're proud of our ancestors and who they were," Celia said, as she looked hard at me, "in spite of what you think. My family, and men and women like them, were the backbone of the Great Cause, not like those pansy-ass élites who paraded around in fancy uniforms and got drunk, made too much noise, and avoided danger, while sending their men out on impossible missions to die. If you'd asked, I'd have told you straight out about them," she said.

She looked over at Caleb, shrugged, then looked back at me. "So what's that have to do with anything?"

"It has to do with what happened to your family after the War, what happened during Reconstruction, and how you, and people like you, are treated today by the descendants of the old aristocracy and by privileged Confederate membership groups like the Golden Knights."

I watched as she and Caleb briefly looked at one another, then back at me.

"What're you talking about?" Celia said. Her voice had

STEVEN M. ROTH

acquired a reptilian hiss. "What do you think happened? And what do you think happens to us today?" She stiffened. "I'll be damned if I'm going to sit here and let you insinuate insults."

Caleb looked from Celia to me and back again.

I took a pull on my bottle of beer, collected my thoughts, and looked directly at Celia, ignoring Caleb now.

"I've learned some interesting things, Celia, mostly about how your ancestors fared during Reconstruction. Apparently that period of history has great importance to you," I said.

"Like many people, your family lost its small farm during the War. It was burned out by invading Yankee troops, crops were not planted, and the land was allowed to erode over four years. When your ancestors returned to their land, there was no way they could start over without financial help."

Celia looked at Caleb, then picked up her tumbler of *Jack* and took a drink. She slowly and very deliberately placed the glass back on the table. She stared at the glass for a full half minute before again looking at me.

"Like you said, it was a common problem for small farmers in the South," she said. "What's it prove?" She turned to Caleb and nodded once, sharply. Then she turned back to face me, a look of triumph now on her face.

"Stay with me on this," I said. "Your family couldn't make it on its own and couldn't get financial help from the occupying Northern Carpetbaggers because their money was being used to help the freed slaves, not white, small, struggling farmers like your ancestors.

"Your family was forced to turn to the plantation owners for financial aid, and so they became tenant farmers on their own land. Forced to become economic slaves while the blacks

348

they once had dominated now prospered from free financial aid and other help."

Celia took Caleb's hand and held it. She looked briefly at him, then turned back to me. She shrugged her seeming indifference.

I continued. "As time passed, your ancestors fell more and more in debt and more and more bound to the aristocratic family that had staked them to their own farm. They also became more and more bitter as the gulf widened between the indebted whites — which they were — and the freed, subsidized black men and women."

"Interesting tale," Celia said.

"I should have picked up on it when you repeatedly referred to the people at the Museum as élites," I said.

"Assuming you're right, what's that have to do with the theft of the documents?" Caleb said. Anger had departed his voice and curiosity had replaced it.

"Everything," I said. "This forms the basis for everything that occurred." I took another long pull on my beer, emptied the bottle, and signaled the waitress for another.

CHAPTER 98

C ALEB TURNED AWAY FROM ME and faced Celia. "We don't have to listen to this crap if you don't want. Let's go." He started to stand up.

Celia squeezed his hand and held up her other palm. "No, let's stay. I'm curious to hear what this fool thinks he knows."

Caleb looked at me and scowled. He turned back to Celia, and nodded. His body language signaled *fight or flight*. I didn't think he was inclined at the moment to engage in flight.

"So," Celia said to me, "what do you think you know?" She smirked as she asked this. Without taking her eyes off mine, she raised her glass and swallowed the last drop of *Jack*. Then she turned away from me and signaled the waitress to bring another.

I paused to collect my thoughts. I had several objectives here and didn't want to blow achieving them by how I approached this. I didn't want to seem pompous because I'd figured it all out and I didn't want to seem to be talking down to Celia. I needed to be just accusatory enough to incite her to defend herself by filling in the blanks, and deceptive enough to lure her in so she would participate with me out of a sense of pride or superiority. I wanted to make this a memorable dialogue, not a forgettable monologue.

"As I said, I should have picked up on this before, on your attitude, by how you referred to the Museum's trustees and members of the Golden Knights as élites."

"That's what they are," Celia said, her voice barely audible. "They have no truck with the likes of me and Caleb. Think they're too good for us."

"I think you're probably right about that," I said. "They're not the best group of people I've ever encountered." I smiled and nodded. "That's my feeling, too, having recently dealt with them myself. But that didn't incite me to commit crimes against them. Not theft, not murder, no matter how much I don't like them and their supercilious attitudes."

"Me either," Celia said. "There were no crimes against them by me."

I glanced over at Caleb to see if he still was perched to fight. He seemed relaxed now, almost curious and inviting, as if he wanted to see how this would play out. As he looked at me, he nodded several times. I interpreted this to mean he was resigned to hearing my tale.

I turned back to Celia. I would now work with the information Zhao had given me.

"It seems all your life you've loudly and indiscriminately railed against the wealthy and privileged in society around you, often losing jobs because of it. That was your reputation in college, too. Your life, it was said, revolved around unrelenting resentment against the so-called *haves*."

Celia shrugged and raised both eyebrows as if to say, *You did your homework. So what? That's not a crime.*

She articulated this thought. "So what? That's not unusual

in this kind of place where people separate themselves based on something they had no influence over — their dead ancestors.

"It's not unusual for some people to resent this, not when you grow up like I did, hearing stories all your life about the land stolen from your family and how your ancestors were practically enslaved by their rich neighbors. But resentment's not a crime."

"No, it's not," I said. "But what I can't figure out is why you tolerate Caleb's idolization of Robert E. Lee." I looked at Caleb. He seemed puzzled by my statement. I turned back to Celia.

"Lee was the *crème de la crème* of Southern élites," I said, "both by reason of his purported birth into Virginia's aristocracy and by virtue of his rank as the senior military officer in the Army of Northern Virginia." I looked back at Caleb. He'd stiffened and seemed prepared again to fight. I nodded at him, then turned back to Celia.

"In fact," I said, "Lee was an incompetent butcher who time and time again sent his men to fight against overwhelming odds when they had no chance of winning. Forcing his men to die rather than retreating and living to fight another day in some other, some friendlier milieu."

Celia seemed to ignore my statement, although I thought it had been fairly provocative.

"What's to tolerate?" she said, referring back to my earlier statement concerning Caleb's fixation with Lee. "Lee's important to Caleb, so, therefore, Lee's important to me." She winked at Caleb. He stared at her, but didn't respond. His forehead was furrowed.

I decided to up the ante.

"When Caleb told you, as he surely would have, what he learned from his customer about Lee's secret, you saw the opportunity to expose Lee, and thereby undermine the myth of the South's greatest hero. You saw an opportunity to kick sand in the collective faces of the people at the Museum who had been suppressing the information."

"I wouldn't do that," Celia said. She turned to Caleb. "It would hurt Caleb."

"I think you not only would do it, but you did do it," I said.

Celia slowly, almost sorrowfully, shook her head. "You're assuming, even if I wanted to, I could steal the documents," she said. "How would I do that? The documents were in a museum, a secure, protected building. It looks like a fortress from the outside."

"I doubt you pulled off the burglary yourself," I said. "You probably had someone do it for you, likely with the aid of a Museum insider."

"Like who," Celia said, "assuming you know what you're talking about?"

"Like Hervey Beauregard," I said. "He's the same person who told Caleb about Lee's secret and later told you that the documents were forgeries. You, in turn, misled Caleb, telling him you were the one who'd had the documents authenticated, and that they turned out to be fakes."

"Why would this Beauregard person help me?" Celia said.

"He didn't do it to help you, Celia, believe me. He did it to help himself. You were as much Beauregard's pawn in this as Caleb was your pawn." I turned and looked at Caleb, when I noticed him start to rise from his seat. Celia put her hand on his arm and stopped him. He frowned, but sat back down.

I continued, turning slightly and facing away from Caleb now, looking steadily at Celia.

"Beauregard didn't give a damn about you or Caleb. You were his tool, Celia. He wanted to use you to embarrass the Museum's director," I said.

"Beauregard wanted to become the next director when the trustees would finally learn about the theft and fire the director because he'd kept that information from them."

"Assuming this isn't all bullshit, why would I want the documents?" Celia said.

"To expose Lee's secret, is why. To make the Golden Knights and the Museum not only look like fools, but also look like liars who were willing to hide the revelation about Lee, men who were willing to continue to deceive everyone to maintain Lee's public image and their own power and influence."

"But the documents are forgeries," Caleb said, "so how could that happen?"

"We don't actually know they're forgeries," I said. "We only know that Beauregard told Celia they were fakes, and that she told you, without revealing her source of that information. Celia misled you into believing she'd had the documents authenticated, but she hadn't. It was the director and his colleagues who authenticated them. For all we know, Beauregard started the rumor the documents were forgeries, using you to spread it via me, after things got out of hand, after the director and Starr had been murdered."

"That doesn't make sense," Celia said. "How would that fit into your theory?"

She seemed to me to be genuinely puzzled. I looked

severely at her, staring coldly into her eyes. She looked back at me without flinching. She was tough.

"The director's and Starr's murders were crimes of opportunity brought about and taken advantage of by Beauregard. He probably hired someone for that. I doubt he did it himself, given the nature of the crimes and my impression of him as a self-indulgent, stuffed-shirt who wouldn't want to dirty his own hands.

"He probably arranged, too, for me to be mugged, since my fountain pen and money-clip later showed up at crime scenes related to the murders. He probably also arranged for Caleb here to monkey with my vehicle when he had it in the shop, so some hacker could take over its computer system."

Caleb leaped from his stool and faced-off with me. "The fuck you think you are, accusing me of that—"

Celia put her hand on Caleb's arm. "Sit, Dear," she said, "while we hear him out. He's just shooting-off his mouth. He doesn't know what he's talking about." She leaned in and kissed Caleb's cheek. "We'll hear him out, then split."

Caleb sat again and glowered at me. I faced Celia.

"So you're not saying I killed anybody then?" she said.

"I'm saying you stole the documents with Beauregard's help, and that Beauregard had the director and Starr murdered to advance his career, using the theft as a cover and opportunity." I paused before I said what really was on my mind. "I'm convinced it was Beauregard who tried to have me killed, not you, Caleb."

"You can't prove what you said about me. You're guessing," Celia said.

"Actually, I'm not guessing, just fitting the pieces together. It's the only scenario that makes sense, based on what I know."

"So what if I did have something to do with the theft. You'll never prove it. It'll be your word against mine. I'm not worried."

She looked at Caleb, nodded, then faced me again.

"Caleb wouldn't turn me in or say anything against me, would you, Dear?" She looked again at Caleb. He shook his head slowly as he frowned.

"I think we'll be able to prove it if we look in your home," I said. "You had the motive — the mind set — and the opportunity and the means. A search of your home should turn up the stolen documents."

Celia's face darkened. "Good luck there. You can't search our home at all since you're not a cop, and the cops can't either unless they get a warrant." She nodded her point sharply, once, and smiled at her apparent victory.

I nodded, too, and smiled.

"You're right on both counts. But the cops will soon have their warrant based on your admission to me just now. Some cops and forensic technicians are waiting outside your home as we speak. They're ready to run the search as soon as Detective Stella calls his partner, who will go to the judge, who is on standby ready to sign the warrant that's sitting on his desk."

Celia and Caleb erupted from their seats. "You can't—" Celia said.

"We can," I said, "and we did." I pointed across the room toward the door, as Detective Stella entered, followed by two uniformed police officers.

"You're done, Celia," I said. "Maybe you, too, Caleb. We'll see once it's all sorted out." I then pointed to my shirt, and said, "I'm wearing a wire, Celia. We have you admitting your part in the theft in your own words."

CHAPTER 99

Detective Halpern, at my request, had prepared an advance warrant to search Celia's and Caleb's home. This would become effective as soon as Detective Stella called him to say we had caught probable cause on the wire I wore. Halpern had already had a friendly judge review the warrant — a judge who agreed to sign it as soon as there was probable cause. Meanwhile, a group of uniformed cops and a forensic team stood by at Celia's and Caleb's home until Halpern showed up, warrant in hand.

The search yielded little, but what it did produce was damning.

The stolen journal and letters were found stored in a strong box behind the couch in the living room. A note from Celia to Beauregard, with Beauregard's return note to her, both found in the strong box, disclosed that Celia had believed the documents were genuine until Beauregard informed her, perhaps intentionally misleading her, that the documents were forgeries.

Detective Stella arrested Celia based on the evidence found at her home and her admission against interest, captured by the wire I wore. They also pulled in Caleb.

The cops arrested Beauregard at the Museum. At first he

refused to leave with them, acting the role of the indignant aristocrat, so they handcuffed his hands behind his back and roughed him up a little. His perp walk from the Museum's entrance to the patrol vehicle parked at the curb caused a sensation among locals. I had tipped off the press about the upcoming events at the Museum so Beauregard could have his fifteen minutes of fame.

I took the position with the cops that Caleb wasn't guilty of anything other than being naïve, that he had been used by Celia and Beauregard as their foil. I actually believed this.

Halpern said he tended to agree, but wanted to question Caleb first before cutting him loose, to sweat him a while before he made it official, one way or the other.

The cops were less successful with Beauregard, owing, perhaps, to his prominent place in Richmond society. They charged him with obstruction of justice and conspiracy to commit burglary. They were not able to tie him to the two murders or to the attempt on my life, although Halpern, Stella, and I thought he had orchestrated all three.

Beauregard was tried and convicted of obstruction. He skated on the conspiracy to commit burglary charge. The court sentenced him to a short jail term at a minimum security prison where he found Jesus and learned to play chess during his brief confinement.

The two murders and the attempt to kill me by crashing my SUV remained unsolved.

Caleb was not charged with anything since there is no statute against being naïve or stupid, or both.

Celia, like Beauregard, was convicted of obstruction. She also was convicted of conspiracy to commit burglary —

clearly with Beauregard, although Beauregard had walked on the charge. Celia was sentenced to ten years for her role.

The slave Isaiah's journal, as well as Anne Carter Lee's letters and Elizabeth Van Lew's letters, were returned to the Museum after the trials. The disclosure at trial of Lee's secret — which was neither proven to be true nor disproven as false — stirred up much controversy among Richmond's high society, among Civil War historians, Lee-family descendants, genealogists, African-Americans, amateur Civil War buffs, Confederate wannabes, philatelists interested in the Confederacy and its postal history, and Civil War reenactors — both Farbs and Hardcores. No one in Richmond seemed untouched by the revelation.

The Museum's personnel officially refused to cooperate with anyone wanting to study the documents, declaring them off-limits and unavailable for the present time. It officially took the position that Isaiah's journal and the letters were genuine artifacts.

One matter continued to puzzle me until I raised it with Halpern. I asked him if he or Stella had come across anyone who had been investigating me? I described my conversation with Toula Xandereas, and the mysterious visitor who had made inquiries about me at the Mount Parnassus Condominium.

Halpern shook his head. "No one we came across. Can't help you there," he said. He speculated it might have been the same person who had taken control of my vehicle and tried to kill me. I tended to agree with him, but never actually found out.

I still work as a PI and still am partnered with Harte. Most of my work these days occurs behind a computer, searching databases, as I continue to heal from my vehicle-wreck. I still take physical therapy, but only two days each week now. I look forward to returning to the field and our next case.

THE END

ACKNOWLEDGEMENTS

I thank, as always, Dominica. Her continued support is my bedrock.

I also thank Gary Griffith for his valuable comments on an early version of the manuscript.

As part of my research for this book, I read twenty-eight published journals (memoirs) written or dictated in the nineteenth century by ex-slaves. This sad and stressful (reading) undertaking by me served the purpose of giving me a sense of the language (diction, vocabulary, and syntax) used by these poor souls.

In creating Isaiah's journal, I tried to be true to what I'd read in terms of the language used, but occasionally I modernized grammar, phrases, and/or punctuation in an effort to make my fictive passages intelligible to a current-day reader.

While the events I portrayed in Isaiah's journal were fictitious, they were inspired by the memoirs I read.

Please Review *THE COUNTERFEIT TWIN*

If you enjoyed *THE COUNTERFEIT TWIN*, please leave a review on Amazon at www.Amazon.com.

Reviews will help me, as an author, and also will help other readers decide if they want to read my book.

FREE BOOK

The first Socrates Cheng mystery
Copy and paste this link into your browser to download a free copy: http://www.stevenmroth.com/FreeBook.aspx

For more information on my other books,
Visit my web site: www.stevenmroth.com

Coming soon!
NO PLACE TO HIDE
The second Trace Austin suspense novel

Trace Austin is back and is in the cross-hairs of the president of the United States who intends to clean up all loose ends from OPERATION TESTING GROUND before he leaves office.

Visit me at:
www.StevenMRoth.com